PROTECTING OUR FOREVER

A BLACKTHORNE SECURITY NOVEL

NICOLE VIDAL

COPYRIGHT

Cover design by Designs with Sass
Developmental Edit by Virginia Cantrell of Hot Tree Editing.
Final Edit by Kim Deister of Hot Tree Editing

ISBN 978-1-7371689-5-9

TABLE OF CONTENTS

KEEP IN TOUCH WITH NV

Visit me on social media or online to learn about my newest releases:

Facebook (http://fb.me/NicoleVidalAuthor)

Instagram (http://instragram.com/nicolevidal_author)

My website (www.nicolevidal.com)

Goodreads (https://bit.ly/NVGoodreads)

Amazon (https://amzn.to/2XCLSlR)

Pinterest (http://pinterest.com/NicoleVidal_Author)

CHAPTER ONE

MADELEINE

"Madeleine, Mr. Stockton on line three. Also, as a reminder, you're scheduled for a meeting uptown in less than an hour, and then you have the rest of the afternoon blocked off," my assistant Simon informs me.

"Thank you. This call with Mr. Stockton won't take long." I pick up the phone and jump right in. "Stefan, it's a pleasure to hear from you. I'll keep this brief as my time is valuable. At the end of this contract, you'll need a new agent."

Stefan is one of my musician clients. He's obstinate, belligerent, and refuses to heed my advice regarding projects to accept. I refuse to allow my name to be associated with his entitled behavior.

"Madeleine, please don't do this. I need you!" Stefan whines through the phone line.

"That may be true, but I'm no longer willing to put up with your inconsistency and inability to follow simple direction to keep your image clean. I wish you the best." I exhale and hang up the phone. This isn't the first time I've let a client go, but it is the first time it's so overdue. "Si, please call for my car."

"Already done. Have a great afternoon, Mads."

"Thank you." Exiting my office, I descend to the lobby and slide into my waiting car.

I plan on it. My... I don't even know what to call him—lover, booty call, friend with benefits—will arrive tonight. Our initial introduction was at Callie's final concert in Atlanta. Callie has been my client since she turned eighteen. She found her forever when Connor was assigned as her bodyguard. Not only was he able to thwart all her security concerns but win her heart as well. Callie makes Connor stronger but can also bring him to his knees. Right before her final meet and greet, Callie introduced Christoph and me. When his hand surrounded mine, a prickle of awareness shot straight up my arm and nestled in my chest. Aside from a few longing glances, nothing happened between us.

The next time I saw him was at Callie's elegant wedding. I arrived immediately after him. Christoph's manners are impeccable. Not only did he open my car door, but he escorted me to my seat. The same awareness coursed through me when I wrapped my arm around his. At first, I thought it was in my head. He never acknowledged any attraction to me at that point. I decided to take matters into my own hands and ask him to join me for a drink. I'm not forward when it comes to dating, not even a little bit.

As much as it pains me to admit, I spent Callie's entire wedding with my gaze locked on his. I was a terrible acquaintance on her special day. Once his obligatory groomsmen duties were complete, we shared a few drinks at the bar. At my invitation, we spent all night and the entire next day setting the sheets in my hotel suite ablaze. We have been meeting as frequently as our schedules allow ever since. Perhaps what we share isn't the healthiest of relationships, but it's all we can handle right now. Speaking for myself, I have no expectations aside from mind-blowing orgasms as often as we can see one another.

My driver pulls me out of my thoughts. "Miss Wilton?"

"Yes, sorry, Jack. I have a lot on my mind." Complete lie. My mind is already past this meeting and recalling with precision the caress of Christoph's tongue along the seam between my thighs and my core—a spot that makes me shudder in anticipation. One only he knows exists.

I exit the car and make my way into the restaurant. I rarely find myself unfocused at a business meeting, especially one where my compensation depends on the details being discussed. Yet today I want nothing more than to be with him. It makes no sense. Nothing is different since the last time I saw him. Nothing major changed in my life. I know the score. Our lives are incompatible for a relationship. We live too far from one another, and neither is able or willing to quit our jobs.

"Madeleine?" a deep voice asks.

"I'm sorry. Could you repeat your question?"

My immediate boss, Stavros Scala, repeats, "Will our client be able to follow those rules?"

"He should be willing to follow those rules and anything else we set forth. If he wants this company to represent him, behaving like an adult instead of a petulant child shouldn't be a deal breaker."

The table of men laugh. I'm accustomed to being the sole woman at the table. I'm the only senior agent at The Scala Agency who is female. Hell, I started over eight years ago; most women don't make it past year two. *Focus, Madi!*

"Always straightforward in her requirements of our clients," Stavros chimes in.

I nod and wish the rest of this meeting to hurry to completion. More than an hour later, I slump into the back seat of my car. Jack notices.

"Bad meeting, Miss Wilton?"

I shake my head. "No, thanks, Jack. Merely ready for the work week to be over."

"I understand. I'll have you home as soon as traffic allows," he assures me.

"Much appreciated." After a few settling moments, I scan through the emails and texts that have arrived since I left the office. There are two emails from Simon regarding my schedule for early next week. I handle those and continue down the list. There are two contracts to review for clients and a few text messages.

Estelle: Hi, sweetheart. Wanted to check on you. Love you, ladybug.

Me: Hi I'm done for the day and taking the weekend off.

Estelle: Good for you. I can't wait to see you soon.

Me: Me too. Love you.

I'm looking forward to spending the holidays with her this year. I may be a successful agent, and I love what I do, but Grams is all I have left, and she won't be here forever.

CA: I'll see you in an hour.

I glance at my watch and realize he'll probably be waiting for me when I get home. Against what my head is telling me, butterflies take flight in my stomach. Developing real feelings for Christoph isn't an option. The car stops in front of my building.

Jack opens my door. "Have a good weekend, Miss Wilton."

"Thank you, Jack. You've been driving me around for the last five years; please call me Madeleine." Only Simon knows more about my schedule than Jack.

"I'll try. Have a nice weekend, Madeleine."

"You too, Jack."

The moment I open my door to my townhouse, I know Christoph is already here. The makings of some delicious dish is spread on my island, and a bottle of wine is breathing as well.

CHAPTER TWO

CHRISTOPH

Meeting her was sheer circumstance. When Connor was injured protecting his now wife, Callie, I stepped in to provide security while he healed. I met Madeleine during the assignment in Atlanta. The moment her hand slid into mine, my world stopped spinning. Not only is she a powerful and successful talent agent, but she's jaw-droppingly gorgeous as well. She's tall without her luxury red-soled shoes, with thick, long blonde hair and the most piercing blue eyes I've ever seen. Her eyes are windows into her true feelings if you look hard enough. I'm confident the list of people she allows to read her is infinitesimal. Thankfully, I'm on the list.

The next time I saw her at Connor's wedding, the awareness returned when I escorted her to a seat. After their reception was our first time together, and epic isn't even an apt description. Ever since, we've been seeing each other whenever our hectic schedules and geographical locations allow.

Her New York apartment mirrors her outward demeanor completely. It's modern with clean, sharp lines, and expensive. Her apartment has two terraces, one for guests and one attached to the master suite. It's a gorgeous outdoor space in the heart of the city. Inwardly, Madeleine isn't hard or disinterested. The small glimpses of the real her when she lets her guard down will be my undoing.

I arrive before her with an armful of groceries for dinner. I love arriving before Madeleine. As far as I can tell, she's on her own. We may have been spending time together over the last six months, but we don't truly share much with one another outside of work and our bodies. Her independence is fiercely attractive. It's partially why I seize every opportunity to take care of her. So far, she hasn't balked.

My profession affords me finely honed skills, including seeing things people try to mask. Madeleine is no different. I only read the portions of her information that were necessary to protect Callie, nothing more. If there is ever a time we're able to be in a relationship, I'm confident she'll share the rest of her story with me like I will with her. For now, we're two consenting adults who have incredible chemistry and life-altering sex.

I'm well into preparing dinner when she steps through her front door. Well, that's not exactly accurate. All the prep work is done, I simply need to cook. As usual, she looks beautiful after a long day of moving and shaking for her clients. Her suit is navy with a pencil skirt and emerald blouse. The colors make her eyes darker and more intriguing.

I approach her with a glass of her favorite red wine in hand. "Hey. How was your day?"

Madeleine accepts the glass and lightly presses her lips to mine. "Not too bad. How was your assignment?" She swirls the wine and takes a satisfying sip.

"Same. I've worked with this client before. Frankly, I'm not sure she needs security in place for this event. It happens once per quarter. She's discreet, and there's limited to no press coverage."

"Any chance you could finish dinner later?" She points toward the food on the island.

I try to recall how long it's been since I saw her last. Honestly, I don't have to try. It's been slightly less than two weeks. "Oscar not doing enough for you?" Oscar is her battery-operated boyfriend.

"He's nowhere near an acceptable substitute for you."

"Glad to hear I won't be replaced anytime soon." I slide my hand along her jaw. Her mouth tastes like pinot noir, and her curves melt against me as our tongues tangle. By the time we reach her massive bed, there's a trail of clothes on the floor. Not only does her apartment and her shoes scream luxury, but her lingerie costs more than I spend on rent in a month. This set matches her suit, and the navy silk and lace feel decadent beneath my fingers. It's almost as soft as her creamy skin.

I hover over her and mark her skin with my mouth, savoring her breasts with my tongue. Rolling and plucking her nipples with my fingers has her on the cusp of begging.

"Christoph…."

My name falling from her lips sounds like a prayer wrapped in desire. Her voice makes my chest tighten. Falling for Madeleine is not an option, despite the coma-inducing sex. Her plea makes me slow my pace and drive her to the edge of taking control. Sex with her is never boring.

Her hand slides between us, and her fingers circle the bundle of nerves at the apex of her thighs. I drag my tongue along the underside of her breast and wet a path down her arm, past the tips of her manicured fingers, and spear her core.

"How does it get better every damn time?" Her question is rhetorical.

I smile against her as she moves faster. Her hips bow off the duvet as she closes in on her first release of the weekend. She increases the speed of her fingers and shudders beneath me. Before her climax subsides, she wraps her other arm around me and rolls us.

Within seconds of landing flat on my back, she aligns herself and takes my shaft deep into her center.

"Damn, babe."

"You make me feel so good."

I grin up at her, set one hand on her hip, and draw circles on her clit with my thumb. She moves along my length ferociously until she's on the verge of splintering. Leaning forward, she increases her pace with her lips plastered against mine.

Her inner muscles clench, and her body convulses around me. I thrust upward twice and fall off the edge immediately after her. Once our breathing regulates, she moves beside me and curls against me.

"You realize I don't come visit you only for sex, right?" I care about Madeleine, but our lives aren't conducive to a lasting relationship given the demands of our professions.

She nods against my chest. "Same for me, but sex with you is spectacular."

I've never had better than her, but the sex isn't what keeps me coming back. It certainly doesn't hurt. There are two distinct sides of Madeleine Wilton: the successful talent agent who refuses to take no for an answer and the soft, warm woman who visits her grandmother as often as she can. The issue isn't wanting a relationship; it's giving her—giving us—the time necessary to thrive. Truly, it isn't possible right now.

"Dinner?" I suggest.

"Sure. What did you decide on for tonight?"

"Spicy shrimp and linguine."

"I don't have any shrimp." She lifts her eyes to mine.

"I grabbed the ingredients at the market down the block on my way here."

"Oh." She presses a kiss to my lips and starts to move away from me.

I tighten my hold on her and draw her against me again. I almost don't ask, but I can't help myself. "Did I overstep?"

She shakes her head. "No, being taken care of isn't something I'm used to anymore."

I nod. I heard what she didn't say—*I like being taken care of and it scares me*—and brush my lips across hers again.

I'm growing attached to you too, Madeleine.

After cleaning up, I gather our strewn clothes and my bag. Dressed in long-slung sweats, I return to the kitchen. Once the water is boiling, she joins me as well.

"How can I help?" she asks.

"Do you want to sauté the shrimp or handle drinks and setting the table?"

"I'll take the drinks and table."

A flicker of uncertainty crosses her gorgeous face. This time I leave it alone. Once the pasta is al dente and the shrimp is cooked through, we sit at the island and eat.

"How's Grams?" I ask between forkfuls. We haven't shared many things that would make a solid foundation of a relationship at this point. One substantial thing we have in common is we were both raised by our grandmothers. Her parents took off for good when she was six. Mine... I have no clue about my family history other than what my grandmother told me. The story goes something like my mother showed up with a baby on her doorstep, and the next morning she was gone.

"Pretty good. She texted me earlier today. She's happy and spry. I miss her every day. I'm looking forward to visiting her for Thanksgiving. What about you?"

"I'm working with Jake to carve out some time soon." Jake is my boss and friend. When he formed Blackthorne Security, I jumped at the chance to leave the military for the private sector. "Is Estelle coming here, or are you going to her?"

"I'm going home."

It dawns on me I don't know where she's from originally. Not surprising but unsettling. "Where is home?"

"I was born in Pennsylvania, but Estelle raised me in Maryland where she still lives. What about you?"

"I'm from North Carolina, but Betty lives in Delaware now. She moved us there when I was ten."

"How far is it from your home?" She knows I live in Connor's condo since he and Callie built their dream home at the farm.

"About forty minutes. It isn't far, but I need to be off the clock to visit and truly be there."

She nods. "I understand completely."

"I know." After cleaning up our dishes, we curl up in the corner of her sectional with our wine.

Once she reaches the bottom of her glass, Madeleine sets it aside. She nips and bites her way up my abs to my cleft chin—a feature she admittedly loves. "Ready for round two?"

"Always. Are you?"

A devilish twinkle materializes in her eyes. "Have I ever let you down?"

"No, never."

Taking my hand in hers, she leads me back to her bedroom for a night of sheet-tangling, orgasm-inducing pleasure I only achieve with her.

CHAPTER THREE

MADELEINE

On weekends we aren't together, I lounge around and relax. Rarely do I go out alone anymore. Eating alone in a crowded restaurant has never been comfortable for me. I have room service when I travel for the same reason.

The weekends we're together in New York have been similar to mine alone except for the sex. When we meet in a different city, we typically order dinner in and spend the time we have together in bed. This morning is no different. I burrow deeper into his corded arms. His hold tightens in sleep. With Christoph, I feel safe and cared for even though we haven't said the words or made any commitment outside of our geographically convenient sheet time.

I feel the moment he wakes.

His mouth travels along my skin from my shoulder to the curve of my neck. Hovering over me, he lowers his lips to mine. "Morning, beautiful."

Only he has ever seen me as beautiful fresh from sleep. "Morning."

"What do you feel like doing today?"

"Can we go out?" I suggest.

If he's surprised, it doesn't show in his ocean-colored eyes—ocean blue of the northeast not the turquoise of the tropics. If we ever break up, it won't be because we weren't honest. He truly understands the demands of my job like I do his. "Sure. Do you have somewhere in mind?"

"No. I'm thinking, other than leaving here, we figure it out as we go." It's completely against who we are in our professional lives. Everything is planned down to the minute for both of us.

"Sounds fun and completely unlike our daily lives."

Or how we usually spend our time together. "Exactly," I reply and attempt to get up.

"Not yet." He lowers his mouth to mine. We may not have labelled what we are to one another, but we feel like a couple when we're together.

After a sexy shared shower, I opt for skinny jeans and a slouchy sweater with tennis shoes. Christoph in a tux is equal parts dashing and sexy, yet casually dressed in dark jeans and a fitted, ivory Henley, he's downright delicious. After a quick breakfast, we ride to the lobby. Once we reach the sidewalk, I turn left, and we start walking.

He leans in close and murmurs near my ear, "This is freeing."

"Yes, it is." About six blocks away from my front door, inspiration strikes. "Ever been to the zoo?"

"Not that I recall. You?"

"Same. What do you think?"

"No rules today. Let's go to the zoo." He throws his arm around my waist and draws me closer. I would be lying if I said it doesn't feel right and welcome.

We cross the street and meander down the path to the Central Park Zoo.

"What's your favorite animal?" he asks after paying for admission.

"Zoo animal? Don't know. Domestic animal, I would say a dog. I haven't had one since Estelle's lab, Spot, died when I was twelve. What about you?"

"I'm going to pick a favorite zoo animal today with you. Betty always had a dog. She still does. Her golden retriever is named, Huck. Her stable manager has two as well. That said, if I had space, I would get a dog or two."

I smile and stop at the red panda enclosure. Christoph sidles beside me with his hand gripping my hip. I didn't notice the possessiveness in his touch until we stepped outside of my apartment. He has an ardent need to always have his hands on me. Secretly, I love it. His desire to have space and a dog or two makes me wonder what else he wants in the future. I mentally chastise myself for attempting to label this. We work as we are right now.

"Ready to move on?" he suggests.

"Sure."

He sets his hands on the curve of my hip and shifts me in front of him so I'm on his right, and we continue through the exhibits. It dawns on me he shifted our positions while we were walking on the sidewalk as well. He made sure I was away from the street. I'm not sure what to call it, protective or… chivalrous perhaps.

Next are the snow leopards. So far these are taking my favorite vote. They're super cute and look cuddly, at least from far away. Then we visit monkeys, sea lions, and an array of birds. Each exhibit is awesome, but the leopards are still in the lead for me. Our last stop at the zoo is the penguins. The tuxedo-wearing animals are zooming around their enclosure while others splash around near the surface, their cute little feet paddling above our heads.

"This is our last exhibit," Christoph informs me. "Which one are you picking?"

"Can I pick two?" I almost whine.

"No, gorgeous. You can only have one favorite of each thing."

There's a sinful undertone when he says my full name, but "gorgeous" and "beautiful" falling from his lips about me is equally appealing. I lean into him and frown. "I choose the penguins. What about you?"

"I'm going with the snow leopards. The baby looks like it would be a great cuddler, except for the whole wild animal part."

Like he is. "Yay! I get both choices." I plant a kiss on his cheek and circle his waist with my arms.

His arm surrounds my shoulders as he pulls me in closer and kisses my temple. *That feels…*

"Where to next?"

"Fall Food Festival?" I suggest.

"Where did you see that?"

"There was a flier on the board at the entrance to the zoo."

"Lead the way." We move back to the entrance and check the address. We walk to the subway and take the train to the closest stop.

Once we step into the neighborhood park, glorious aromas from the fifteen booths waft in our direction.

"What's our plan here?" He glances over at me, a grin on his face. His dimpled grin makes me swoon.

"One lap around, and then we choose a few options," I recommend.

"Sounds good." He tucks me against him as we weave through the vendors. The food choices range from tacos to kabobs to barbeque and cannoli. We move off to the side after a lap through the food trucks.

"What are you voting for?" I figure we may pick some of the same foods. This way I can try everything I want to try.

"I'm leaning toward the taco sampler and a chocolate-dipped cheesecake. You?"

It's as if he read my mind. "Do you share your food?"

"With you, I will."

"You don't normally?"

"Never had anyone I was willing to share with until now." His reply reveals so much more than he thinks. "What are your choices?"

"I narrowed it down to the tacos, the chicken kabobs, and the cannoli. If you're willing to let me try the tacos, I'll get the chicken."

"Deal."

"Where shall I meet you?"

"I'll go with you." The look in his eyes conveys it isn't an option for him to be more than an arm's length away unless absolutely necessary. Protective and affectionate Christoph is hot as hell. He slides his arm around me, and we move to order our lunch.

With our meals, two desserts, and drinks in hand, we grab one of the benches past the vendor area. He offers me the first bite of his tacos.

"You go first; it's your choice."

"Ladies first, always."

"Thank you." I lean forward and take a bite from the beef taco in his hands. "Ohmigod! Have some; it's so good!"

A sly smile graces his face. He takes a bite as well. "You're right. These are good, but not the best I've ever had."

Now I'm intrigued. "Where did you get the best tacos ever?"

"In Mexico with Connor a few years ago," he replies and moves on to the pork taco in the sampler.

I wonder how far I can push to learn more about Christoph. "Were you friends before working together?"

"Unit mates first, then friends, then coworkers. It comes with being thrown together and surviving some harrowing times."

"Did you enlist as soon as you were able?" I don't know how deep he will let me dig. This feels like a first date, not two people who have incredible sex hanging out. I offer him a taste of the chicken kabobs.

He savors the bite. "Yum, it's tasty too. Yes. I didn't see any other way to support myself and Betty. What about you? How did you become a successful talent agent?"

I shake my head. "Truthfully, it was an accident, and I owe it all to Callie."

"How so?"

I take the last bite of my chicken. While I collect my thoughts, he offers me a taste of the pork taco. A soft moan falls from my lips, making Christoph shift in his seat. I smile inwardly.

"I was a measly intern for Stavros Scala when I heard Callie sing for the first time. For almost three months, I piped Callie singing into his office, changed the ringtone on his phone, and made his driver play a CD I created every time he got into his town car.

"Wow, you're tenacious."

I laugh softly. "Stavros equated it to a dog with an everlasting bone. He made a deal with me: if I signed Callie, she could be my first client. If I got her a record deal, he would promote me to junior agent. I signed her the next day and a record deal three weeks later. Within three months, I was working with three music clients and one actor. Actually, I cut him loose yesterday."

The expression on his face is hard to read. Gorgeous, but not giving anything away.

"What are you thinking?" Generally, I wouldn't ask such an open-ended question, but I'm dying to get into his head a bit more.

"I'm trying to reconcile tenacious, successful, and sought-after talent agent with the woman who asked me for a drink at Callie and Connor's wedding."

Christoph truly sees me. I am two different people. The hard shell necessary for handling unruly, uncooperative clients goes up the moment I slip on my Louboutins. When I'm not working, I'm not forward or tenacious in going after anything except him. Asking him to share a drink with me was the first time in as long as I can remember when I reached out for something I wanted.

"I don't know if there's anything to reconcile exactly. My profession is cutthroat and hard-nosed. If you miss a call, you could miss out on the next big star. Once I'm at work, I exude the confidence to handle everything. I'm not as unyielding outside of the office. Only two people see the out-of-office me."

Laying it out there for him isn't as difficult as I thought it would be. We both know the score. Hell, this is the first time we've ventured out of the bedroom since we met. We don't have any long-term prospects. Incredible sex is the only thing truly on the table. It was a conversation we had with brutal honesty the second time we were together. Neither of us is looking for anything more than a safe, regular booty call.

"I'm honored." He presses a kiss to the back of my hand.

"Who said you're one of the two people?" I wink at him and gather our trash.

A sexy smile materializes on his face. *No, you can't fall for him.* I rein in my growing desire to change our relationship and focus on today. A boyfriend doesn't fit into my life, and a girlfriend doesn't fit into his. It's why we work.

"Am I wrong?" His voice is soft and slightly insecure.

Christoph unsure of himself only adds to his devastating appeal. "No, you're not. Only you and Estelle know the real me."

"Ready for another stop, or do you want to go home?"

I don't want this day to end, but I know it will. In less than twenty-four hours, I'll be alone again. We won't see one another until we're both in Los Angeles for the Grammys with Callie. Since she sang at the September 11th twentieth anniversary celebration as herself, she wrote, produced, and laid down an album in her new state-of-the-art studio in her home. She's not only up for four Grammys as a singer but two as a songwriter as well. It's a momentous day for both of us. Her husband, Connor, will accompany her, but Christoph will act as her security with probably one other member of Blackthorne.

"Definitely not ready to go home. What do you have in mind?"

He smirks. "I may have gone a bit outside of the rules for today and googled activities."

"I see. I may be willing to overlook the inherent planner in you. What did you find?"

He turns his phone toward me, open to tickets for a sunset cruise on the Hudson. There's no way for him to know I love sailing, despite not having done it in while.

"Yes, let's."

He secures tickets online, and we take the subway across town to the port. We grab seats on a bench near the pier while we wait for the ship to board. After we board, we take seats on the top level. As soon as the captain gives us permission, we move to the railing. Christoph traps me with his hard body against the railing and surrounds me with his arms. I grip his forearms in front of me.

For almost the first half of the cruise, we don't really talk. The silence is comfortable. Honestly, it's keeping me from sharing the fact I might need to end our relationship because I'm starting to miss him when he's not around. It's the absolute last thing I want to do.

"I had a wonderful time with you today," he whispers in my ear. Prickles of awareness streak down my side.

"Me too."

"Any chance you're free next weekend so I can see you sooner?"

Oh how I wish. "I'll be here, but I have an artist launch party on Saturday night in the Hamptons."

"No problem." The rejection in his tone makes my heart hurt.

Maybe he is interested in more like I am. *No, it wasn't our agreement.*

As we round the Statue of Liberty, the sun casts ribbons of red, orange, pink, and purple across the sky. As the boat taxis into the slip, I turn in his arms and flatten my hands on his sculpted back. I have so many things I want to ask him, but I remain silent. I can't break our agreement. Hell, it was my suggestion in the first place. Yet I've never been as honest with any man ever before. Even Estelle knows about him. I've never told her about anyone. Maybe sharing with her is more telling than anything else.

CHAPTER FOUR

CHRISTOPH

I'm well on my way to my next assignment with Miss Forrester, but my mind is still with Madeleine. The last few days were different than any other time we've spent together. We spent the entire day together outside of her luxurious apartment. It felt like a date, and it was one of the best dates I've ever been on. Catching feelings for Madeleine is not what we agreed on. Yet, I am. Her rejection for this weekend hit me harder than I anticipated.

I agreed to our arrangement fully intending to stick to it. Now I'm not sure it was the right choice.

Once the plane lands in Chicago, I turn on my phone, and a flurry of notifications comes through. I tackle the easy ones first.

Connor: Everything set for L.A.?

Me: Yup. I'll travel with you from home.

Connor: Would you prefer Maia or Alex?

Me: Who would Callie prefer?

Connor: Good point. Maia it is.

Until recently, Maia was the sole female member of Blackthorne. Many would think she's a pushover based on her stature, but nothing is farther from the truth. Alejandra, who prefers Alex, joined the team right before Connor stepped away from field work. Alex is great, but Maia and Callie are friends as well. This is Callie's first event after revealing her true self to the public. Connor and Callie are working on adopting a child and having one the old-fashioned way. Since Callie was orphaned by the September 11th attack, she wants to provide a loving, stable home for children like herself—the type of home the foster system didn't provide for her. Connor also has similar sentiments because of his mother Joyce's profession and Jake.

Our former unit mate and now boss, Jake, was adopted with Joyce's help, along with his siblings Jill and Cameron. At one time, I thought Jill and I would try dating, but since I started seeing Madeleine, I know Jill isn't the one for me. The trick is going to be to convince Madeleine we can pull off a real relationship.

Jake: Hey, can you give me a call before you meet with the client?

Me: Sure.

The last message concerns me.

Anamchara*: I don't like the way we left things.*

Anamchara is Gaelic for soul mate. It's what Gramps called Betty. I have never called her the term of endearment out loud, despite feeling its truth deep in my soul.

Anamchara: *Do we need to talk about us?*

Neither do I. Maybe we do. I can't answer her right now. I pull open the door for my rental car and drive to my accommodations for the next few days. My mind is swimming with ways to answer Madeleine. Since Connor's wedding, we started seeing each other casually but exclusively. I realize it sounds impossible, but we only see each other. It works because we don't have a lot of free time. We agreed to spend our free time with each other only. It sounds like we're in a long-distance relationship. I suppose we are, but we don't typically text or talk on the phone when we're apart either. Her text is an anomaly. I resolve to think more after I see what Jake needs. He answers after the first ring.

"Hey, Jake."

"Hi. How was your flight?"

Jake knows I'm not a fan of flying. I would prefer to drive. "Bumpy, but I'm here. What's up?"

"I received an alert from Blaine a few hours ago. A photo of you and Madeleine was posted in a local New York newspaper." Blaine is a white hat hacker and our private investigator. He's one of the best in the world.

"Okay. I'm photographed all the time with high-profile people."

"True, but someone is actively looking for you. Blaine found a bot specifically searching for images of you."

"Who?" I have no family other than Betty, my Blackthorne family, and my green family. Each group was vetted carefully and thoroughly.

"I don't know yet, but I wanted your permission to have Blaine keep digging."

I drag my hand down my face. "Yes, you have my permission. Do I need to warn Madeleine?"

"What is your relationship to her?"

I push out a harsh breath. "After this past weekend and her text from an hour ago, I'm not sure." I need to talk to her.

"Let's give Blaine some time and then reevaluate."

"Okay."

"Do you want to talk about her?"

No. Yes. "I don't know what to say. Until Saturday the lines were clear—just sex."

"What happened Saturday?" Jake prods.

"For lack of a better term, we went on a date."

I hear the levity in his voice. "Now you like her, like her?"

"Eloquent, Jake. I care about her. I did before, but I never got any indication she might be on the same page as me or the notion our arrangement wasn't working for her anymore."

"As someone who waited too damn long for the right woman, I suggest talking to her and soon." It took Jake over two years to share his true feelings with Norah. I'm sure her needing Blackthorne protection played into it as well.

"Thanks, Jake. I'll consider it."

"Anytime. I'll contact you when I have more info."

I end the call, chuck my phone onto the bed, and set my face in my hands. *What do I want?* It's not an easy question to answer. At some point, I want a woman who can bring me to my knees but make me stronger as well. Madeleine very well could be that woman. I want a family despite being an only child raised by my grandmother. The larger question is can I work for Blackthorne and have it all. Unfortunately, the answer is likely no.

I'm not sure how this conversation will go, but I know it shouldn't wait.

Me: Can you talk now?

Anamchara: *Give me a few minutes to get upstairs. I'll call you.*

Me: Okay.

I strip out of my clothes and tug on a fresh shirt and shorts. I pull my suit out of my luggage and hang it. Now I won't have to iron before Miss Forrester's first event. My phone rings in my hand, and I'm instantly nervous.

"Hey."

"Hi. How was your flight?" Her voice is softer than normal.

"Fine. Chicago isn't far from New York, especially direct." Silence stretches between us. She wanted to talk, so I wait her out.

"I'm not sure where to start," she murmurs.

"Why are you upset about how we left things?" My tone is cautious. Truly, I'm not sure I want to hear her answer.

"I heard the disappointment you tried to hide."

No one other than Gram has ever been able to read me as well as Madeleine, not even Jake or Connor despite our time in the trenches together. "I understand your reason for saying no. Our agreement doesn't include me adding more time."

"Do you want more time?"

Own it! "Yes. I realized we're kind of in a long-distance relationship without the best part of getting to know every detail about one another. I want ... a real relationship with you. If you don't, that's fine."

"Are you serious?" A note of giddiness comes through in her question.

More than I have been about anything ever before. "Yes, completely serious. Is it going to be easy? Hell no. It'll be harder than normal because of our jobs and the distance between our homes. Are you in?"

"Absolutely."

A weight I didn't know I was carrying lifts off my chest. "How was your day, gorgeous?"

A sexy sigh zips through the phone line. *Noted, sweetheart.* "Busy. Are you still free this weekend? Would you be willing to attend my launch with me?"

"Yes. What is the dress code?"

"Really?" Sheer joy and relief lace her voice.

"Yes, of course. Why wouldn't I want to attend with you?"

She laughs softly. "You do realize you would be following me around all night and people will ignore you, right?"

"I understand completely. It also means everyone will know you're with me." Silence falls between us again. "Madeleine?"

"Uh-huh?"

"Not the response you expected?"

She pushes out a harsh breath. "It's what I wanted to hear, but I wasn't sure."

I push the video call button on my phone. Within thirty seconds, her beautiful face fills my screen. "Hi there."

"Hi."

"Allow me to be absolutely clear. Madeleine—I don't know your middle name yet—Wilton, I care about you and would like to court you properly. It will include dates, work functions, lazy Sundays, and everything else we want to add. Still in?"

"Yes, all in. My middle name is Grace. What's yours?"

"Nope, not sharing. Not even Jake and Connor know my middle name." Probably not entirely true since they did my background check for Blackthorne. I didn't purposefully share it though.

"Cross my heart never to share with anyone." She literally crosses her heart.

"Callie?" I question.

"Especially Callie. She tells Connor everything. Plus, we aren't besties. We're friendly and work together for her career, but we don't have Margarita Mondays or any girls' nights."

I laugh. "Fine. I trust you. It's Murphy."

"It isn't awful. Why don't you share it?"

"From what little Betty has shared about my parents, it's my father's name."

"Oh. I'm sorry for pushing." Her shoulders slump a bit.

"Don't be. I caved on my own. What perfume do you wear? I considered snooping but decided against it."

"Usually I wear Acqua di Parma Arancia di Capri. If I'm feeling especially frisky, I wear Kilian Good Girl Gone Bad."

Her response is more intriguing than I anticipated. "I see. How might I tell the difference?"

Her nose wrinkles up. It's endearing.

"You need to spill the details now, gorgeous."

She smirks. "When we first met, I was likely wearing the Acqua. At the wedding and anytime thereafter when I knew we would be together, the Kilian."

"Miss Wilton, are you saying I make you feel frisky?"

Her face turns bright red. "Always."

"I wish you weren't so far away right now."

"Me too."

Pushing away my thoughts, I refocus on the screen, which doesn't help either. Her sleeping attire leaves little to the imagination. She chose a silky set of pajamas with a lace hem in an emerald green. My imagination doesn't need assistance. I have a complete, detailed, mental and tactile picture of every dip and curve of her flawless body. Madeleine could easily be a model if she wasn't a successful talent agent.

"What is your schedule this week?" she asks.

"My client has a luncheon with her agent and a new studio. Then the next evening she has a dinner with a director for a film she's considering."

"What about Thursday and Friday?"

"I have a meeting with Jake and Connor on Thursday morning at ten. Otherwise, I'm free."

"Any reason you can't fly here instead of home?" Her voice decreases in volume as she asks.

"What happened to forward Madeleine?" I quip.

"Christoph, will you come here instead of home?"

"I would love nothing more than time with you. We should get some sleep."

She smiles, but she isn't ready to end this call. "Sleep is overrated."

"Maybe, but the faster we sleep, the sooner we can sleep together."

Her expression perks up a bit at my statement. "Deal. Good night."

"Good night, beautiful. I'll call you tomorrow." With the weight of my feelings now out in the open, I charge my phone and turn in for the night.

CHAPTER FIVE

MADELEINE

At the end of lunch, my assistant Simon enters my office with a large arrangement of flowers. I reel in my excitement. No one has ever sent me flowers to the office before. Well, not a suitor. Clients send them all the time, but these are special. I don't need to look at the card to know Christoph sent them.

"Dare I ask who these stunning boudoir peonies are from?" Of course, Simon knows the type of flower.

"You can ask, Si, but I won't share."

His finger makes a circle around my face. "Oh, Mads. The blush is fierce with this man. You should keep him. Happy and flush looks spectacular on you." As always, Simon doesn't hold back.

"Thanks, Si. It's kind of new. Well, not really."

"The elusive booty call is now the elusive boyfriend?"

I shake my head. I should know better than to say anything at all. Simon handles my schedule with an iron fist. "Thank you for bringing these in. Bye, Simon."

"Fine, Mads. I won't push for more… yet."

"Much appreciated." Once my door snicks closed, I push the privacy screen for the glass and bring the flowers to my nose. The fragrance is light but still lovely.

Me: Thank you. These are gorgeous.

CA: You're welcome.

Me: Did I tell you my favorite color?

CA: No, but my attention to detail is keenly honed.

Me: Yes, it is. Shouldn't you be working right now?

CA: Almost. It's earlier here.

Me: I forgot. I'll talk to you later.

CA: Later, beautiful.

Butterflies threaten in my belly, and I attempt to push them down. Then I realize I don't have to push them away anymore. We are a couple. Smiling, I settle into my chair and revel in how good I feel right now. Luxuriating in my feelings is short-lived when Simon breaks in with an urgent call regarding the launch party of Saturday.

"Good afternoon, Stavros. What is the issue?" He's in the Hamptons setting up for the launch party at his estate.

"Madeleine, thank goodness you're there. Unfortunately, I'm stuck here in the Hamptons until the road reopens—there's some kind of major accident snarling traffic—and one of the vendors for the launch party went out of business effective immediately. I need all the décor from the centerpieces to the VIP suite repurchased today. I would have Regina handle it, but she's here already."

"I'll take care of it, Stavros."

"Thank you. I can always count of you."

I end the call and buzz Simon. "I need a florist to take over the launch party for Stavros on Saturday evening in the Hamptons."

"On it."

Simon is magic. His connections surprise even me. I wouldn't doubt there's a network of high-profile assistants who help each other out in these types of situations. Turning in my chair, I catch a glimpse of my flowers and sigh. I don't know how we'll make this work, but I'm willing to give it everything I have. We may not have started out in a conventional way with phone calls and dates complete with question-and-answer sessions, but I'm excited to do all those things now.

Within an hour, Simon has a consultation set up for me at a downtown florist who has a location in the Hamptons. "Can you have Jack here in time for me to make the appointment? Then I'll go home."

"Already done. Have you chosen your attire for Saturday yet?"

I shake my head.

"I'm thinking the navy suit with the beaded lapels and the Louboutins with the open toe."

"Sounds good to me. I'll check it out when I get home. You should go home too, Si. You work too much. Maybe there's a beau for you to spend time with as well."

"Not at the moment. Only me and Fluffy."

"I'll add it to my to-do list: Find a good man for Simon."

He laughs and returns to his desk. I tidy up my desk and meet Jack in the lobby. While he takes me to the florist, I call Callie.

"Hey, Madi. How are you?"

"I'm well and you?"

"Good, all good." She's hiding something, but I don't have time to press her on it.

"How is the adoption process moving along?"

"Connor and I are approved. We're simply waiting for a child who needs a loving, permanent home."

"I'm so happy for both of you. All set for the Grammys?" I ask, hoping to get this call completed before we arrive.

"As far as I know, we are. Connor and Jake set up the security. I believe Maia and Nolan are joining Christoph. Seems a bit extra in my opinion, but it's their area of expertise."

I shake my head though she can't see me. "It's your first public event since the anniversary performance. It doesn't seem over the top if you ask me."

"Huh. Maybe you're right. I didn't see it from that point of view. When will you be arriving?"

"I'll be there for meetings a day before the show. I'm sure Jake will contact me with your information in plenty of time."

"You're right, Madi. I'm worrying for no reason. I'm sure my husband—still getting used to 'husband'—and Jake are ready like they always have been."

My mind gets stuck on "husband." Does Christoph want to get married? Does he want a family? We don't know very much about one another other than bedroom and food preferences—although our date was stellar without any planning. Honestly, spending time with him is perfect without anything else.

"Madi?"

"Sorry, Cal. Precisely. I need to get inside to a meeting. I'm crazy proud you put the real you out there. Your new album and songs are insane. Old fans and new fans simply love them."

"Thanks, Madi. Are you okay?"

"Yeah, I'm on my way to fix an issue for the launch this weekend. Nothing to worry about. See you soon."

Christoph is detrimental to my focus even when we aren't in the same time zone. I push my thoughts aside and hustle to my meeting for flowers and centerpieces. Three excruciating hours later, I pile back into my car and slump down into the seat.

"That bad, huh?" Jack settles into the driver's seat.

I shake my head. "All it tells me is I want a small, simple wedding. This is for a launch party, not a royal wedding."

Jack smirks. "Knowing what you want is more than half the battle."

"What about you? What was your wedding like?"

A look of nostalgia crosses his face. "Nancy and I eloped at the courthouse and flew to the Bahamas before anyone knew we tied the knot. It was downright perfect."

"See, it can be done." I smile and gaze out the window. As if he heard our conversation, Christoph texts me.

CA: I'm finished for today. Call me when you're free.

Me: I'm headed home. Should be free in an hour.

CA: Perfect. Talk to you then.

Will the flutters always be present when he calls or sends me flowers? I hope so. Learning more about him moves to the top of my to-do list, in addition to finding a partner for Simon. If anyone deserves to be happy, it's Simon. He works tirelessly, never complains when I keep him too long, and his fashion sense is always on point. My scattered thoughts consume my entire ride home.

Jack pulls along the curb and opens my door. "Have a lovely evening, Miss... Madeleine." He escorts me to the lobby door.

"Thank you, Jack. You too."

I grab my mail from the concierge and ride up to my apartment. I pull off my high-heeled shoes as soon as the door clicks closed. A tray of leftover food is warming while I pour a glass of white wine. While I strip out of my work attire and into silky pajamas, I consider waiting to call Christoph until after I eat but decide against it.

CHAPTER SIX

CHRISTOPH

After I escort Miss Forrester to her suite for the rest of the day, I hit the gym. A few miles later, I shower and change after texting Madeleine. Before she agreed to date me, she was on my mind when we were apart. Inexplicably, it's more now. I'm excited to learn everything we haven't shared yet.

A view of her tufted couch fills the screen. "Hi, gorgeous. How was your day?" After some movement, I see a glimpse of her black, silky cami and matching shorts. She has no idea how easily she turns me on, and usually it has nothing to do with sex.

"Hi. It was busy, and I'm glad it's over. The morning went smoothly. Your delivery piqued Simon's interest. Then Stavros sent me on a mission to fix a floral mishap for the launch on Saturday."

"My intention wasn't to reveal more than you wanted to share. I was thinking about you, and I sent flowers. How is your perpetual ray of sunshine?"

"I love them. Simon is great, but too smart for his own good. As you know, I'm a private person. Very few people know many details about me. I barely mentioned anything, and Simon pinned the flowers were from you. Something about the elusive almost-monthly booty call turning into a still elusive boyfriend."

I laugh. "Would you prefer I send them to your apartment?"

"No. Feel free to do whatever you want. You're the first man to ever send me flowers."

"Who have you been dating?"

"It was always me and Estelle. I never wanted to spend time away from her unless it was necessary. Finding a lasting relationship wasn't something I looked for since my last one ended."

"When did it end?" My voice comes out low, even though, now, I have a right to know.

"My last relationship of any consequence ended soon after college. Parker and I were a couple since high school. Everyone seemed to think we would marry, myself included. Once the expectations of running his father's company were thrust at his feet, he changed almost overnight. My attentive, loving guy was gone, replaced by a man with a short temper and no time for me. It took me a month to gather the courage to walk away. Since then, no one has lasted more than a few dates, until you."

"Because of your ambition and success?"

"How do you see me with such clarity?"

"I see the private you, always have. You command attention and respect the second you walk into a room, from men and women alike. The woman who was forward enough to ask me to share a drink is the woman I always see. Maybe it's because I have the same walls as you. Perhaps it's our similar childhoods. Whatever the reason, I see all of you. I have no problem not being the more powerful or successful person in a relationship. Hell, I spend my workdays and nights escorting rich and famous people to and from events to protect them from the public. True, they have more money, but otherwise, they're people with insecurities, hang-ups, and flaws like everyone else. They simply have the means to hide them. You have never been able to hide your true self from me. Have you tried?"

"No, I never felt as if I needed to with you."

"You don't." I never hid anything from her.

"How was the luncheon?"

"Boring, exactly how I like them. My client is overly cautious due to some stalker issues in the past few years. Dinner tomorrow will likely be the same."

"Good. Are you flying out after the dinner or in the morning?"

"I wanted to talk to you first. Generally, I prefer to go home once my client is safely tucked away. Normally, I go home to an empty condo. This time is different. As much as I want the time with you, even asleep, I respect I'm going into your home in the early hours of the morning."

Her face gives nothing away. "I meant all in when I said it."

"Okay. I'll fly there immediately after the client's event."

A smile graces her gorgeous face.

"What about you? When was your last relationship?"

"I met Lucy in high school, but her parents forbade her from seeing me because I lived with Betty. To her parents, a nuclear family was required for success. Lucy was a rebel. We started sneaking around as often as possible. For three years we hung out, but never labelled what it was. There was no way a girl like her would ever go public with a guy like me."

"What does that mean?" The anger in her voice is evident.

"Her family was rich, and mine wasn't. They would never accept me as good enough for their daughter had I been given the chance to meet them."

"That's awful."

"Maybe, but true nonetheless. As you know, I served with Connor and Jake. When I enlisted, she cut all ties with me until about five years later. She reached out and apologized for her behavior and was looking for a chance to rekindle whatever we had. At the time, I wasn't going to be stateside anytime soon, and I shared the information with her. I never heard from her again."

"I haven't met her, and I despise her."

"She made her choice, and it wasn't me. Since then, no one has made it more than a date or two, except you."

"Thank you for taking a chance with me."

"I should be thanking you. You opened the door for there to be an us."

She laughs and takes a sip of her wine. Watching her tongue lick the stray drop off the rim of the glass stops my thoughts and makes my heart rate spike.

"You can't do things like that when I can't touch you."

"Do what?" Her voice sounds innocent and sweet.

It wasn't purposeful. Damn! "Never mind." I shift in my seat and hope she doesn't notice.

Fire in her eyes flies through the screen. "What did I do to make you uncomfortable?"

"Uncomfortable, not exactly." *Not the kind I'm willing to discuss right now.* "Wishing I could taste the wine you licked off the glass with your tongue, absolutely."

Redness creeps into her cheeks. "I'll try to pay more attention."

"Don't, especially when I'm close enough to kiss you. I want the you I see. The you you hide from the rest of the world."

Her eyes widen, and she attempts to speak but fails twice. "I'm not sure of the appropriate response."

"You don't have to say anything."

She shakes her head. "I do. You make me feel unbalanced, but in a good way. I'm sure it doesn't make sense. Professional me takes no prisoners. I get the best deal for my client, which in turn makes me successful. Private me is more reserved. I rarely go after what I want…." Her gaze pins to mine.

I would give almost anything to be beside her right now. To take her into my arms and kiss her breathless.

"Until you." She attempts to stifle a yawn and fails miserably.

"Get some sleep. I'll be there as soon as I can tomorrow night."

She nods. "Good night."

"Good night, beautiful." I end the call and amble to bed. The moment my head hits the pillow, my phone rings again with Jake's designated ringtone.

"Yeah, Jake?"

"Hey. I'm sorry for calling so late, but Blaine found some more info."

Now I'm on high alert. "Meaning?"

"According to this report, someone has been stalking you for quite some time."

"I've missed tails? Impossible!"

"No, you haven't missed tails. They're following you digitally through published photos with clients."

Is Madeleine safe? "Is Betty safe?"

"Yes. As far as Blaine can tell, they're actively searching for only you."

"Can you have him monitor Madeleine too?"

"I assume your relationship status with Madeleine has changed since we last spoke."

"Yes. Does he have any idea who?"

"I'll have Blaine monitor the three of you. He's still working on the who and why. When do you plan to see her again? What do you plan to tell her?"

His question is for information only. He's my boss and my friend. He knows my schedule. "I'm going to see her tomorrow after my job ends with Miss Forrester. I'll be available for our meeting by phone or video conference if necessary. I'm not telling her anything yet. As far as I know, she's perfectly safe. I'll be with her as much as I can in case the situation changes."

"Okay."

I drag my fingers through my hair. My heart falls to my toes. "Am I putting her at risk?"

"Nothing in this information points in that direction."

The information Jake provides doesn't loosen the knot in my stomach. "Jake, give it to me straight. If we were talking about Norah, what would you do?"

"The only way I feel comfortable is when Norah is within arm's reach, even now with no threat."

"I'll get to her as soon as I can. Please call if Blaine finds anything else, day or night."

"Of course. I'm sure it will be nearly impossible, but try to get some sleep," Jake suggests.

"I'll do my best." I barely resist the urge to call Madeleine and wake her. There's nothing I can do from here. My mind is racing. Jake said she's fine, yet I'm still worried for her safety—her and Betty. It's a foreign feeling, worrying about someone other than Betty who isn't a client. It's unnerving but not unwelcome. The bigger question is who's following me and why.

I mentally run through my list of clients and come up empty. Jake vets each client thoroughly before taking a contract. True, we are hired to protect them, but never once has anyone been injured or, worse, in our care. Nothing from my time in the service would lead to anything like this. The only remaining potential culprit is my family.

I consider calling Betty to dig for more information, but I don't want to wake her either. Truthfully, I haven't asked about my family because I don't want to know. Betty raised me, and she's my family. I have no interest in my biological parents. They wanted nothing to do with me from the time I was about a month old. With nothing left to do but try to get some sleep, I flop onto the soft bedding and close my eyes despite knowing rest won't come.

CHAPTER SEVEN

MADELEINE

My alarm hits differently this morning knowing Christoph will be back tonight—late tonight, but still we'll be in the same time zone. I hurry through my morning routine, including a short yoga session, and get into the office early. I have three contracts to finish negotiating and a meeting with Stavros about my yearly review.

"Morning, Si."

"Morning, Mads. You're awfully chipper this morning. Were you alone last night?"

I cast a sideways glance at him as he follows me into my office. "You know my schedule, so what do you think?"

"Your response would lead me to believe you were alone, but it wouldn't explain your smile and overall demeanor."

"Take it for what it is, Si. I have a lot of work to do today. Please give me a warning twenty minutes before my meeting with Stavros."

"You got it." He closes the door behind him.

I settle into my cushy chair and make my first call of the day. "Jimmy, how are you?" I don't wait for his reply. "Good. I'm calling about the dressing room clause and the access to my client in your proposed contract for the venue in Denver."

"Madeleine, you know I can't give you want you want for Lady M."

I shake my head. "Yes, you can, and you will or she won't play at your venue. You're the sole holdout for the entire tour, Jimmy. She doesn't need to make this stop. My client has already conceded the number of seats you plan to provide. You can make sure she gets what she needs backstage."

"What does she absolutely need?" His voice comes out resigned.

"She needs a dressing room at least twelve feet by twelve feet to accommodate the costume changes and her stylists. Lady M will attend a meet and greet with fans before her show for two hours, not three. Final offer or she removes Denver from her tour stops."

He huffs through the phone. "I'll get you a final answer by close of business today."

"Thank you, Jimmy. You won't regret it."

He grumbles something I can't make out before he ends the call.

I spin in my chair and take in the cityscape out my window. There's only one view better than this one, and Stavros won't be giving it up anytime soon. My cell buzzes on my desk.

CA: Good morning. How many contracts have you slayed so far?

Me: Morning. LOL. Only one so far, but two on deck.

CA: I have no doubt you can secure what your clients need.

Me: I'll do my best. I can't wait to see you.

CA: Me too. Crush those contracts. I'll be there as soon as I can.
Me: Deal.

I turn back to my desk and tackle both contract calls before my meeting with Stavros. I've secured the necessary changes for these two contracts. I'm still waiting on Jimmy to confirm the third.

"Mads, this is your twenty-minute warning," Simon croons through the intercom.

I grin. "Thanks, Si. Could you order a late lunch for me in an hour?"

"I've got you."

"You're the best, Simon."

"Awww, you love me. You really love me." Simon mimics Jim Carrey from *The Mask*.

I shake my head and gather the files for my meeting. Once outside his office, I knock on the doorframe because his assistant isn't at her desk. Stavros waves me in and ends his call.

"Madeleine, thank you for coming."

"Of course. I brought the active files you requested."

He shakes his head, passes behind me, and closes his office door but leaves the glass clear. "You can set those down. It was a ruse, so to speak. I won't keep you in suspense. I'm retiring in three months. I want you to replace me."

OMG! Ohmigod! Clearly, I knew Stavros was older and at some point would retire, but I didn't think it would be this soon. "Thank you. I'm floored."

"You earned it. I've never met anyone as tenacious as you for their clients."

"I assume this is hush-hush for now."

Stavros shakes his head. "Yes, at this point, only those in this room and my wife are aware."

"When do you plan to share this wider? Where would I be based?" Concern ricochets through me. New York is already far enough from Maryland. *Wait, what? Of course, he would cross my mind.* The other offices are in Los Angeles and Washington D.C. *Focus!* This is a huge promotion.

"I want to take some time to bring you up to speed and figure out the best base for you. I chose New York, but it may not be the right fit for you."

"Thank you again. I'm ecstatic!"

"As you should be. I appreciate your discretion. We want to do this properly and preserve continuity as best as possible."

"Of course."

The intercom breaks our conversation. "Mr. Scala, your wife is on line two. She indicates it's urgent."

"We'll talk more soon, Madeleine."

I nod and leave his office. Balancing my giddiness with my concern about the possibility of moving clear across the country is tempering my reaction a bit. I take the long way back to my office simply because Simon will know something is up based on my demeanor.

"Your meeting was short. Your lunch will be here in twenty minutes," Simon informs me as I pass by.

"Thanks, Si."

"I got you, Mads."

I close myself inside my office, blur the glass, and consider this epic promotion. My time to ponder my newfound fortune is short-lived. I have more clients who need updated contracts. Three hours later and a coffee drop-off from Simon, I have successfully negotiated updated contracts and riders for two additional clients today instead of tomorrow.

Near six, I close my laptop and wrap up for the day. A secret celebratory glass of wine and some decadent sheet time with Christoph is in my future. Well, in the morning hopefully. Tonight sleeping some of the night curled against him is more than enough.

Wine poured and power suit dropped in the laundry, I curl up on my terrace and revel in my insane news.

Me: Please wake me when you get here. I have big news.

CA: I would prefer to slide into your luxurious sheets and around you without waking you.

Me: Not a chance. I need to kiss you so much I ache.

CA: I was being respectful. I'll accept as many kisses as you want to give.

CA: I'm coming for you, Madeleine.

Me: I'm waiting.

I polish off my glass of cabernet and turn in for the night. If I attempt to stay awake, I'll fail miserably. I set my head on my pillow and allow myself to drift off to sleep knowing in a few hours, I won't be alone anymore.

CHAPTER EIGHT

CHRISTOPH

Every moment we're apart seems like an eternity since we decided to move forward as a couple.

The flight attendant finally finishes the deplaning announcements. Thankfully, I only use a carry-on when I travel for Blackthorne. I sprint to my uber, one stop closer to her. Near two in the morning, the car pulls along the curb. I ride the elevator to her apartment, disarm her alarm, reengage it, and move toward her.

At the threshold of the master bedroom, I pause to take her in. Her long locks are spread across her pillow, the sheet draped over her hips, and the thin strap of her lace and silk pajamas is halfway down her left arm. I strip off my clothes and round the bed. She shifts, and her sky-colored eyes flutter open.

"Hi."

"Hi." I lift the sheet and slide into her huge bed behind her. I press a kiss to her bare shoulder and raise the strap of her camisole back up.

A soft moan surrounds me as she snuggles deeper into my arms. "I missed you."

"I missed you too. Go back to sleep. You're stuck with me now."

"Not stuck at all." Her voice trails off, and her breathing shallows.

I catalog her curves against me and fall asleep. Barely four hours later, I wake in the exact same position. Only now I plan to wake her with my mouth. Adding enough space between us, I start at the nape of her neck and kiss along the back of her shoulders. She tries to squirm away, but I brand her left hip with my fingers.

"A girl could get used to being taken care of in the morning. I love waking up with you knowing you don't have to leave."

"Every morning?" I push up on my arm but maintain my hold on her.

She cranes her neck to look back at me. "Not *every* morning. A girl needs her beauty sleep."

"You don't. You're stunning."

"You don't need to compliment me. I'm a sure thing."

This woman. "You're mine now. You deserve to hear it frequently. Not only because it's true, but it's how I feel."

The look in her eyes changes. She very well may be in this as deep as I am. I grip the hem of her camisole and tug it over her head. Then I lower back down to the bed and continue my quest to kiss every inch of her skin. I crisscross down her toned back to the curve of her ass before climbing over her and drawing her shorts and panties down her long, sexy legs.

"You're going to make me late for work, aren't you?"

I grin against her hip, moving downward. "I'll stop exploring your gorgeous body if you need to get to work on time."

"No, hell no. I'm soaked with need, and my body is aching."

"How soaked?"

She sighs heavily. Despite my intention to continue down to her toes, I bracket her waist and lift her to her knees. I draw the flat of my tongue along her folds. Goose bumps erupt across her skin.

She wasn't lying. "What's different this time?" Before waiting for an answer, I taste her again and again.

She casts a look over her shoulder after I plunge two fingers into her center. Desire clouds her eyes. "I don't know, but don't stop." Her voice comes out desperate and needy.

As if I would stop. Giving her pleasure is equally as pleasurable for me. Her muscles tighten around my fingers, and her nub pulses against my thumb.

"Christoph!" My name falling from her pouty lips in the throes of passion is a shot to my heart, especially now. Now I know we could make us work long-term.

As the waves of her climax diminish to ripples, I withdraw my fingers, shuck my boxer briefs, and slide into her hot core to the root. When I thrust forward, she pushes back. In a perfect rhythm, we chase our release.

"You feel so good."

I swipe my fingers between us and soak them with our combined arousal. "Baby?" Our sheet time is adventurous to say the least, but I always ask first.

"Yes, fill me." Her voice sounds like a plea for relief.

I push two fingers into her tight hole and fall back into a tantalizing rhythm until she clenches around me. Spirals of pleasure take hold of me from the base of my spine as I explode inside her. Every time we're together, it's nothing short of spectacular. Yet somehow this felt different, bigger as if it were more than before. The only difference is she's mine, and I can't wait for everyone to know. I withdraw slowly, gather her against me, and lower us to the bed on our sides.

"You make me wish I could play hooky."

I press a kiss to the sweet spot behind her ear and whisper, "I wouldn't be opposed to spending the entire day in bed with you."

"Can we plan for it on Sunday?"

"I'm in. What time do you need to leave for work? I'm asking because I know playing hooky truly isn't an option."

She twists to check the clock. "I need to leave in a little over an hour. My first appointment is at eleven today. The later I am, the more questions Simon will ask though."

"Tell him I rocked your world and you couldn't bear to leave me alone longer than necessary."

A breathtaking smile graces her face. "While your statement is true, I won't share with Simon."

"I appreciate your boundaries. What was the big news you needed to share?"

She lights up again. "You are sworn to secrecy. I'm not supposed to share with anyone. I'll cut you off if this gets out and I can trace it back to you."

Damn! "I didn't know you had a sadistic streak."

She laughs. "I don't, but this is a big deal, and I don't want to mess it up."

I would never betray her trust. "The secret you're about to share is safe with me."

"Stavros is retiring in three months, and he handpicked me to replace him."

"That's huge, gorgeous! Congratulations!" I turn, hover over her, and lower my lips to hers. She opens for me, and I kiss her breathless like I plan to each day as long as she'll have me. I draw her lower lip between my teeth and bite lightly.

She groans. "You know what it does to me."

"I do. I don't want you to forget about me while we're apart today." I grin at her.

"There's no chance, not with the burn from your stubble on my inner thighs."

"I kind of dig when you share exactly what you feel. No, I kind of love it."

"Good. You won't like this next part though. I need to get into the shower like ten minutes ago."

"I know, sweetness. Go, I'll make you breakfast." If she's surprised, it doesn't show. Reluctantly, I rock back onto my heels and allow her to move into her bathroom. Her walking away from me naked is branded forever in my mind.

I pull on my clothes and pad to the kitchen. Thankfully, my phone has been silent since I arrived incredibly early this morning. I'm sure Jake will wait until our meeting to update me. I peruse her barren fridge and start on a veggie scramble. It's pretty much all I can make with the options she has. I'll order some groceries later and prepare a celebratory dinner for her.

When I turn back to the island, she appears wearing a red sheath dress and sexy-as-hell heels that make her legs look a mile long. My instinct is to throw her over my shoulder and strip the suit from her body and make love to her again. I know it isn't an option, but it's still what I want.

"You can't look at me like you want to devour me," she accuses.

"You look sexy as sin, and I want to devour you excruciatingly slow. Can't though or your food will get cold." I set the plate and a cup of coffee in front of her.

"Thanks."

"You're welcome." We finish eating in silence, and she rushes out the door. I fix her bed and luxuriate in her massive shower. Carrara marble adorns the walls for the double shower with a rainforest showerhead and wall jets too. I have minutes to spare after ordering some groceries to make my meeting with Jake and Connor.

The laptop alerts me one of them joined the call.

"Hey, Connor."

"Morning. Where are you?"

I turn and see the cityscape through the French doors leading to her terrace. "At Madeleine's."

He cocks an eyebrow but says nothing else.

"How are the plans for the Grammys?" I ask to move away from his unstated opinion as to why I'm at Madeleine's.

"It may be over the top, but I plan to have you, Maia, and Nolan with us."

I shake my head. "You have to do what makes you comfortable. It could go either way. Three plus you seems sufficient for the event and the afterparty if she still wants to attend."

"Thanks. Are you going to say anything about your current location?"

"No—"

"Hey, guys, sorry I'm late," Jake interrupts.

"No problem. I was grilling Christoph on his current location."

"Nice view," Jake adds.

I shake my head. "Can we address what we need to, not my relationship status or where my other half happens to live?"

Silence settles. I replay my words in my head and... *They're never going to gloss over my words.* "Go ahead. Get it over with. I said '*my.*' Is it accurate? Not yet, but it could be. I want it to be."

"I've got nothing more to say than what I already said the other day. C, what about you?" Jake asks.

"I've got nothing other than I'm happy for you," Connor replies.

"Thanks. I appreciate it. Do you have an update from Blaine?"

Jake shuffles the papers in front of him. "As far as he can tell, someone paid a midgrade private investigator to locate and surveil you digitally. Neither Madeleine nor Betty have been searched. The PI must think Madeleine is a client. I suppose it isn't an awful assumption. It makes her less interesting."

"It puts her at risk. I let her go to the office alone."

Connor smirks. "You let her?"

"Couldn't keep your comment to yourself?"

"No, not a chance. Madeleine isn't at risk," Jake assures me. "Our clients roam about freely when their events are private. Her going to work isn't a public thing. Are you attending the launch on Saturday?"

I shake my head. "How do you know about the launch party?"

"Callie."

Madeleine was right. Callie shares everything with her husband. "Yes, I'm going. What can I do?"

"Personally, don't do anything rash. Use cash when you can and don't go out unnecessarily. If you do go out with Madeleine, it wouldn't hurt to act as if she's a client you're interested in. It'll keep up the ruse if the PI genuinely believes she's a Blackthorne client," Jake suggests.

"Do I need to tell her?"

"No," both men answer unequivocally.

Yet I'm still not sure it's the right call. We go over my schedule for the next few weeks, which includes the Grammys with Callie and then a stint in Maine to be available in case something goes wrong while all husbands go on a deep-sea fishing expedition. I don't foresee any issues. All the threats to any of them have been eliminated more than a year ago. Considering my growing feelings for Madeleine, I understand why the guys are willing to go toe-to-toe with their wives to allow my local presence, just in case. Despite their substantial wealth, it'll still take half a day to get back home at best.

"You good, man?" Connor asks.

"Yeah. I need to know who is searching for me and why now. My life isn't interesting." *Until Madeleine made me feel like a real family is a possibility for someone with a childhood like mine.*

"I understand your perspective. Someone is clearly interested enough to pay for the information. Blaine will find out what you need to know. I'll update you as soon I know more. If you need anything from the condo, have Gemma send it to you."

"Thanks, Jake. I'll call her." More clothes from home would be a good thing, especially if I'm staying here until my next job. I'm crazy excited about more time with Madeleine.

"See you in L.A, Connor." After the call ends, I inform the concierge about the order of groceries.

"I'll send them up when they arrive, Mr. Anderson."

"Thank you." I consider what to do with the rest of my day. First, I need information, and only one person can give it to me without ruining my plans.

"Good morning, Scala Talent Agency. How may I direct your call?"

"Morning, Simon Dumont, please."

"One moment, sir."

After a brief stint with classic hold music, Simon answers. "Good morning, Madeleine Wilton's office. How may I help you?"

"Good morning, Simon. This is Christoph Anderson."

I hear giddiness in his response. "Nice to connect a voice to a name on her calendar, Mr. Anderson. Would you like to speak with the boss lady?"

"Not right now, actually. I need your help."

"Ooooh! I love subterfuge for a noble cause. What can I do?"

"I'm planning an intimate dinner for tonight. What time is her last appointment?"

I hear Simon tapping away. "Her last appointment today is at three but block…. Please hold one moment, sir." The classical music abruptly returns. Within two minutes, he returns to the line. "Sorry for the interruption."

"No problem."

"It's blocked off for two hours. It shouldn't take the entire scheduled time, but I can make sure to shoo her out the door within thirty minutes of it ending. It'll take an hour to get her home. Jack is good, but no match for uptown traffic. You're looking at 6:30 at the earliest."

"Thanks, Simon. Mum's the word."

I imagine him zipping his lips shut. "You've got it. Anything else?"

"Not for today. She's lucky to have you."

"I could say the same for you. She's less edgy, at least with me."

I smile. "Thank you. I appreciate your help."

"My pleasure."

I end the call and lace up for a long run around Central Park. After showering, I start preparing dinner.

CHAPTER NINE

MADELEINE

My workday drags on. I have one more appointment, and then I can go home. The fact a chiseled, blue-eyed man will be waiting seems to make the time pass slower. Is this what it feels like to be balanced with work and home? I truly love it.

"Mads, Ms. Mayhew is on line three."

"Thanks, Si. I hope to finish this up in less than the blocked-off time."

"Of course you can. You're a rock star."

"Flattery will get you far, Si, even if you aren't interested in me."

"If I were straight, I would be. You don't need me. Mr. Peonies is doing an excellent job making you happy."

Yes, he is. I smile and take the call. "Ms. Mayhew. Thank you for taking my call. I've spoken with my client. He understands how the producers feel his behavior is unacceptable but doesn't believe it rises to the level of breaking the conduct clause in his contract with your production company."

"Madeleine, we've worked together before, and this isn't the first time your client has made a significant misstep."

"I'm aware. However, you knew he wasn't a boy scout when you signed him. It's why the clause is in his contract. The clause requires him to show up on time for filming days, keep his composure with his costars, and maintain a clean image in the press. He's done everything to the letter." Mikhail is a gorgeous action star, but his behavior doesn't become his status. He's a playboy and a demanding man. He's gotten into enough scrapes with the press and his costars, which caused the production company to require a behavior clause for this film.

"You have got to be kidding me, Madeleine. He danced on top of a bar with his costars."

I smirk even though Beatrice can't see me. "You said the keyword, Bea. *With.* He was dancing with his costars. Nothing about his behavior over the weekend rises to the level of termination in the contract as worded."

"The producers aren't happy," Bea presses.

I shake my head. "For the first time since I started representing him, Mikhail has done nothing wrong. If the producers need to speak with me, fine, but he toed the line and doesn't deserve to be fired."

"I'll see what I can do, Madeleine. How much longer will you be at the office this evening?"

I consider saying I'll be available, but don't. My life outside of these walls is worth getting home to now, and I'm not willing to encroach on it. "I'm leaving as soon as we're done." I pull up my calendar. "I have an opening tomorrow morning at eleven. Otherwise, my next opening is next Wednesday at eight in the morning before I travel."

"Good evening, Madeleine."

I end the call and close out my email for the day. I settle into the car after greeting Jack and let the day melt away during my ride home.

When we arrive, Jack opens my door. "Have a great evening, Madeleine."

"You as well, Jack."

I step into the lobby, and the concierge greets me. "Good evening, Miss Wilton."

"Good evening."

"This arrived for you this afternoon." Theo hands me an ivory envelope and a single rose.

"Thank you." I accept them and step into the elevator. As I open the envelope, I smell the rose. Being taken care of and romanced is…. I didn't know what I was missing. Christoph is damn good at it. The envelope contains an invitation to an intimate dinner this evening.

I open the door to my apartment, and I'm greeted by Christoph. He takes my attaché case and handbag and sets them on the island. Then he presents more flowers and a sensual kiss, which knocks me on my heels.

Then he adds some space between us. "Hi. How was slaying contracts and squeezing every incentive out of your opponents today?"

I smile. "Not too bad. I think Mikhail might be able to keep his major movie role. I didn't stay to find out though. I came home instead."

"Good for you."

I eliminate the space he added between us. My body melts into his as if it were my sole purpose. "You're very good for my work-life balance. I really love having you here. Though I'm afraid to get used to it."

"I love being here. I would say don't be afraid, but I am too, for different reasons. I'm in, all in, to navigate this with you."

I nod. "What smells delicious?"

"Dinner. Do you want to change?"

I pull back and brush my lips across his. "If I change, we won't eat. Plus, you're dressed too." He looks sinful in black slacks and a crisp, white dress shirt with the sleeves rolled up to show off his muscled forearms.

"That's disturbingly accurate." With an arm around my waist, he guides me into the kitchen, and we put water into a vase. While I snip the ends and arrange the flowers, he pours two glasses of white wine.

"Can you carry these, and I'll bring out our salads?"

"I can, but there's a small carrying fee."

He grins at me. "If you want a kiss, you can take one or ten."

I press my lips to his, scoop up the wine, and wink at him over my shoulder. I attempt to set the glasses at the dining room table, but he stops me.

"We're eating outside," he informs me.

When I step onto my private terrace, I'm floored. The table is set with a floral centerpiece, my dishware is in an arrangement I would've never thought of, and string lights hang on the pergola. "This is gorgeous. You didn't have to go to all this trouble for one dinner."

"It wasn't any trouble. I like taking care of you. Gram taught me to cook and made sure I knew it was the best way to show someone you care. Also, I'm fairly certain you don't eat well when you're alone."

"Betty is a wise woman. You're not wrong." It's impossible for me to fathom. He's everything he seems and so much more. I can't wait to learn the more part. Yet I'm terrified.

"She's the best. She can't wait to meet you."

I wrinkle my nose. "Betty knows about me?"

"I told her about you before I got home from Atlanta."

I told Estelle at the same time. "Really?"

"Yes. I've never felt drawn to any woman like I am to you, and we only shook hands. The same feeling, only stronger, happened when I saw you at the wedding. Every time since then it…."

"Increases," I supply.

"Exactly."

"What other hidden talents do you possess, Mr. Anderson?"

He laughs. "If you're impressed by the salad, wait until you actually eat dinner and dessert."

Sheer glee courses through me. I believed him when he said we could do this. Now we need to put in the work. After polishing off our salads, Christoph presents chicken with marsala risotto and roasted asparagus.

I savor the first bite. The appreciative moan falling from my lips earns me a smirk across the table.

"It's awful, isn't it?"

I laugh softly. "No, it's perfect. Do you cook like this for yourself?"

"No. In fact, I've only cooked for you and Betty. I refuse to let her cook for me after handling it my entire life. Although, there are some recipes she's much better at then me."

I'm intrigued. "Such as?"

A sheepish smile crosses his face. "I can cook. Baking, not so much."

"You said you made dessert."

He shakes his head. "I did, but if any part of this meal flops, it'll be dessert."

"I have confidence in your baking even if you fail. This meal is delicious." I lean over and kiss him softly.

He drags his thumb across my lips. "Thank you. Do you have any hobbies?"

Only Estelle knows my passion hobbies. "I have two actually. I take photos, and I'm an avid stargazer."

"Those hobbies must be difficult in the city. Do you photograph landscapes, people, something else?"

"They are. Most of my photos are landscapes, but I have photographed people as well, usually when they're unsuspecting. The photography is more difficult because I don't like people in my personal space. Renting a studio for the limited amount of time I have to spend on my hobby isn't a wise business decision."

"Will you share some with me?"

My chest tightens, and my heart beats harder and faster. He truly sees me. "Sure."

"Madeleine, it's fine if you don't want to."

Clearly, he heard the hesitance in my response. "It isn't you. It's me."

Christoph turns our chairs so we're facing one another. He slides forward, brackets my waist, and pulls me into his arms. "Please explain."

"We... this"–I motion back and forth between us–"scares me. How I feel scares me."

"Good."

I lift an eyebrow, link my fingers around his neck, and lean back to look at him directly. "Good?"

"If it isn't scary, it isn't worth chasing. Weren't you scared out of your mind to pipe music into Stavros's car or change his ringtone?"

"Of course, but this is different."

He cups my face with his hands and skims his lips across mine. "Why, gorgeous?"

"This isn't only about me. It's both of us. How can we possibly know what we're doing given the examples we have?" His hold on me tightens more. Ignoring his delicious scent and how I feel safe and cared for despite this vulnerable conversation is increasingly difficult.

"Gram may have raised me mostly on her own, but I remember Gramps. I remember the way they looked at one another despite my age. I saw it in the photos around my childhood home every single day. We have current examples too."

"Like who?" My voice comes out soft and barely audible.

"Jake and Connor have each successfully found a wife who makes them better men. You haven't met them yet, but their parents are also excellent examples of stable, long-lasting marriages. Did you ever meet your grandfather, Estelle's husband?"

A flicker of sadness passes through my mind.

"You don't have to tell me."

Damn him and his observation skills. "You should know the reasons why I'm scared. It's… everything about you breaks the hard armor I put up when I leave my private space. No one else has ever made a hairline crack. You cracked me open with one touch, only you didn't know."

"I felt it then. I still do."

I take a deep breath. "Gramps left with my parents. As Estelle tells it, something about making a killing in real estate and promises of money within a month. As far as I know, my parents, Gramps, and Grams went destitute. Ironically, the plan was for them to live like this and come back for me and Grams. Did they live like this?" I motion to my luxury apartment and clothes. "No, not even close, but Grams does now as much as she'll let me pay for things."

"Can you promise me one thing?"

Anything. "What?"

"Always tell me when you're scared. If we're honest with one another, we can figure out the best way forward together."

"I will. Will you promise the same?"

"Absolutely. I would never ask something of you I wouldn't agree to myself."

I curl deeper into his embrace, which I didn't think was possible for a long while. No man has ever made me believe a strong, stable, long-term relationship was possible. I have no reason to doubt Christoph.

He has done everything, and more, than he promises every single day. His lips press against my forehead.

I never realized how intimate a forehead kiss feels.

"Dessert or sleep?" he murmurs against my skin.

I smile and lift my gaze to his. "Dessert in bed, then sleep?" I suggest.

"Perfect plan."

We hurriedly clean the dishes, change, and eat almond tangerine panna cotta in bed.

"I think you may be shortchanging your baking prowess, babe."

"Nah, I got lucky this time."

Maybe so, but I appreciate it nonetheless.

CHAPTER TEN

CHRISTOPH

We're leaving in the morning for an event this evening. The ride to Stavros's Hamptons estate will take about three hours, maybe more with traffic.

"Ready?" Her voice sounds shaky, and she's fidgeting.

I draw her against me and set my lips on the curve of her neck. "Breathe, beautiful. Why are you nervous?"

She whispers, "I've never brought anyone to a work event before. Are you sure you don't mind following me around and being ignored by almost everyone?"

I grin at her. "Only two people matter outside of us tonight, Stavros and Simon. I'm secure enough in who we are and in myself to follow around my smoking-hot, successful girlfriend at her high-profile work event."

After the shock dissipates from her face, she kisses me lightly and drops a set of keys in my hand.

I foolishly assumed Madeleine didn't have a car because she uses a car service in the city, which I vetted once I learned about it. "I'm driving?"

"I don't let *anyone* drive my car. Will you drive?"

"Sure. Do you not like driving?"

"I don't dislike it, but it's our first opportunity to ride together."

Whether it's traditional couple norms or she prefers being a passenger, I'm driving. I grab her bags and follow her to the garage. She stops next to a white Audi RS 5 Coupe. My surprise must be evident on my face.

"Not what you expected?"

I shake my head. "I'm not sure what I expected. Honestly, I'm surprised you have a car at all." I open the trunk and set the bags inside and then open her door.

"Thank you."

"You're welcome." I'll always hold the door for her. Yet when she wears a dress that rides up her toned thighs a bit higher when she sits like the fitted sheath dress she's wearing now, the view is worth as much as her appreciation of my manners. Of all things, Betty made sure my manners are impeccable. I know which fork to use at a formal dinner. She taught me using the scene from *Pretty Woman.* I round the car and slide into the butter-soft leather seats and start her car.

She inputs the directions, and we set off for an overnight in the Hamptons. Despite my work with the rich and famous, I've never been there before. Once we're out of the city, the traffic eases a bit but then comes to a screeching halt in Queens. Her foot is tapping on the floor mat the longer we fail to move closer to our destination. It's been about thirty minutes of standstill traffic at this point. I set my hand on her leg right above her knee. Her eyes snap to mine.

"We'll get there in plenty of time for you to check everything and change."

"Okay."

I slide my hand up a little higher, and she relaxes a bit more. An inch further and her eyes flutter closed. I haven't touched her yet, and her body is vibrating with need.

She lifts her hips off the seat as I push the fabric higher, baring her to me.

"No panties?" It isn't the first time I've found her bare beneath her clothes, but I wasn't expecting it for a work function. She's going to keep me on my toes.

She shrugs and drops her hand between her thighs, her thumb drawing circles around her already swollen nub. I bury two fingers into her hot, wet core and move with her. Madeleine tightens around me as I add a third finger and grinds against my hand.

"Chris… oh my…." Shudders course through her as her release crests. Her muscles clench around my fingers in taut waves, then slowly loosen into ripples. Her rocking slows, and her breathing regulates. "Never did that before."

As I withdraw my fingers, she grasps my hand and sucks my fingers into her mouth one by one. *Holy fuck!* She's never done that before. "I've seen you get yourself off before when we were apart."

Somehow her faces flushes more red. She bows off the seat again and adjusts her dress. "Not what I meant. Our video chat when you were in

New Orleans was exceptionally satisfying considering you never touched me."

"I completely agree. What do you mean never before?"

"This was the first sexual anything I did in a car."

I raise an eyebrow. "No making out after a date, nothing?"

"Nope."

My mind is now spinning with options and dark, private places I can park her car and have my naughty way with her. Unfortunately I don't know any on Long Island.

"Where did your mind go?"

I consider keeping my dirty thoughts to myself, but I share them anyway. Nothing about our sheet time would lead me to believe my musing would be over the top. "I want to find a dark, private, secure spot to strip you down and have sex in your car."

Her eyes widen as her gaze rises from my cock straining against my pants. "I'm game whenever you find such a spot."

"I'll hold you to that."

Her voice is raspy and nearly desperate despite her recent orgasm. "Please do."

Less than an hour later, I pull in front of a monstrous mansion with the most spectacular water view I've ever seen. I open her door and offer her a hand up.

"It's stunning, isn't it?" Madeleine asks, gazing out at the ocean.

"You are." I wrap my arm around her waist and draw her against me.

"Thank you."

Dropping my lips near her ear, I promise, "I'll say it every day until you believe me without a doubt."

"I believe you. I'm just not used to hearing it."

I drag my tongue along the shell of her ear. "How do you feel about public displays of affection at a business function?"

Surprise graces her flawless skin as she pulls back to look at me. "I'm not against it, but we need to keep in mind the people around us and the top-secret info."

"I'm glad you're taking some of the weight of our mutual lack of self-control in the bedroom."

She laughs softly. "And my car."

"I'm just getting started with your car."

Her hands fan her face. I offer her my arm, and we step into Stavros's Hamptons home. Immediately, we're greeted by his staff.

"Miss Wilton, right this way." The butler leads us to the backyard. After pointing Madeleine to the planner, he addresses me. "Mr. Anderson, would you care for a drink?"

"Thank you. I'll take a water and one for Miss Wilton as well, please."

"Of course, sir."

I nod and move closer to Madeleine.

It would be a lie for me to say I haven't done my research on her boss. His agency grossed the most money for its clients for the last ten years worldwide.

The moment Stavros steps into the room, he calls out to her.

"Madeleine, thank you for coming early. I appreciate your attention to the last-minute details for my event."

"Of course. Stavros, Christoph Anderson. Christoph, my boss, Stavros Scala." Stavros is a short, portly man with thinning hair—although most people are shorter than me. I love how tall Madeleine is. Our mouths align when she has her highest heels on.

"Pleasure to meet you, Mr. Anderson. I would say I'm surprised I haven't heard about you, but Madeleine maintains a hard line between her professional and personal life."

"Likewise." I don't plan to address the details about our relationship with her boss.

The server returns with two waters. I open one and offer it to Madeleine. She accepts, thanks me, and continues going over the last-minute details with her boss.

"Ah, my love. Please come say hello to Madeleine and her guest." An older woman perfectly coifed in business casual attire approaches and takes Stavros's outstretched hand.

"Leanna, you remember Madeleine, and this is her guest, Christoph."

She extends her hand to Madeleine. "Pleasure to see you again." Mrs. Scala then extends her hand to me. "Nice to meet you, young man."

"The pleasure is mine, Mrs. Scala."

"Please, it's Leanna."

She beckons Madeleine closer. Madeleine bends down to listen. I can't make out what she says, but it made my woman blush. *I love calling her mine.*

As they draw apart, Leanna pats Madeleine's hand. "You must get going to dress for the party."

"We will return as quickly as possible," Madeleine assures her.

Leanna shakes her head. "Take your time, dear."

As we step away from them, I slide my hand around her waist, pull her flush against me, and whisper, "Are you going to share what she said to you to make you blush so fiercely?"

Madeleine nods but says nothing as we head back out to the car. As I round the back of the vehicle, I note Leanna is watching us from the balcony above the front door.

"Please share. Your blush was insanely sexy, and I need to know how to replicate it."

She shakes her head while she inputs the address to our accommodations for tonight into the GPS. Based on the arrival time, it isn't far away. I pull forward and follow the directions. "You probably need more background before I share. The first time I met Leanna was about three months after I started working for Stavros. She was a frequent visitor to the office and called at least twice a day. Fast forward over the last decade or so, I've seen her at least once a month, mostly at company events or in passing since I started handling my own clients." The fading blush starts to creep back into her skin as she gathers her thoughts. "The last time I saw Leanna…."

I take her hand in mine and thread our fingers together. Her palm in mine feels perfect. I've never held her hand until now. As twisted as it sounds, it seemed too intimate when I knew we weren't truly a couple. Now we are. Her eyes drop to our intertwined fingers and then lift to mine.

She continues, "I saw Leanna three days after returning from Atlanta. She said, 'Whoever he is, hold on to him.' When I returned from Callie's wedding, I saw her again. She was more forceful with her opinion. Leanna said, 'Marry him.'"

I park in front of a small cottage about five miles away from Stavros's compound, kill the engine, and twist toward her. "And today?" I urge her to continue.

"She asked what I was waiting for, and said, if you don't ask and soon, I should stake a claim myself."

I grin at her. "Leanna doesn't mince words, does she?"

"No."

"We've never discussed marriage. Is it something you want?"

Her fingers tighten around mine. "I'll answer you, but this is the first time we've held hands."

"I know. It felt too…."

"Intimate," she supplies.

I lift our hands and kiss the back of hers. "Precisely."

"To answer your question, the notion of marriage doesn't scare me regarding the monogamy and building a life with someone, despite the fact I've never made it past a few months with anyone, but you. My previously mentioned lack of good examples terrifies me. What about you?"

"I agree with you, except for the examples part. However, I should add I never met any woman I could see myself with far into the future until you." I could see Madeleine beside me for the rest of my life without hesitation. "I would like to continue talking, but you have an event to get to."

"We should talk more."

"We will, beautiful." I release her and move to her door. Once she's standing, I take her into my arms and kiss her breathless. I could kiss her for the rest of my life and be deliriously happy. Together we walk to the quaint cottage, which is probably worth a million dollars given its location and water view.

Under an hour later, we're ready to return to the party. "You look gorgeous." She's wearing a navy suit with a pencil skirt and a jacket with beaded lapels.

"You look hot yourself."

I chose the black suit I had for my assignment. Gemma plans to contact me tomorrow when she's at my condo to send some items to New York.

The moment we arrive at the party, a swarm of people greet her. I realize Madeleine wasn't lying when she indicated people would ignore me. I didn't think she was. The entire time we've been here so far, she has refused to let go of my hand and has introduced me to everyone she's spoken with. Right now is the only time she hasn't been within arm's reach, and that's only because she went to the restroom. I take the time to check my messages.

Jake: Your evasive actions seem to be working. Blaine hasn't found any new images.

Me: Glad to hear it.

Jake: I plan to keep the monitoring on.

Me: Yes, thank you.

Jake: We'll talk about Los Angeles at our next meeting.

Me: Okay.

Jake's update is a relief. Eventually, either Blaine will locate the person who is searching for me, or they will make themselves known. It doesn't matter much to me either way. If Madeleine and Betty are safe, I'm fine, even more so waking with Madeleine's lush body in my arms.

As I'm putting up my phone, Simon happens upon me waiting outside the bathroom door. "Mr. Anderson, it's a pleasure to meet you in person." Simon looks me up and down. He's about five eight, bicyclist fit, and dressed impeccably. His suit screams, "I know a good tailor and it's worth every penny."

"Likewise, Simon. Please call me Christoph. I appreciate your assistance. The surprise was successful."

"You're welcome. I heard. Well done. Merely to solidify my timelines, when did you meet Madeleine?"

"We first met last September. The answer to the question you really want to ask is about eight months ago after our mutual friend's wedding."

I see Simon's brain working. "I see. Either way, she's happy and you're the reason. Don't hurt her, or I will come for you."

Stifling the laugh proves too much. I laugh heartily, and Simon joins in. "I won't hurt her, Simon."

"Glad to hear it."

Madeleine joins us from the restroom. "Hi, Si. Did you arrive fashionably late again?"

He chuckles and kisses her cheeks. "You look gorgeous! You know it. These parties don't get started until the bigwigs like yourself leave."

"Can I already? It would be wonderful to call it a night. I'm kind of tired."

Simon looks at his watch and whispers loud enough for me to hear, "I'm sure your need to leave has nothing to do with this man who appears to be carved out of granite."

Madeleine glances at me, winks, and replies, "No, nothing at all."

Within thirty minutes of our conversation with Simon, Madeleine has made her final rounds and bid Stavros and Leanna goodnight. After the short ride to the cottage, I strip her out of her suit and explore her body with my tongue on the chaise lounge on the patio. Her screaming my name is loud enough I would worry about the neighbors if there were any. Afterward, we slide beneath the sheets until the morning.

CHAPTER ELEVEN

MADELEINE

After a wonderful time in the Hamptons and spending the majority of Sunday in bed with Christoph, the work week is back upon us. I have four days before flying to the West Coast to support Callie at the Grammys. Upon our return to New York, I have a few more days before Christoph is off to Maine for an assignment. I'm not a fan of him leaving at all.

I step into the lobby and ride to my office. Simon accosts me with files and messages before I make it to my desk.

"Ms. Mayhew called twice already this morning. Mr. Stockton is requesting a meeting to discuss a new contract. Callie Michelson reached out to discuss her event this weekend."

Hearing Callie's married name makes my heart skip. Christoph and I never really talked more about marriage over the weekend, but I could see myself changing my last name to his. "Thank you. Breathe, Si. Give me ten minutes to get more coffee and then call Ms. Mayhew back. Then I'll consider speaking with Mr. Stockton, although I'm not keen on taking him back. Please have Callie call back early this afternoon."

"Fine. Have anything to share about the rest of your weekend after I saw you?"

"Nope, not sharing any private details with you, Si, not now, probably not ever."

He frowns at me as I step into my office.

CA: You left your lunch. Are you free to have lunch with me?

Me: Always. I can meet you in the lobby at one.

CA: I'll be there.

With fresh coffee, I lift the receiver to speak with Beatrice. "Good morning, Bea. What can I do you for this fine morning?"

"Are you okay, Madeleine?"

I smile. I'm happy, and it's clearly spilling over into my work demeanor and word choice. I'm not sure if it's a good thing or a bad thing. "I'm fine. What have the producers decided?"

She sighs heavily. "You were right. Your client didn't break his contract, and the producers are going to stick by him."

"Thank you. As they should. The early reviews of the tapings are promising."

"You're welcome. I merely hope he can keep this up."

"Don't worry, Bea. He will." *Or he won't have me as his agent anymore.* Ending the call, I swivel in my chair and gaze at the buildings. I love my job, and I'm spectacular at it. However, I miss the farm where Estelle raised me. The peace and quiet is certainly lacking in the big city. Yet with Christoph here, I feel less isolated.

I spend the next hour reviewing Mr. Stockton's file and upcoming roles. Given the studios he's set to work with and the contracts currently in place, I have no plans to take him back.

I push the intercom. "Simon, could you call Mr. Stockton and inform him I don't plan to change my mind. I'm no longer willing to act as his agent. Also, I'm heading out for lunch in a few."

"Okay. Please say hi to your gorgeous man for me."

How does Simon know? "I will."

I see him air fist bump me from his desk. I shake my head and grab my handbag. When I step off the elevator and turn toward the lobby, Simon's words echo in my head. From behind, he's gorgeous. Christoph is facing out the narrow lobby windows toward the street. With his arms crossed in front of him, his shirt is taut over his sculpted back. Don't get me started on how good his ass looks in those dark jeans. I sidle beside him and wrap my arm around his back.

He presses a kiss to my temple and then brushes his lips over mine. "Hi. How was your morning?"

"Not too bad. I missed having breakfast with you."

"Me too, but you seemed to need the sleep more." We turn right out of my building and walk a few blocks to a deli. The sandwiches here are the best in a two-mile radius. After we order, we grab a table in the back corner.

"How was your meeting with Jake? Everything set for Callie?"

The manager delivers our food. When Christoph unwraps his, he offers me the first taste. "Thanks."

He chose the Italian combo, and I went with turkey. "You're welcome. Everything is set. I'm going to fly out with you, and the team is going to meet us there by early Saturday—something about Callie needing to meet with Kelly for some alterations to her dress."

Kelly Barnett is the owner and founding designer of a couture dress boutique in Maine. She met her husband, Hollywood's most sought-after actor and director, Ellis Barnett, during her first costuming job. Since then, they married and had two children. Now Kelly is sought after for her costuming work as well as her unique couture designs.

"Okay."

He reaches across the table and sets his large palm over mine. "What's on your mind?"

"You."

He grins at me. "I love where this is going."

"Shouldn't you be flying with Callie?"

"Not necessarily. As you know, Callie was already in Orlando when Connor was first hired. It depends on the situation. Connor, Maia, and Nolan will be with her when she flies to LA. What is worrying you?"

"As much as I want you here, I don't want our relationship status to affect your job."

"Madeleine," his voice is husky and low, "look at me, please."

I lock my eyes to his. I've never seen this look before. Concern and fear dance in his blue eyes.

"Our relationship and how much time I spend with you in New York won't affect my job. If I weren't with you the last week, I would have been home alone. With you is preferable."

"Are you sure?"

He swivels his chair around the table and cups my face. "Yes, I'm sure."

"Together is preferrable for me too." I lean forward and kiss him slow and deep, pulling back at the brink of being inappropriate for our surroundings.

"We can continue this when you get home tonight."

Our lips still a mere inch from one another. "We absolutely should."

We finish our food, and he walks me back to my office. "I'll see you tonight."

I steal another kiss and slowly make my way upstairs. Luckily, this afternoon only includes a call with Callie.

"How was lunch with Lover Boy?" Simon sings as I walk by.

I smile and reply, "Don't call him that, Si! When the time comes, I will torture you and your future boyfriend."

"I would expect nothing less, my fierce boss lady."

"Glad to hear it. Please put Callie through when she calls in for our appointment."

Simon nods and plops back down into his chair. Once inside my office, I pull up the schedule for the rest of the week to see if I can get ahead on anything. There are two contract reviews set for Wednesday. I search for the files and get started. About an hour later, both are marked up with questions and language issues that need to be addressed.

"Mads, Callie is on line two."

I settle back into my chair and twist to face the city. "Hi, Cal. How are you?"

"Good. I assume Connor or Jake talked to you about our trip?"

"No, but Christoph shared the plan with me."

"Oh, is he still there with you?"

I don't like the concern in her voice. "Yes, is everything okay?"

"Yes, of course. I saw the two of you in Atlanta despite my increased worry for Connor at the time. Then again at our wedding. Have you been seeing him since then?"

"On and off until recently." I consider stopping my answer there, but Callie will see us together at the Grammys in a few days. "Now we're dating."

A loud squeal comes through the phone. "I'm so happy for you. It saves me the trouble of searching for someone for you. Both Norah and I have been trying to get Maia to share her true feelings with Nolan. As far as I know, she hasn't yet."

"I see." I'm glad Callie nor anyone else is matchmaking for me anymore. Estelle tried a few times and failed miserably. She inadvertently set me up with a man I met on a dating app. Our date was the previous weekend, and I left before dinner was served.

"Your relationship status isn't the true reason I called. We're having twins!"

"Wow! Congratulations, Callie. Does your pregnancy impact the adoption?""

Callie laughs. "We want a large family with a mix of both."

"That's why your dress needs to be altered."

"Yup. Very few people know, but you can share with Christoph if you want."

"I don't want to spoil it for Connor."

"What a nice gesture. I'll have Connor call him as soon as we hang up."

"Thanks. He should share the good news first. I'll see you in a few days. Take care of yourself."

"Bye, Madi."

I end the call and immediately dial Estelle. I haven't been the best granddaughter lately.

"Hi, ladybug. Is everything good?" Estelle sounds winded.

"Are you okay?"

"Of course. I left my phone downstairs. I rushed when I heard your ringtone. Is everything good with you?"

"Yes, it is. I'm going to the Grammys this weekend, so I wanted to talk before then."

"Oh, how sweet of you. I'm feeling healthy, Madeleine. There's no need to worry about me."

Stubborn woman. "I always worry about you. You're all...." *She isn't all I have anymore.*

"Is it the man you met in Atlanta, ladybug?" Of course she noticed the pause. She never misses a thing.

"Yes. We started officially dating recently."

"I can't wait to meet him."

"Would you mind if he crashes our holiday dinner?"

I hear glee in her response. "Oh no. I would be delighted to meet him then."

"Love you."

"I love you too, ladybug." I end the call and sigh. Holiday dinners with Estelle are always amazing. Adding Christoph might make them better.

After clearing my desk, I gather my bag and the contracts I reviewed early. I stop to talk with Simon. "Did I miss anything during those calls?"

"Nothing at all. Your schedule is clear for the rest of the day."

"Perfect. Can you call Jack if he isn't already waiting?"

Simon taps a few keys. "He's already downstairs."

"Great! Here are the contracts set for review on Wednesday. Please make sure they get into the appropriate hands."

"On it, Mads." Noting my bag is slung around my forearm, he states, "He's really good for your work-life balance."

Hiding the huge smile on my face at the mention of Christoph is virtually impossible. "Yes, he is. He cooks too."

"Oh, girl! You need him in your life. He's a keeper!"

He is. "Good night, Si." I twist on my red-soled heel and move to the elevator. Less than an hour later, I'm joining Christoph in my already steamy shower enclosure. I'm tempted to watch the water sluice down his impressive abs a little longer, but he startles me instead.

"I can feel you when you're near me. Come closer, beautiful."

"Your ninja skills are impressive."

He shakes his head, sending water droplets toward me. I slide my arms around him and press hungry kisses across the top of his back. It's rare he doesn't take control when we're together. I glide my hands downward and tease my fingertip along the side of his length before gripping him with both hands. Two strokes later, I'm against the tiled wall with my hands in one of his above my head. I hook my leg around his hip to draw him closer. He sucks one nipple into his mouth, biting down while his hand slips between my thighs to my hot center. The decadent pain from his teeth combined with the slow, sensual strokes of his fingers sends spikes of pleasure radiating through my body.

Grinding against his hand, I chase the orgasm building in my lower abdomen. *That feels....* "You are...."

He grins against my breast. Each nip of his teeth makes my pleasure spiral closer and closer. My climax thunders through me as I shudder against his sinful form. When my leg gives way, he releases my hands and shifts us to the bench along the wall. Now straddling his thighs, I meld our mouths together and surround him with my still pulsing core.

His arms climb up my back and cup my shoulders. As I thrust downward, he lifts, hitting deeper inside me than ever before. Lowering one arm, he surrounds my waist and paints circles with his thumb over my throbbing nub.

"You feel—"

"So do you." My words muffled are by the increasing pace of our bodies.

We feverishly chase our release, neither wanting to let go before the other. *Well, again.*

"I'm so close."

"Me too."

The moment those words leave his lips, decadent ribbons of pleasure cascade through me while he lengthens and throbs inside me. His hold tightens around me as I collapse against his chest.

After rinsing off, he teaches me how to make an easy parmesan chicken and roasted veggie dinner. The last thing I remember is curling up on the couch against him.

CHAPTER TWELVE

CHRISTOPH

The moment we land in Los Angeles, Madeleine is in work mode. The two sides of her are distinct. This Madeleine is tenacious, always early, and ready to tackle any problem her clients might get into. I'm busying myself people watching while she attends a preshow meeting on Callie's behalf.

When she emerges from her meeting, I find the other agents and executives with their heads hanging as she walks toward me. A huge smile graces her face a mere moment before she kisses me softly.

"How was the meeting?"

She smirks. "Callie is going to be pleased. Her former record company, not so much."

"You're amazing!"

She shrugs. "Yeah, I kind of am." A soft giggle escapes her lips.

So hot! "What's next, Miss Wilton?"

She laughs. "I'm free until I meet with Callie tomorrow for the preshow interview circuit."

I slide my arms around her and tug her lush curves against me. "What do you want to do?"

"I'm fairly certain there's a secluded area of the pool we can use."

I'm momentarily speechless. A vision of her in the red, string bikini she packed rushes through my brain and sends all the blood in my body plummeting south. She isn't suggesting... no, of course she isn't.

She rises on her toes so her mouth is even with my ear. "Wherever your thoughts just went, it's a near certainty I'm willing to join you."

"Are you sure?"

She drags her tongue along the outer edge of my ear. "I'm a fierce negotiator; I said 'near.' My limits with you are basically nonexistent. However, legal limits apply, so no nudity in the pool."

I frown.

"At least this pool." Her voice is laced with sultry undertones.

I eliminate every bit of air between us and whisper, "I'll build you a completely secluded pool as soon as humanly possible."

Her skin blushes, she threads her fingers in mine, and we race to our suite. Within thirty minutes, my gorgeous woman is ready, wearing a thin coverup over said string bikini and a huge pair of sunglasses. When we arrive at the pool, we're escorted to our own private cabana. By private, I mean it can be closed on all four sides.

I raise an eyebrow in her direction, and she minutely shakes her head.

"If you need anything, please let me know," the steward states as he leaves.

"You can't blame me for trying." I lift off my shirt and her cover-up, casting them onto the chair.

She drags her fingernails down my bare chest. "I'm too vocal when we're together for this amount of privacy."

"You could try to be quiet," I sheepishly suggest.

She shakes her head. "Not possible with how much you make me feel."

My cheeks heat.

"That's hot!" She plasters a blistering kiss on me.

"Careful, gorgeous. You won't get into the pool if you keep kissing me like you want to do sinful things to my body."

Her eyes widen before she replies, "I vaguely recall you agreeing to be my boyfriend."

"True, so?"

"It means I can kiss you however I want and whenever I want as long as no laws are broken."

I lower the panels to shroud us in privacy. "I see. If it's true for you, it is for me as well, correct?"

Nervously, she replies, "Yes."

I lower myself to the chaise lounge and tug at the strings tied on her left hip. Her bottom folds over, exposing half of her bare bikini area. I drag the flat of my tongue along the curve of her hip and inward. Peeling the bottoms out of my way, I continue to move.

Shivers skate over her skin. "Christoph, stop." Her voice comes out breathy and raspy.

I pull back and look up at her.

Her expression isn't what I expect. It's filled with desire and dripping with seduction. "Let's go back to the suite."

I grasp the two strings, retie them at her hip, and link our hands before following her suggestion. We spend the afternoon, evening, and late into the night in various stages of nakedness on numerous surfaces in the posh suite.

My internal clock is off a bit. Near four in the morning, I wake and can't fall back to sleep. I study the sprinkle of freckles at the nape of her neck and the birth mark on the small of her back. When she doesn't wake, I slip out of bed and order breakfast to arrive near nine. She needs to meet with Callie before her interviews. While I wait, I check my messages.

Connor: We boarded a few minutes ago. We're scheduled to arrive near eleven.

Me: Thanks.

Connor: Any change in your situation?

Me: All quiet as of the last check.

Connor: Good. You can review the security plan before the interviews.

Me: Roger.

The next set of messages is from Jake.

Jake: Any concern with still going to Maine?

Me: Not unless Blaine finds a more significant threat.

Jake: Okay, just verifying. I assume you received what you needed from Gemma?

Me: Yes, all set. She deserves a raise and maybe a new title.

Jake: She probably does. Let me know if you need anything else for Callie.

Me: Will do.

The last part is interesting considering Connor is his partner in Blackthorne and he'll be present. Then I think better of it. It makes complete sense. Connor won't be as clearheaded because it's his wife's security.

At a knock at the door, I admit the server and accept our breakfast. When I turn back, Madeleine is walking into the sitting area wearing my white, V-neck shirt. It looks infinitely better on her.

"Morning," she murmurs.

"Morning." I draw her close and kiss her lightly. When I release her, she's a bit unsteady.

"What's wrong, gorgeous?"

She rolls her eyes. "You're a terrible liar."

"Not lying. Fresh out of bed you, especially in my shirt dipping low, is my favorite version of you. Are you all right?"

"Yeah, a bit lightheaded. We didn't really eat enough yesterday considering all the expended energy."

I grin at her, prepare her coffee, and set it in front of her.

"Thanks." We finish breakfast and take a fresh cup of coffee into the bedroom to dress.

"When do you need to leave?" She hangs her head and continues, "Sorry, I sound needy as hell."

I take her hand in mine. "You don't. You sound like we're still working on navigating how we work when our jobs are at the same place. I'm not a fan of giving up my alone time with you either."

"It sounds much better phrased like that."

"I'll escort you to meet Callie, not because I need to but because I'm able and I want to. Then you, Callie, Nolan, and Maia will head into the interviews. After I go over the plans with Connor for tomorrow, we'll join you inside. If I'm lucky, I can review them before the interviews."

She steps into my embrace. "Thank you. How much time do we have?"

I check my watch and catch the cloud of lust surrounding her. "Not enough time for me to worship you properly."

The heat in her eyes quadruples. "The things you say."

"Every word is true and how I feel." My phone vibrates in my pocket.

"Alone time is up, huh?"

I slip my phone out of my pocket and see the preview is from Connor. "Yeah, for now."

She slides her hands up to cup my face and presses a searing kiss to my lips before pulling away.

Damn! I'm never letting her go. It isn't going to be easy, but together I believe we can have everything we want. The bigger question I need to address is, is the private investigator only a blip or something to handle expeditiously? I know better than to hope for the former.

CHAPTER THIRTEEN

MADELEINE

We join the team from Blackthorne, Callie, and Connor in a small conference room they reserved. Nolan and Maia are chatting over near the beverages. I met Maia in Atlanta when I met Christoph. I didn't meet Nolan until Callie's wedding. He's tall with light hair and piercing green eyes. He's fit like a martial artist not a gym rat. He looks at Maia like she hung the moon. I wonder if she realizes he's attracted to her too. Callie and Connor are near the window. All talking ceases when they see us holding hands.

Callie regains her composure first and rushes over to me. "It's great to see you." She's glowing, and her baby bump is obvious to me because I know she's pregnant. The A-line dress masks it adequately.

"I didn't get to ask. How far along are you?"

"Five months. How are things with you?"

I know she means with Christoph. I'm not willing to share very much though. Not only because it's new, but my personal life is still mine. Callie is my client and acquaintance. The line is already blurry because Christoph and Connor are friends, coworkers, and former unit mates. "We're figuring it out." As if he knows I need comfort or support, I feel

Christoph's gaze on me. When I catch his eye, he mouths, *"Are you okay?"*

I reply, *"Yes,"* silently. I love how he's attuned to me so well already. I return my attention to Callie and get down to business. "The first set of interviews are for national entertainment news shows. Then there's a short ten-minute break. The second set is for a few local affiliates. These will focus more on your nominations rather than the shift in your career after the memorial performance and press release."

"Thanks, Madi. I couldn't do this without you."

"You're welcome. Do you need anything before we get started?"

"No, I'm good." She walks over to Connor, and he tucks her against his body. I notice she relaxes as their proximity increases. It's interesting because Christoph calms me as well. I don't think he realizes it though.

I greet Maia and Nolan while grabbing a water from the beverage station. "Nice to see you again."

"You too," Maia replies.

Both Connor and Christoph join us and go over some last-minute information about Callie's security. With Maia and Nolan in front of Callie and Connor, we make our way to the interview set. Christoph and I follow closely behind.

Three exhausting hours later, the team escorts Callie to her suite. She answered the same set of questions for each group and nailed it. Thankfully, no one picked up on her cradling her belly during the local portion of the interviews.

PROTECTING OUR FOREVER 113

"Thank you for your support today, Madi," Callie states before we leave her suite.

"You're welcome. I know we had a difference of opinion about the memorial performance. I'm glad it worked out well for you." I was completely against Callie exposing her true identity and sing as herself instead of her stage persona, Carys, at the memorial. Her adamance exceeded mine given her parents perished in the terrorist attack. She felt singing as Carys was disingenuous. My recommendation was for her to attend but not perform. In the end, she's in control of her career, and her revelation was accepted well by her fans.

"I am too. I'll meet you at the end of the red carpet." Callie hugs me close.

"See you then."

I move to the door and wait for Christoph and Connor to finish discussing the details for tomorrow for the final time.

"All set?" He approaches me.

I nod and walk through the suite door before him. Once we're in the elevator, I ask, "Every detail buttoned up for tomorrow? How are you?"

"We aren't expecting any issues given how today went, but we're prepared for them anyway. Once Callie is inside the auditorium, the pressure will decrease significantly. Other than needing to eat, I'm fine. What about you?"

"I'm hungry, overtired, and deliciously sore in places I haven't been ever before. I wonder who is at fault."

The same blush from the pool creeps into his cheeks again. "It isn't my fault."

"Of course it is. If you didn't rock my world, I would be getting enough sleep."

He slides the key into the reader and opens our suite door. Setting his hands on my ass, he eliminates any space between us before replying, "The feeling is mutual, gorgeous. We found the one person who is willing to put in the work for a relationship. Coaxing pleasure from your luscious curves is worth a little less sleep, isn't it?"

"I'm not complaining about quality. Merely saying we need to balance a bit better because we're more than a once-a-month thing."

He feigns dejection before adding, "I'm sure we can find an appropriate balance going forward." Lifting me, he walks to the bedroom and sets me on the bed. Kneeling before me, he slips my shoes from my feet, brushing his lips on my ankles. "What do you want for dinner?"

"I'm not too picky. Whatever is fastest."

He smiles and moves to the door. "I'll order and be right back."

His broad shoulders showcased in his fitted dress shirt is the last thing I remember.

At some point, I stir and he draws me closer against his sculpted chest. I take stock of my surroundings. Being wrapped in his arms isn't odd given we're at a hotel, but…

"Stop thinking so hard. You fell asleep while I was ordering dinner. I didn't want to wake you," he murmurs against my shoulder blade.

I burrow deeper into his body. "Thank you."

"Always. I'll go order a huge breakfast. Please stay here. You haven't eaten since the fruit between interview segments."

His attention to me is off the charts. "I will."

No man has ever taken care of me as well as him. All I know is I'm never letting him go. About ten minutes later, he returns with a bottled water and a granola bar.

Sitting up slowly, I accept them. "Thanks." I push the wave of nausea down and take a bite of the bar and sip the water.

"What time do you need to meet Callie?" he asks.

"We're meeting at the venue. She will reach the end of the red carpet near four. I need to be ready to leave at two. What about you?"

He twists to look at me. "I need to meet the team at one to escort Callie. Did you arrange for transportation for yourself already?"

"Yes, Si set it up for me. It's the same company Jack works for but on the West Coast."

"Good. Jack's company is solid."

I raise an eyebrow with the water bottle halfway to my lips. "What do you mean?"

"I checked out Jack's company, the concierge in your building, and the security company at your office."

"When?"

"Within the first two months of us being together. Why? Does it upset you? It was the only way I could take care of you from afar."

"I'm not upset. Maybe a little surprised."

"Madeleine, I care about you deeply. It was something I could verify without being intrusive in your life. As terrible as this will sound, Connor being shot was the best thing to ever happen to me."

"What? That's simply ridiculous."

He smirks at me. "I met you covering for him in Atlanta."

Oh my heart. In the brief time we've been a couple, he's everything he seems.

"Connor is my brother and always will be, but you... you're everything I didn't know I needed." A knock on the suite door breaks our discussion. "I'll be right back." A few minutes later, Christoph pushes the cart into the bedroom and against the side of the bed.

I shift my legs over the edge and watch him. "I could say the same thing about you."

He steps around the table and kisses me tenderly. "Eat, beautiful. No other option right now."

I smile and dig in. After eating and showering, I feel much better. My hair and makeup are done. The only thing left is for me to slip into my dress. When I join Christoph in the sitting room, he's already dressed except for his tie and jacket. My man looks amazing in shorts and a graphic tee, but in a tailored suit, he's droolworthy. He's rapidly flicking through the available channels.

"Stop."

He stops scrolling and turns to look at me. "Football?"

I curl up next to him on the couch. "I love football." Surprise registers on his face. "You still have a bunch of things to learn about me."

"I guess so. Do you have a favorite team?" His eyes widen with anticipation.

"The Ravens are my team. I still follow them despite their poor showing in recent years. What about you?"

"Same actually. What other sexy snippet of information are you withholding?"

A wide grin grows on my face. "I'm not hiding anything. I prefer to spend my Sundays during football season undisturbed with an unhealthy amount of food in front of a huge television. My favorite ice cream is—"

"Cookies and cream."

"I never told you my favorite ice-cream flavor."

A knowing grin flashes on his face. "No, you didn't, but I recall distinct disgust when the hotel in Chicago didn't have it on hand for you during one of our late-night dessert room service fixes."

"What about you?"

"I prefer similar football Sundays. Can we make it a standing date if we are together?"

"Absolutely."

"Ice cream: chocolate chocolate chip. My favorite action movie star is—"

"Vin Diesel."

He laughs heartily. "Wrong! Old-school action star: Bruce Willis. Currently, I would say Dwayne Johnson. He's versatile from *Moana* to *Jumanji* to the *Fast* saga. What about you?"

"Old-school action hero, I would say Harrison Ford. Current action star is hands down Gerard Butler. Action movie actress, I would say Gal Gadot. I wasn't happy when Giselle was killed off the *Fast* saga. Han and Giselle deserved a happily ever after like Dom and Letty and Mia and Brian."

His phone rings. "Yeah, Jake." He listens quietly before responding, "I'll tell her now."

I stiffen beside him. The "her" is likely me, not Callie. He ends the call, turns, and pulls me against him.

I kiss his jaw lightly before asking, "What's going on?"

He exhales harshly. "When I landed in Chicago, Jake reached out to me. Blaine discovered someone was following me digitally through published photos. A photo of us at the food trucks was published in a small local newspaper and online earlier the same day."

"Okay."

"Fast forward a week or so, Blaine learned someone paid a midlevel investigator to keep tabs on me. At the time, I asked Blaine to monitor you and Betty as well. The only reason I didn't share with you until now is they were only searching for me. Now, they're watching Betty too."

I sit up a bit straighter. Unexpectedly, I'm not angry. "What does it mean for Betty? What does it mean for today? What about us?" My questions decrease in volume.

"Say that again."

"Us."

He kisses me possessively and deeply. "I truly love a tiny word with a huge meaning."

"Me too."

"To answer your questions, Jake added Estelle to the list of people for Blaine to monitor. Jake is going to visit Betty and leave Finn with her as long as necessary. I'm sure Finn will be heartbroken given Betty can cook like no one else and he's a country boy at heart. Jake and Connor made changes to today's personnel groupings. Maia will be here soon, and both of us will escort you to the venue."

"Why?"

He pauses before answering. "In addition to your importance to me, Jake feels it would make sense to make it look like you're a client of Blackthorne. It would explain my increased proximity to you and protect you at the same time."

"I understand. What about when you go to Maine? I'll be alone."

His face falls, and he tries to recover. He's unsuccessful. "I refuse to let anything happen to you. Our relationship may be new, but it's special. I'm not willing to give up on us now, if ever. As of right now, Jake is taking extra precautions. If something changes, Jake will address my assignments, as necessary."

I never truly considered what his profession entails. A sliver of fear slices through me recalling Connor was shot pursuing Callie's stalker.

"Not only are you going to be fine, but so am I."

I'm speechless. "How?" I manage to whisper.

"I can read you as if you said your thoughts aloud. No one can read me as well as you." He tightens his hold on me.

Holy hell! He smells delicious, which is not something that should be crossing my mind right now. I relax slightly against him and check the time. "Does it change our departure time?" I pull back enough to look at him.

"No, we'll use the transportation you put in place and then meet up with Callie and the team at the venue." Somewhat relieved, I melt into him with the early game playing in the background. Normally, I would be yelling at the television, but today I'm soaking in as much comfort as I can draw from him.

CHAPTER FOURTEEN

CHRISTOPH

If Jake is worried, so am I. I'm confident he shared all of Blaine's information. Jake knows, if I told him about Madeleine, she's important to me. With Blaine's assistance, I'll find out who is looking for me and why. Then, with Jake and Connor's help, I'll handle it.

About twenty minutes ago, Madeleine went to dress for the event. I take the opportunity to call Betty before Maia arrives.

As usual, she answers on the first ring. "Hi, Grams."

"Hi, Christoph. How are you?"

"I'm well. I wanted to give you a heads-up." I share the information Blaine found and inform her of Jake and Finn's impending arrival. "Do you have any idea what this could be about?"

"No. As you know, we live a simple life. Always have."

Only truth in her words. Until Gramps died, the three of us lived on a midsize, self-sufficient farm. Now Grams has a large stable to board horses, a massive personal garden for vegetables and one for flowers, and a dog. "Please heed Finn. Right now, it's a precaution."

"Why aren't you coming yourself?"

"I'm on the West Coast with a client. Finn is closer."

"What about the woman you're seeing?" Grams always gets to the heart of every situation. I didn't think I was going to get out of spilling the recent changes in my life. She knows Madeleine is important to me even if she isn't aware we're a couple yet.

"She's here as well given who the client is." Grams knows Madeleine is Callie's agent. She'll put it together before Jake can share with her.

"Has something changed with her?"

I don't hide anything from Grams. "Yes, very recently."

"I won't pry anymore, but I want to meet her."

A smile materializes on my face. "I'll figure out the details as soon as possible."

"Be safe, Christoph."

"Always, Grams. Love you."

"Love you too."

I exhale noisily. Grams will listen to Finn. Now, I need to focus on getting through this event safely for both Callie and Madeleine. I understand the need to have other people here for Callie's security. I'm on edge for a client. My need to protect Madeleine is exponentially higher.

A soft knock alerts me of Maia's arrival.

"Hi, Maia." Given the nature of this event, Maia is dressed up as well. Her maroon dress hits below her knees with crisscrossing straps over her chest and back.

"Hey. How are you holding up?"

I clasp my hands around my neck and drag them forward. "Not worried about me."

A wide smile breaks out on her face. "Sweet, now Nolan owes me twenty."

I can't contain my laugh. "You two are betting on what? My feelings for Madeleine."

She snickers. "Something like that."

Before I can address it further, Madeleine enters the sitting room. *Holy fuck!* She's breathtaking. This dress surpasses the emerald silk dress from Callie's wedding. Her dress is long with narrow straps and skims over her body. It's nude with a black lace overlay perfectly highlighting her curves. Her back is completely exposed. My fingers itch to feel her ultra-soft skin beneath them again and soon.

"Hi, Maia. You look beautiful."

"Hi, Madeleine. Thank you. So do you."

Silence hangs in the room while I unabashedly stare at Madeleine. I don't realize it until Maia clears her throat.

"All set?" I address her.

"Sure." Her voice comes out low and shaky. She's nervous.

"Maia, could you give us a minute?"

She smiles deviously. I need to know what they're betting on. "Of course."

I open the bedroom door, usher Madeleine in, and close it behind us. Taking her into my arms, I kiss her with every ounce of pent-up desire and passion I have for her. I'll never get enough, and I knew from the moment she shook my hand. "You're breathtaking."

"Thank you. You don't look half bad yourself." She winks at me.

"Still nervous?"

She kisses me again. "I wanted to make sure I got another kiss before we leave. I won't kiss you so boldly in public."

I frown and press a soft kiss to her forehead. "All set now?"

"Yes."

With my hand on the exposed skin of her back, I lead her back into the sitting room and follow Maia to the waiting car. Once we arrive at the venue, we'll be escorted along the outer edge of the red carpet to wait for Callie at the entrance to the auditorium.

Photographers and entertainment reporters are only interested in those walking the red carpet. If you aren't worthy, you're escorted to a cordoned area within five minutes of arrival. Madeleine is tucked beside me with Maia in front of us.

"Care to share what the bet is, Maia?"

Maia shakes her head. "Nope."

"What are you talking about?" Madeleine asks dangerously close to my ear.

"All I know is Nolan owes Maia a twenty spot for something about us."

Madeleine kisses the hinge of my jaw. "Don't worry. I'll find out for you."

I look over at her and revel in my newfound information about my better half. She's as mischievous as I am.

Moments later, I hear "Callie, over here" repeatedly. The throng of reporters pushes back toward us, eliminating the walkway into the venue. I shift Madeleine behind me, linking our fingers at my side. Her other hand grips the back of my jacket.

Maia and Nolan exchange a nod and a few key bits of information through our earpieces. We'll meet them at the secondary point once the walkway clears. I'm not opposed to having Madeleine closer to me than we are right now. However, I would prefer it to be a perfectly safe environment. She isn't in danger, but she isn't comfortable either. I don't like it one bit.

More than fifteen minutes later, we have a path into the building. For a tiny person, Maia commands attention. She steps in front of the next group of nominees and ushers Madeleine inside and straight to the anteroom. Unfortunately, we miss Callie who is already in her seat for the opening host segment. We take our seats in the green room for agents and presenters for the duration of the ceremony.

A flurry of stylish singers, songwriters, and music's brightest minds celebrate one another for the next four hours. In the end, Callie garners four awards out of the six she was nominated for, including best original song.

Connor: Callie wants to return to the hotel suite instead of the after-party. Does returning to the hotel work for Madeleine?

I lean closer and ask Madeleine.

"Whatever Callie wants is fine. The after-parties aren't required."

Me: Whatever Callie wants is fine.

Connor: Roger. We'll meet you at exit point C and return to the hotel.

Me: Roger.

I turn to Maia and Madeleine. "Our client wants to return to the hotel."

Maia nods and Madeleine tightens her fingers in mine. Holding her hand certainly doesn't keep up the façade that she's a Blackthorne client, but I don't see how it could cause harm either. Even more so, I love knowing she's mine.

Upon our return to the hotel, we spend about an hour with Callie celebrating her wins. The good news is we're already back at the hotel. However, our flight home isn't scheduled until tomorrow morning. Along with Maia, I escort Madeleine back to our suite. I know protocol, and Maia's presence falls into it, but I want to scream, "I can protect my woman." Yet a shred of concern slices through me. Perhaps I'm too close to do it.

"Thanks, Maia. We'll see you in the morning for the trip to the airport."

"Of course. Good night, Madeleine."

Madeleine waves politely and continues into the bedroom. After Maia leaves, I lock the door and recheck it—twice. I knock on the bedroom door lightly.

"You don't have to knock." She turns to face me, wearing only her bra and panties beneath an untied silk robe.

"I know. How are you doing?"

She slips her arms around me, gripping the back of my shirt. I surround her and lower us to the chair with her in my lap. "Talk to me please."

"I'm scared, and ironically, I don't know what or who I'm scared of." Her tone is laced with anger at herself and the situation, as if she doesn't have the right to be upset.

"Have you been worrying all night?"

She nods against my chest. She hid it extremely well.

I drop a kiss on her head and lift her chin with two fingers. "I will never let anything happen to you. I wouldn't survive it." I may not have voiced my true feelings yet, but Madeleine Wilton is my other half. I will do anything for her.

"What if you aren't with me?"

Shaking my head, "I trust Jake, Connor, and my teammates with my life and yours. If he says it's a precaution, it is. I won't leave your side if you aren't safe." Every word is true, but it still doesn't ease the tension in her body. "Do you want to take a bath or shower to relax before going to sleep?"

She pauses before responding. "Will you come to bed with me?"

Damn! She's truly scared, and it's my fault. I don't like it, not one bit. "Without question." I press a kiss to her forehead, rise with her in my arms, and set her on the plush carpet on the long side of the bed. After setting an alarm on my phone, I strip off my suit and lay it on the dressing bench. I curl my body around hers and hold her until sleep overtakes us both.

CHAPTER FIFTEEN

MADELEINE

I never considered myself the clingy type, but having Christoph escort me to work and home each day isn't terrible. I love it, except I can't get comfortable with it. Tomorrow he leaves for his assignment in Maine. True, it's only for four days, but I'm not looking forward to it. I was falling for him before we started dating. Now I can't imagine waking up without him beside me.

"Morning, Mads. No escort to the office today?" Simon inquires as I step off the elevator.

I shake him off and avoid further questions. "He has a meeting and needs to get back to the apartment."

"If you say so. Your meeting with Mr. Scala is in thirty minutes. Afterward, you're free until one for the video conference call for the Rodin contract."

"Thanks, Si." I take a seat in my office and attempt to clear my inbox before meeting Stavros. Even though I'm confident my inbox will fill up again in the meantime, I'm successful at least for now.

Stavros waves me into his office as I approach. I latch the door behind me and take a seat.

"I wanted to thank you again for your attention to detail at the launch party. The studio was pleased."

I nod.

"I took the liberty of having the heads of each department pull a comprehensive report for the entire company." He sets a box in front of me and then adds another on top of it. "Please review these so you're aware of the status in each department."

"Of course."

"If you plan to make changes upon taking the helm, I understand. My way of handling issues may not be your way. I suggest you start the process of hiring at least one more assistant. As of last week, I have informed my clients and provided them with your contact information. If they choose to stay on with you after their current contract with me expires, a new contract will be negotiated with you. I have instructed Regina to provide you with the files of my open clients. I will have them delivered to your office. I'll announce your promotion in about a month. You might consider taking a longer vacation for the holidays before I leave."

"Thank you. I will need to bring Simon into the loop if I'm going to add to my staff. He needs to be comfortable with anyone I add to my team. Also, should I schedule a visit to the DC office to make a decision where I want to be based?"

"Understood. A visit to the DC office would be wise. The LA office is satellite. Other than a receptionist, it varies how many people are in the office daily. You can work remotely whenever you need. Would you prefer to warn the staff or show up?"

"I would prefer to show up. If I announce I'm coming, they will know something is up."

He grins and hands me another file. "This is a proposed contract to replace me. Review it and we'll discuss further."

"Thank you."

"Choosing you as my replacement was the second easiest decision I've made in my life."

"What was the first?" I wonder if he'll answer me.

A wide smile grows on his face. "Choosing Leanna."

His answer warms me. I can see myself answering the same way about Christoph at some point in my life.

"I hope I'm not overstepping, but you and Mr. Anderson look happy together."

"We met a while back but only started seeing each other recently."

"I see. Either way, he seems comfortable not being the center of attention. It'll be useful as you establish yourself further in this job."

I nod, rise from my chair, and grab one of the boxes. Stavros isn't wrong. It's one of the qualities that makes Christoph different. He's willing to be beside me and doesn't feel diminished by my success. It's one of the reasons I love him. After my second trip to my office, I ask Simon to join me.

"Hey, Mads. What can I do for you?"

I close the door and turn on the privacy screen. Generally, I prefer to keep the glass clear when I'm not alone, but experience has taught me Simon will freak out when I share this news.

"Please sit. I have some news to share with you."

"Mads, you're making me nervous, and it isn't an easy feat."

I shake my head. "Everything I say must stay in this room, or I'll fire you. Understood?"

Simon sits up ramrod straight in the chair and nods furiously. Of all people, he knows I follow through.

"Stavros is retiring at the end of the year. He has chosen me to replace him."

Simon's hands cover his mouth and barely contain his squeal. I give him a few minutes to process, especially considering I've already had a few weeks. "Ohmigod! You rock, Mads! Congrats!"

I smile, and he fangirls a bit more.

Finally containing himself a bit, he asks, "What do you need from me? What happens now?"

I explain what I need from him regarding another assistant and let him know I'm checking out the other offices. Then I drop the biggest ask ever. "Si, if I choose not to stay in New York, would you be willing to relocate with me?"

"Oh, Mads. I'm flattered you can't live without me. I think the answer will depend on if you choose DC or LA."

My heart sinks a bit. "Meaning?"

"I'm more than willing to be a short flight away from my family, but cross country would require some thought."

I knew LA would be a stretch for Simon. Frankly, I don't want to move far away from Christoph. Even without visiting the office, I'm leaning toward DC, but I won't share with Simon outright, at least not yet. "I understand. I'm in the same predicament." I hope Simon catches I'm leaning toward DC without me saying the words.

"I understand. I'll draft an ad for an exceptional junior assistant for you."

I smirk at him. "I see what you did there. I kind of love it, Si. Mums the word."

He rounds my desk and hugs me tight. His hugs are the type that make you feel loved and cared for but not in a sexual sort of way. When Simon hugs me, my chest screams in pain. What the heck is happening there? After he releases me, he scampers out of my office and gets to work.

I take a moment and check my inbox again. Not too bad, only three new messages. Expeditiously, I clear them and check my phone.

CA: How is your morning? Everything is set for my next assignment.

Me: Pretty good. I'll share more details later. Do you know where you're going after this weekend?

I'm not expecting an immediate answer, but I'm pleasantly surprised when I get one.

CA: I asked Jake for some time to visit Betty for the holidays.

Me: Okay. Can we talk about my day and the holidays when I get home?

CA: Sure. When do you want me to pick you up?

Me: I'm aiming for three. I'll let you know if I can't make it happen.

CA: More time with you. Perfect!

He may not realize it, but he always knows what I need to hear. I buckle down and finish the phone calls and reviews until my video conference. I have plenty of time to clear my desk before Christoph arrives.

"Si, I'm heading out for the day."

A devilish grin appears on his face. "Have fun. Don't do anything I wouldn't do."

"What would be eliminated?"

He winks at me. "Not much! Don't forget you have a personal appointment tomorrow at lunch, and it isn't Lover Boy this time."

I glare at him for calling Christoph "Lover Boy" again. "Si! Thanks. See you in the morning."

I push the down button for the elevator. When the doors open, my gorgeous man is ready to step off.

"Hi, beautiful." He kisses me lightly as the doors close, then threads his fingers in mine.

"Perfect timing."

As we step onto the sidewalk, he asks, "Do you want to go home or…?"

Home. I love hearing him call my apartment home. "I want to share everything, but it needs to be in private. Can we walk in the park and then go home?"

"Of course. Will you be warm enough?"

"You won't let me be cold."

He's over-the-top gentlemanly. Betty taught him well. "No, I won't."

We stroll through Sheep Meadow in Central Park, enjoying our time together, before taking a taxi to my apartment.

"How does takeout sound?" he suggests.

"You have somewhere in mind?"

He nods.

"Sure. You know what I like."

He raises an eyebrow. "We're talking about dinner not whether you like me to drag my tongue along the shell of your ear or your preference I take you from behind after we've been apart too long."

My cheeks heat. "Order the food. Maybe later you can learn something new I like between the sheets."

"Challenge accepted, gorgeous."

About an hour later, we're setting our food on the terrace table. These Italian dishes from Romano's looks delish. I clearly didn't consider the chill in the air when I changed after work when I opted for his white V-neck and yoga pants with crisscross cutouts to midthigh. Inexplicably knowing I need more layers, he grabs his hoodie beside him and throws it over my shoulders. Immediately, I slip my arms into the sleeves. Not only is it warm, but it smells like him—a heady combination of amber, cedar, and perhaps a hint of vanilla.

"Before we get into all the stuff we need to discuss, what cologne do you wear?"

"Eros. Why?"

"I meant to ask when we talked about my perfume before but didn't. Want to go first or…?"

He gestures for me to continue while shoving a forkful of lasagna between his full lips.

"I met with Stavros again today. He gave me a report for each department of the company for review as well as a proposed contract for my new role with the company. He suggested I visit DC and hire another assistant. He also recommended I take a longer vacation around the holidays."

"It makes sense. Are you going to take him up on it?"

This is one of the best meals I've ever eaten. "Where did you say this was from? It's amazing!"

"Romano's."

"To answer your question, yes. I plan to visit the DC office. Afterward I'll determine where I want to be based."

"Wait, you don't have to stay in New York?"

I hear the hopeful tone in his question. "No, I don't. Stavros chose New York. I can opt for New York, LA, or DC."

"Is it a good thing or not?"

"It would be nice to be closer to Estelle… and you."

He sets his fork down and slides his fingers between mine on the table. "You should do what's best for you. I can leave from any airport to get to my assignments. I'll be with you as much as possible, regardless of where my truck is parked."

He's in as deep as I am. "Are you sure?"

"Yes. I want you, Madeleine. I want to build on what we already share through good days, bad days, and every day in between."

"Thank you. Will you join me for dinner at Estelle's for Thanksgiving?"

A huge grin breaks out on his face. "I was going to invite you to Betty's. Where does Estelle live exactly and what time would dinner be?"

We determine our grandmothers live about forty minutes away from one another and we could easily make both if we stay at his place in Maryland. I haven't been there yet. We went to my hotel after Callie's wedding because he was in the process of moving out of the bunkhouse and into Connor's condo. Maia and Nolan were also offered the option but declined.

"Well, that's settled. How is Simon taking the news?" he asks before clearing his plate of the last swipe of sauce.

"With Stavros's consent, I shared the news with Simon and asked him to start a search for a second assistant. I also asked him if he would be willing to move with me if I leave New York."

"I can't imagine him saying no, although I don't know Simon personally. Professionally, he's solid and a great coconspirator. Does he have a significant other?"

I snicker a little. "I should fire him for helping you."

"You loved our celebratory dinner. Don't fire him for giving me a little additional insight into your schedule to make sure the timing was right."

I wink at him. "Fine. Finding him a partner is on my to-do list. He said he would consider DC but doesn't want to be across the country from his family. I completely understand where he's coming from."

"Did you already eliminate LA as an option?"

His ability to see me is unsettling and comforting at the same time. "Pretty much. I can't be so much further away from Estelle." Or him, but I don't add it again. *Get it together, Madi! He told you he's in.*

"When do you plan to go to DC and for how long?"

"It depends. What is your plan after your assignment in Maine?"

"I plan to come back here, but I'll be on call if Jake needs me for a week. Then I'll be on vacation for two weeks, including Thanksgiving. What are you thinking?"

I gaze down at our still linked hands. "I'm considering going after your assignment. We could fly there sometime on Monday, and I could take almost a week in DC. Then I'll take two weeks off. Work for a few weeks and then take the rest of the year. Other than a farewell for Stavros, it should be no problem."

"I love your plan."

"Can I stay with you?"

He rises from his seat and lifts my hand to his lips. "You don't ever have to ask. Ready to share something new with me?"

"You're searching. I'm not simply going to tell you."

"If you need something, you have to tell me, sexually or otherwise."

I throw a sultry look over my shoulder. "I need you to explore every inch of my body until you find a new spot that will make me come."

"There's one I haven't found yet?"

"Perhaps."

"Game on." He follows me to the kitchen.

I push the sleeves of his hoodie up above my elbows and attempt to wash our dishes. He spins me around, tugs the zipper down, and drags his tongue as low as the vee of his shirt will allow, then pushes the hoodie to the marble floor and lifts his shirt over my head.

"My clothes look hot on you, but they look even better on the floor." A wry smile breaks out on his face before he draws one nipple between his teeth and rolls the other between his thumb and fingers.

I grip the cool edge of the granite, and a low moan falls from my lips as he travels down the valley between my breasts, and he drags his tongue along the underside of my breast. "You already found that one." I wince when he pushes my breasts up to lick the most tender spot.

"You okay?" No way he would have missed me flinch.

I nod. *Why am I sore?* Shaking off the thought, I thread my fingers through his soft, thick hair as he travels down my abdomen.

He turns me away from him and explores upward from the small of my back to the nape of my neck. "Follow me," he whispers and extends his hand to me.

Tingles run from the spot his breath hit my skin over my entire body. Taking his hand, I let him lead me to the chaise in front of the fireplace in the bedroom. His hands on my hips guide me to the cushion. An open hand splayed across my chest lowers me to my back. Grabbing the waist of my leggings and panties, he peels them down and casts them aside. Painstakingly he kisses his way from the top of my foot and up the outside of my leg. Each press of his lips and slide of his skin over mine forces slivers of pleasure cascading through my veins. A sultry sigh escapes my lips as I squirm beneath him before he moves back down and rising again from my ankle until he reaches the seam of my leg. His breath on my dripping and achy core could send me over the edge.

After one swipe of his tongue, he murmurs against my skin, "Shall I keep going or use this one?"

"Are you sure you checked everywhere?" I ask in jest.

He drags his tongue along the space between my core and my other thigh. "I'm thorough."

My fingernails dig deeper into his shoulders. "Yes, you are."

"So much so I know I didn't miss anywhere on your perfect body. I'm also certain I would have found every sweet spot to make your toes curl since we met."

I push up onto my elbows and look down at him. His gorgeous cerulean eyes meeting mine. "Yet you searched anyway?"

"Worshipping you and coaxing pleasured moans and orgasms from your body is one of my favorite things to do."

Sweet mercy, the things he says to me. "Let's chase one together."

Without another word, he nudges my thighs wider and flattens his tongue along my folds and continues climbing until he reaches my lips. Setting my calf on his shoulder, he buries his hard length into my center. Our rhythm is steady and matched by our fingers intertwined teasing my clit. My release tightens in my lower body. I increase my pace, and he meets me with equal measure. His face scrunches up, and his fingers dig into my hip even deeper.

"Go over with me…." As the words leave my lips, the now taut spiral unravels faster than ever before, and we fall into bliss together.

A mere breath later, Christoph lowers himself to hover over me. "It was more intense than usual." He presses his lips to mine and rolls us onto our sides.

"What time do you need to leave?" I ask, even though I don't want him to leave at all.

He frowns for the briefest of moments. "I need to leave at five. I'll try not to wake you."

"No." My answer comes out more forceful than I intend. "Please don't leave without waking me. I need at least a kiss to tide me over until you come back."

"Okay, I'll wake you before I leave. I'm going to miss you."

"Me too." *More than I've admitted to him.*

We clean up and slide beneath the sheets.

CHAPTER SIXTEEN

CHRISTOPH

Never before her have I wished a job away. I set my bag near the door and retreat to the bedroom. Somehow, I was able to slip out of bed without waking Madeleine.

I would give almost anything to stay with her instead of babysitting in Maine. My opinion of this assignment sounds terrible even in my own mind. This job isn't difficult or taxing in any way. I'm going to make the husbands feel better about leaving their wives and children alone for four days—all six of them.

You would think the women would bristle. They have each other, but given the past security issues with Billie, Kelly, Noelle, and Savannah, they have compromised on having me nearby with a few check-ins during the long weekend. Hired photographers and private investigators followed and harassed Billie. Kelly had a previous boyfriend and former employee of her husband stalk her. Noelle was harassed by the paparazzi, not only because of her brother's big-shot Hollywood status, but marrying Cash, New York's most eligible bachelor. Billie is Cash's little sister. Ellis is Noelle's brother and Kelly's husband. When Cash married Noelle, Sam took his place on the list. Then he started dating Savannah.

Not only was she followed but kidnapped for ransom as well. I understand why they want me there. Being away wasn't unpalatable until I had someone waiting for me at home.

Lowering myself to the edge of the bed, I draw my hand down the side of her flawless cheek. "*Anamchara*, I need to go."

She stirs, and her eyes flutter open. "Already?"

"Afraid so. I set the alarm for you. I'll be back as soon as I can." I consider asking her to only go to work, but I don't want to alarm her any further. There have been no developments since Blaine found images of Betty. He will alert me if there's a breach. I lower my mouth to hers and kiss her tenderly. Her warm hand cups the side of my face. As I pull away, she drags her thumb across my lower lip.

"Call me when you can," she whispers as if she has no right to ask.

"I know you're scared. I meant what I said. If Jake felt you were in any danger, he would replace me on this assignment."

She nods. I press a kiss to her forehead and push off the bed. If I don't, I won't leave her. The hold she has on me is strong and deep into my soul. At the threshold, I pause and look back at her. Madeleine blows me a kiss, and I move to the door. Bag in hand, I ride down to my car destined for the airport.

A bumpy flight later, I land at a nearby airport and turn my phone back on.

Anamchara: *Thank you for breakfast. I miss you already.*

Me: My pleasure. Have a great day at work. I miss you too.

I fetch the keys to the rental at the counter and drive into York Beach. Instead of heading to Norah's townhouse first, I make a stop at So Elegant where Kelly and Billie should be. Norah is originally from York Beach. When she moved in with Jake, she kept her townhouse because it's paid for and it's useful for jobs like this one given how many of our clients live nearby.

I ring the bell, and Billie answers the door. She's a tiny blonde who creates amazing couture dresses. "You're here early."

"Hi, Billie. I came straight here. Getting my visits out of the way. Then I can simply call later."

She rolls her eyes. "We can take care of ourselves."

"I'm sure you can, but given the sheer number of you and the children, the guys and Jake felt a little backup wouldn't hurt. How many children are there now?"

"Between all of us, there are six plus two on the way." Billie sets her hand on her belly.

"You?"

She nods.

I lean down and hug her loosely. "Congratulations!"

"Thank you."

Kelly breezes into the room. "Good morning, Christoph. Did you sleep at all?"

"Of course. I left at six this morning. The flight isn't long. How are you?"

"As I told my husband, we're fine. All of us, but we appreciate you being here just in case. Where is your next stop?"

I smile. "The Perk, then Noelle's office, Caroline, then Savannah's, and lastly the townhouse. Call me if you need anything." They won't call unless there's an absolute emergency.

"We will," the ladies reply at once.

I shake my head and exit the store. Around the corner, I step into the Perk and grab a coffee and one of Kelsey's delicious scones. Kelsey is the owner of the Perk and a member of the girl gang. She has attended many of the girls' nights at Kelly's or Noelle's.

"Hi, Scarlett." Savannah's younger sister Scarlett is at the counter to take my order.

It takes her a moment to place where she knows me from. "Christoph, welcome to the Perk. Nice to see you again. Is my sister okay?"

Her concerns are legitimate. The last time she saw me was when Savannah was taken by an unscrupulous loan shark to get repayment for their father's debt. "Yup. She's fine."

"What can I fetch for you?"

I give her my order and wait off to the side. While I wait, a few customers stroll in. It's the off season, so it isn't as busy as the summer months.

"Christoph?"

I turn to find Captain William Ramirez, Kelsey's husband, and Sergeant Grant Washington, Kelly's brother-in-law, approaching. I extend my hand to both. "Morning, gentlemen. Nice to see you again." Previously when Blackthorne provided security, we interfaced with the local authorities, including William and Grant. I'm sure Jake informed William about my presence though we don't expect any issues.

"Fishing trip?" Grant asks.

"Yup."

"I'm sure the women will be fine," Grant adds.

Considering my stomach is in knots leaving Madeleine alone, I understand how the men feel. There isn't a threat to her, but there is one to me. My presence, though likely unnecessary, makes them feel at ease. "You're probably correct. I understand their position though."

"Same. I refuse to leave Kelsey, Benjamin, and Valentina alone if I can help it," William adds.

I would prefer to be significantly closer to Madeleine, threat or not. "I understand."

"What's her name?" Grant asks.

"Madeleine," I respond without a second thought.

"Damn! I was kidding around. Good for you, man!"

I fail to hide the smile talking about her brings to my face. "Thanks."

Scarlett returns with my order.

"Thanks, Scarlett."

"Anytime. Have a nice day. Please say hi to my sister for me."

"Will do. Have a nice day, guys."

"Let us know if you need assistance," William offers.

"I shouldn't, but thanks." I wave to everyone and step outside. The salty air hits me given there's a strip of beach a block over. I inhale deeply and take the long way around to my rental. Even without the salty scent, the riverbank at Jake's compound soothes me the same.

I drive over to Noelle's office. She owns a daycare, but her focus is creating specialized plans for kids who need assistance in reading or math and implementing the individualized plans at their schools. She recently hired her sister-in-law Caroline to work with her. When I push the doorbell, the young girl behind the desk asks for my name before buzzing me in.

"I'll get Mrs. Morgan for you." Her voice is shaky considering she's at most five feet tall and I tower over her. Minutes later, she returns and escorts me to Noelle's office.

"Morning, Christoph."

"Morning. Is that Emme?" A raven-haired toddler is playing with blocks on the floor. She grew so much since the last time I saw her. Emme is Sam and Savannah Morgan's daughter. I would be guessing if I said she's a year and a half old.

Noelle smiles. "Yes. All the children are here. It'll save you a trip to Savannah's."

I chuckle. "I appreciate you trying to make my day easier, but I'll visit Savannah all the same. I'll be able to say I saw each of you today when your husbands call."

Noelle shakes her head. "We're getting together tomorrow night at Caroline's."

"Speaking of Caroline, is she here?" I ask. It'll save me another stop.

"She'll be here in the next fifteen minutes." Noelle advises the young receptionist to have Caroline stop by her office when she arrives.

"Great," I reply and take a seat.

Emme toddles over to me and sets her hands on my thigh. Once she's steady, she lifts her arms up.

"She wants you to pick her up," Noelle informs me.

I lift her into my lap, and she smiles widely.

"Dis?" She looks at Noelle.

Noelle replies, "This is Christoph."

"Tof, tof," Emme repeats before throwing her arms around me as best she can and setting her head on my chest.

"She likes you."

I grin at Emme. "What's not to like? Although I'm surprised she isn't scared given my stature."

"True, you are taller than her father and uncles."

Emme hasn't moved since she set her head on my chest. Her eyes are closed, and her breathing is slow and measured. I don't have much experience with babies, but I want to be a dad someday. I wonder if Madeleine wants children.

"Where did your mind go?"

I glance up from Emme to Noelle. "Why?"

"Your features softened, and you smiled."

"I smile." My voice adequately portrays my disagreement with her statement. Madeleine makes me happier than I've ever been. Logic would suggest my smile is bigger or different because of her.

"You do, but not in a wistful and happy manner. Have I met her?"

I hang my head. "You are the second person today to pin I'm dating someone. I don't think you could have met Madeleine."

"She makes you happy. Hold on to her."

"I plan to."

Caroline lightly knocks on the door, and Noelle's finger goes straight to her lips. Caroline rounds my chair to stand beside Noelle. "Awww! You look hotter with a baby sound asleep on your chest. As you can see, I'm fine."

"I'm only doing my job, Caroline," I whisper in an effort not to wake Emme.

"I know, but these men of ours are overreacting."

"Perhaps, but a visit from me now and tomorrow evening isn't too bad. Plus, you'll be together so it'll be simple."

Caroline pinches the bridge of her nose, clearly annoyed by my presence. "Fine. We'll see you tomorrow night."

I tighten my hold around Emme and cradle her in the crook of my arm as I rise from the chair. "Where should I set her down?"

"Follow me," Noelle states.

I follow her out of the office into the center. All talking ceases and every eye in the place is watching me intently. I set Emme down in a small crib in a darkened room and back out. "Thanks for letting me stop by Noelle. I'll see the entire girl gang tomorrow night."

"Sounds good."

I exit the center and take a short ride to see Savannah. I left Savannah last for a few reasons. One, it's the furthest away, but also her home is near the Nubble Lighthouse.

I bound up the steps and ring the bell.

"Hi, Christoph." Savannah answers the door and gestures for me to step inside. She's comfortably dressed and visibly pregnant. She runs Morgan Insurance with Sam out of their home office.

"Savannah. How are things?"

"Great. Ever since the move here, everything has been quiet."

Their home is a newer build and has modern furniture and a spectacular ocean view.

"Scarlett says hello by the way. I saw her at the Perk this morning after I stopped by So Elegant."

"Thanks. She's come a long way since we left New York. I'm sorry to cut this short, but I have a conference call in ten minutes."

I wave her off. "No problem. I'll see you tomorrow night at Caroline's."

"Have a nice day, Christoph."

I close the door behind me after replying, "You too, Savannah." Effectively dispatched and finished with my work for the day, I park in the lot before the majestic lighthouse. In the summer months, this park teems with cars and tourists. Given the time of the year, the park is desolate.

Before I get out of the car, I check in with Betty.

"Hello there."

"Hi, Grams. How is everything going?"

"I'm fine. Don't worry about me. Finn is a good kid. His weeding skills are exceptional."

I chuckle inwardly. Finn is going to despise me when this situation is resolved. "Glad he's offering you some assistance."

"Will you still be able to visit for the holiday?"

It isn't optional in my opinion. "That's the plan. I would like to bring Madeleine if it's okay with you."

"Oh my old lady heart! You finally told her how you feel."

I smirk. "I did."

"Of course. I can't wait to meet the woman who captured your heart all those months ago."

"I'll see you soon. Go easy on Finn. He's there to keep me sane."

"Any leads?"

"Nothing that helps me determine who is looking for me. Any chance it's my parents?"

Betty exhales sharply. "I have never lied to you, Christoph. The afternoon your mother showed up with you in her arms was the last time I've ever heard from her. Perhaps I should have looked for my daughter, but in my heart I knew being here was the best thing for you."

"I'm not suggesting you lied. Not everyone is as lucky as I am. You willingly raised your grandson, and you did it without complaint or making me feel like a burden. You didn't have to do any of those things. I'm forever grateful."

"You're a good man, Christoph."

"You raised me well. I may not have had the latest sneakers, but I had what I needed. I love you, Grams."

"I love you. I'll see you soon."

I end the call and stare out my windshield for a few moments before I take a seat on a large rock. The waves are crashing below me, and the soothing sound of the water settles me. Every time my mind is clear of work, I think of Madeleine. That isn't accurate; she's always in the front of my mind. I knew when we met, she is special. Now thoughts of her consume me. Unlike Connor, I'm not a partner in Blackthorne, but I could request to change my role in the company. Travelling this much and being away from Madeleine isn't going to work for me much longer.

I suppose it will depend on which office she chooses to use as her base. Would a New York office be a solid addition to the company? Is there work I could do only at the compound? A lot of possibilities swirl in my head, each one centered around Madeleine. She's the first woman who has captured and held my attention. I refuse to let her go.

Me: How was your morning?

Anamchara: *Busy. You?*

Me: I finished my first set of visits. Now I'm sitting at the lighthouse.

Anamchara: *Sounds beautiful.*

I take a picture of the lighthouse and the ocean to my right and send it to her.

Anamchara: *Wow! It looks peaceful.*

Me: It is. We can come for a visit if you want.

Anamchara: *I would love to visit. I'll talk to you tonight.*

Me: TTYL.

I was hoping our texting would center me more. The reality is I need her within arm's reach as much as possible. After some more time passes, I drive to Norah's townhouse and settle in for the rest of the day.

CHAPTER SEVENTEEN

MADELEINE

I hurry out of the office and into the waiting car. "Afternoon, Jack."

"Afternoon, Madeleine."

I gaze out the window, watching the city pass by.

Shortly thereafter Jack opens the car door and escorts me into the nondescript office building. "I'll be here when you're finished."

"Thanks, Jack. It shouldn't be long." I have an appointment for my yearly physical. About two weeks ago, I had blood drawn per my doctor's request.

The perky brunette behind reception escorts me immediately into a small conference room instead of an exam room.

"Madeleine, it's wonderful to see you again."

"Hi, Dr. Sullivan."

"Give me one moment to review these results again." She takes a minute to look over the papers in my chart. "How have you been feeling lately?"

"Not too bad. A bit more tired than normal. I've had a few bouts of nausea from not eating enough and increased breast tenderness, but that's because I'm due this week."

She looks up at me and says, "You're pregnant."

Each seemingly disconnected thing makes complete sense right now. Everything I've dismissed as unimportant was a huge clue. "Can you repeat that?"

Dr. Sullivan smiles and takes my hand in hers. "I know this is a bit of a shock, but you're going to have a baby."

"I *never* miss my pill. I have an alarm on my phone!"

"Nothing is 100 percent."

I'm sure there are appropriate questions I should be asking right now. Yet only Christoph's gorgeous face is front and center. "How far along?" I manage to ask.

"You're on the seasonal pill, correct? It means you only get a period every quarter instead of every month."

I nod and pull out my phone. "My last period was at the end of the last pack." *Three months ago!*

"Based on your cycle, I would estimate you're about ten weeks along. Small meals will help with the nausea, and the breast tenderness should ease in the next few weeks, along with the fatigue." Her response is soft as she squeezes my hand. "Is there someone I can call for you?"

I know she means the father. "No, I'm fine. Surprised but fine. He's out of town for business until Sunday."

"You'll need to follow up with your gynecologist and schedule an ultrasound. I'll give you a prescription for prenatal vitamins. You should fill it as soon as possible."

"Thank you." I take the prescription from her and push to my feet.

"Congratulations, Madeleine." She exits the room, and I follow close behind. Slowly, I walk toward the elevator.

With each step, I start to wrap my brain around the fact I'm going to be a mom. A baby who is half me and half Christoph. My heart tightens in my chest. I hope he or she has his eyes—stunning and deeply expressive eyes seemingly only I can read.

I've always wanted to be a mom. I would have preferred to be married first. Does Christoph want children? It's one topic we haven't discussed yet. In all fairness, we haven't been literally dating very long. I have no idea how he's going to feel about this development. I'm nervous but ecstatic all at once. The timing isn't ideal given my pending promotion, but I'll figure it out.

"Everything okay, Madeleine?" Jack's voice pulls me out of my head.

"Yes, thank you." I settle into the back seat and set my hands on my lower abdomen. "I've got you, baby," I whisper. Assurance—some for me and some for my child.

"Back to the office?" Jack asks.

"Yes. Thank you."

Before I return to my office, I stop by the break room and grab a few packages of graham crackers and a bottled water. Simon catches me before I get into the safety of my office. Keeping this news to myself until I see Christoph in person isn't going to be easy.

"Everything good, Mads?"

"Yes. How is the candidate search going?"

Simon smirks. "I have three lined up for telephone interviews for next week while you visit DC."

"Perfect. Please set them in my calendar."

He closes himself into my office. "Already done."

"You're my work rock, Si."

Simon opens his mouth with a snappy comeback but pauses.

"Say it."

"Work rock, huh? I'm hurt. I've been replaced."

I chuckle "You have never been my rock outside of here, Si. I'm not your type. I will find you a kick-ass partner and soon."

"Don't worry about me. Your free time is full off the clock. I've seen Mr. Anderson; I completely understand. That mountain of a man has a soft center only you see. He takes care of you. He uses subterfuge appropriately to surprise you, which you deserve more than anyone I know."

My cheeks blush and realization floods my brain. Christoph is nothing short of amazing. He willingly stands beside me and isn't diminished by my success or paycheck. He takes care of me more than anyone, aside from Estelle. *I love him.* I'm in love with the man who is the father of my unborn child. "He is all of those things. Thank you."

"Anything else?" Simon asks.

"Not right now. I'm going to review these reports for the rest of the day."

"No worries." He latches the door behind him.

After Simon leaves, I call to make an appointment for an ultrasound. Thankfully, I can get in on Monday before we leave for DC. I push in my wireless earbuds, set the volume to low, and bury my nose in the first set of reports. A few hours later, I toss two into my bag and head out for the evening. Instead of dwelling on the fact my apartment feels huge without him here, I change, grab my camera, and take a taxi to Central Park.

The weather is gorgeous. The diminishing foliage is shades of crimson, golden yellow, and deep orange. I capture photos near Sheep Meadow. Then I meander to The Lake and take more shots there. As the sun sets and a chill grips the air, I capture more images near the Boathouse, including what appears to be a proposal. Unable to keep these images to myself, I hurry over to the couple.

"Excuse me," I state as I approach them.

They look up at me, sheer joy plastered on both of their faces. "Yes?"

"Congratulations! I was taking landscape images, and I captured your proposal. If you would be willing to give me your email address, I can forward them to you."

The bride-to-be is beaming. "Really?"

"Absolutely. Check them out. I'm Madi by the way." I turn the display toward her, and tears fall down her cheeks.

"Sofie and Greg." She leans forward and checks out the images. "These are amazing! Are you a photographer?"

"No, only for me. It's relaxing."

"You're talented." Greg hands me a card with Sofie's email address on it.

"Thank you. Congratulations, again. I'll clean these up and send them to you." I smile inwardly and make my way back toward a taxi home. Once I'm in the back seat, my phone vibrates in my back pocket.

CA: Hey there. Are you home?

Me: Almost.

CA: Is everything okay?

Me: Of course. The light was perfect. I was taking photos at the park.

I feel terrible withholding information from him. I can't share this monumental news over the phone. I need to look him in the eyes and share we're going to be parents—together.

CA: Please call me when you're home.

Me: No problem.

After tipping the driver, I enter the lobby.

"Good evening, Miss Wilton."

"Hello."

"Here is your mail and a delivery that arrived for you."

I accepted the envelopes and the bags. One looks like there's a cooler inside. I'm giddy and intrigued. Even from Maine, he's still taking care of me. There's no way he knows I'm starving.

Setting the bags on the island, I shrug off my jacket and tennis shoes. What I want most is to call Christoph. No, I want him to be here so I can kiss him and share our incredible, fantastic, and a bit scary news. *Sigh.* I pluck the ivory envelope from the bags.

Anamchara,

He has only called me that once before. What does it mean? I push my thoughts away and keep reading.

I ordered these from the food truck from the festival. It's everything we had on our first date. I would ask you to save some for me, but we both know it would be futile. I'll be back as soon as possible. xoxo, Christoph

I open the cooler and find a cheesecake pop and cannoli. After moving them into the fridge, I pull out an order of tacos and the chicken kabobs I ate. This must have taken a ton of legwork.

Me: Are you free?

My phone rings almost immediately with a video call.

His gorgeous face fills my screen. He looks like he recently completed a workout though. "Hi."

"Hi. How are the Morgan and Barnett women? It sounds like you have a harem or something."

He laughs. "They're fine and marginally miffed by my presence. I see both sides. Each had some form of security issue over the last few years. All the husbands are away together. It's precautionary. Only Emme seemed fine with my presence. She fell asleep on me while I was talking to Noelle."

My chest tightens. "Awww, Uncle Christoph. Sam's daughter, right? How old is she now?"

"Yes, Sam's daughter. She's about eighteen months old I guess."

"How sweet. You don't have to prepare dinner for me from so far away. Thank you. I appreciate it, and I'm sure it was a lot of work, but I can take care of myself." *I'm not against being taken care of though, especially by him.*

"I know you can. I want to. Will you let me, please?"

Oh my heart! I need to tell him. No, not over the phone. I'm not telling him I love him or he's going to be a dad over the phone—video call or not. "I will."

"Glad it's settled. How was the park?"

The joy of taking photos and capturing the proposal brings a huge grin to my face. I share about the images and Greg and Sofie.

"They're lucky you happened to be nearby with your camera."

"Thanks. What do you plan to do this evening?"

"I need to shower, and then I'm going to watch the game. What about you?"

"After I eat the amazing meal you sent, I'll review some more of the reports and the proposed contract for my promotion probably with the game on in the background."

"Eat, sweetheart. I'll call you during halftime."

"I will. Talk to you later."

We end the call, and I warm the food he sent. It's as delicious as I remember. I curl up on the couch with one of the boxes of reports but decide to review my new contract as the CEO and President of Scala Talent.

I review the boilerplate language at the beginning quickly as nothing is out of the ordinary. It provides for car service and business or first-class flights when necessary—both items I already have in my current contract. There's an additional three weeks of vacation on top of the three I already have. Then I get to the compensation portion. Currently, I earn a significant salary on top of the commission from my clients. I'm floored. Not only does this contract almost double my base salary, it maintains the commission I get from my clients, and it also gives me 2.5 percent of every commission in the company.

More simply, if an agent signs a client with Scala, the company has a minimum commission of 10 percent. If it were my client, I would earn 5 percent and the company gets the other 5 percent. If the commission is fifteen, the agent gets ten, the company still five. When Stavros retires, half of the company percent would be payable to me. I would earn seventy-five percent for my clients, plus 2.5 percent of every other agent. *Insanity!* It certainly explains Stavros's numerous real estate holdings.

I live frugally given how much I earn. True, I have a luxury apartment and wardrobe, and I make sure Estelle wants for nothing. Aside from purchasing my apartment, I live off my salary and invest all my commissions. I have since my second year with Scala. There's absolutely nothing in the contract that gives me pause. I would sign it now if it didn't have a draft watermark on it.

My phone chime pulls me out of my thoughts. "Hey," I answer and push the video button.

"Hi. You look shell-shocked. The game isn't a blowout." His observation is on point.

"I am a little. I reviewed the employment contract first."

"That good or that bad?"

"I'm speechless. My current salary and commission structure affords me a lot of things, and frankly, I save most of it. The new one as the president and CEO is insane."

"You worked your ass off to get where you are. I'm sure you deserve everything Stavros is offering you."

"Thank you. All quiet there?"

"Yes. I have sufficiently annoyed the Morgan and Barnett women with my visits and calls today."

I giggle. "Except Emme."

"Except Emme."

I can't contain a huge yawn.

"Get some sleep, *anamchara*. I'll call you in the morning."

"What does that mean?"

He inhales deeply. "It's Gaelic for soul friend. In English, it translates to soul mate."

"Oh, Christoph. It's beautiful."

"True too."

"I wish you were here."

"Why?"

I love you, and we're going to have a baby. "I would prefer to show you how much you mean to me instead of going to sleep alone."

"Me too. I'll be back as soon as I can. Good night, *anamchara*."

"Good night, Christoph." I end the video and curse the timing of my appointment. I hate this. Then I remind myself news like this requires hand holding and eye contact as well as the ability to be held afterward. I sincerely hope he isn't angry with me for waiting until we're together.

I clean up and curl into my bed, which feels so much larger without him here, and sleep fitfully until the wee hours of the morning.

Instead of languishing in my inability to sleep, I head into the office. It's desolate and deathly quiet this early in the morning. A few hours later, Simon taps on the doorframe of my office.

"Morning. You're here early. Lover Boy out of town?"

I give him the side-eye but answer anyway. "Please don't call him that." *It isn't like the other option is better—baby daddy. Ugh!* "I couldn't sleep, so I came in early. What's your excuse?"

"Same except for the boy toy in my bed part."

"Si, don't come up with more names. He has one; please use it."

"Touchy, this morning."

I glare at him.

"Your day is light. I added one more phone interview for next week to your schedule."

"Thank you. I'm sorry for being snippy. I got used to sharing my space, and now I'm alone and it feels...."

"Lonely, for lack of a better word," Simon suggests.

"Exactly."

He nods, steps into my office, and the door snicks closed. "I've been thinking about your offer. I'm willing to move to DC if you'll still have me. I can't do LA though, I'm sorry."

I rise from my chair and hug him. "Thank God! I can't do this without you. LA is certainly at the bottom of my list of bases. Stavros hasn't been to the LA office in the last three years for more than a meeting or two. I plan to make a final choice by the end of my vacation."

"Perfect, Mads."

He leaves my office, and I turn my attention to the report for individual agents. Whoever compiled this report is thorough. It lists each agent, their highest year, lowest, and the average over their entire career with Scala. I'm not surprised the top two are Stavros and myself. I'm shocked by the third person on the list—Mitchell Kennedy. According to this, he's been with Scala for the last five years. Yet I've never met him. He's based in LA. He's third on the list, but his average commission is about half of what I pull in. The rest of the agents are incrementally lower.

Near eleven, I look through the glass of my office and a vaguely familiar Latino man steps into view. His hair is dark, almost black, and his skin is still darkened from the summer sun. He's about my height and built like a boxer—broad shoulders and a lean waist.

"Mads, there is a Lt. Cruz here to see you." Simon's voice crackles through the intercom.

Even though I still can't place him, I have Simon send him in. "Good afternoon, can I help you?"

"Hello, I'm Javier Cruz. C-top sent me." He shakes his head. "Christoph sent me."

Fear slices through me. "Is he okay? Is Estelle? Is everyone okay? How do I know you are who you say you are? Even though you look familiar, it isn't enough for me to go with you."

He pulls out his phone with a grin on his face.

A familiar voice immediately answers, "Yeah, Cruz."

Christoph.

"You were right. She's cautious and suspicious." He turns the phone toward me, and Christoph's face fills the screen.

"*Anamchara*, there have been some developments overnight. I need you to go with Cruz. He's going to take you to the Morgan's New York home. I'll be there as soon as I can."

"Okay. I need to pack up. Is there any rush?" It's awkward having Cruz hold the phone in front of me. "May I?" I point to his phone.

"Of course. I'll be right outside the door."

"Thanks, Cruz," Christoph states.

"I've got your six, brother. Always." Cruz leaves my office.

I turn the phone, and the pained look on his face is almost too much. "Madeleine, I'll explain in more detail later. Please listen to Cruz. I need you to call Estelle and give her a heads-up. Jake is sending Maia to her, and Connor is on his way here to replace me."

I nod furiously. "Please hurry, we need you here."

"I love you. I'll be there soon." He ends the call before I can respond.

He loves me. Does he realize he told me he loves me? I said "we."

I inhale sharply and use the intercom, "Si, could you come in here with Cruz please."

Moments later both men step into my office. I hand Cruz his phone back. "I need about fifteen minutes to gather what I need for my trip to DC next week."

I don't miss the noncommittal shrug from Cruz.

"Si, please reschedule my conference call on Monday morning for the Rodin contract to later in the week, maybe Wednesday. Also, can you make a file of the resumés for my interviews next week and print the latest data for my client list, please."

"On it, Mads." He dutifully leaves to do what I asked.

"Is there anything I can help with?" Cruz offers.

"Not yet, but thank you. You were at the wedding, right? Mostly chatting with Jill if I recall correctly."

A tight smile graces his face. "Yes, I was. I served with Jake, Connor, and Christoph."

I wonder how Jake feels about Cruz cozying up to his little sister. I ignore my stray thought and pack what I need.

I finish going through the files and then call Estelle as requested.

"Hi, ladybug. How are you?"

"I'm fine. There has been a potential security breach with a client. There's no need to panic. However, Blackthorne Security is sending a woman named Maia to stay with you. It's only a precaution. Maia is great. I've worked with her before."

"What about you?" Estelle's tone is concerned. Little does she know there's two of us here.

"Christoph sent someone here as well."

"Where is he? Shouldn't he be with you?"

I love Estelle's feisty side. Everyone should have at least one person in their life who fiercely protects them. *I've got you, little one.* "He's on his way back to me. He was on an assignment."

"I'll do what you ask. Please be safe. Will you still be here for the holiday?"

"I certainly hope so. Love you, Grams."

"I love you, ladybug."

I end the call and close my eyes briefly.

"You did a good job," Cruz praises me.

"Thanks. Nothing I said was a lie, but I could've given her a bit more information."

"For Estelle, it is only a precaution. However, it seems as if whoever is looking for C-top is branching out slowly."

I acknowledge his words as Si returns with the information I requested. In under twenty minutes, we in the car on our way to the Morgan's.

CHAPTER EIGHTEEN

CHRISTOPH

"Yeah, Jake." My phone wakes me from a sound sleep in Norah's guest bedroom. There's no chance this call is a good one. I glance at the clock. It's near nine in the morning.

"Blaine called. Now they're also following Madeleine. I forwarded the photos to you from yesterday afternoon. She was in an office building on the upper west side and then Central Park. She spoke with a couple there as well."

"She was taking photos and caught a proposal. She wanted to share the images with them."

Jake continues, "Blaine is still looking for who is behind all of this. He believes one of his contemporaries handles cyber security for the private investigator. According to Blaine, only a few people in the world know how to hide information extremely well. He reached out to her a few hours ago."

My brain is spinning, searching for someone I trust who lives in New York City. "Is Cruz available?"

"I called him first. He's waiting for someone to come in to cover his shift. Christoph, I've been in a comparable situation with Norah. We'll figure it out. Cruz will take care of her for you. Connor is on his way there. Please leave the notes from your assignment on the island and get to the airport."

"Thanks, brother."

"You did it for me. You're family. If Madeleine is yours, so is she."

Mine. Completely mine. I hang up, hustle through the shower, hurriedly pack, scribble notes for Connor, and leave for the airport. As I park the rental, my phone rings.

"Yeah, Cruz."

After talking to Madeleine, I settle into my seat on the plane. Once we're airborne, it hits me—she said, *"We need you."* I also shared how I truly feel about her. I would have preferred to tell her in person. I ponder my misstep and attempt to placate the fear gripping me.

Someone is searching for me and not only put Betty but the woman I love at risk and, if I heard her correctly, our child. I need to get to Madeleine, and then I can focus on whether I'm going to be a father. I won't be calm until her fingers are threaded between mine.

Right before five, I hurry into the lobby of Cash's building. "Good evening, Arthur. How are you and your wife?"

"We're well, Mr. Anderson. Thank you for asking. Lt. Cruz and Miss Wilton arrived a few hours ago. A food delivery is planned near six this evening."

"Thank you." When the elevator doors open and I see Madeleine sitting at the island, I finally take a breath. Only once my arms are around her do I breathe normally again. I draw back and kiss her until I'm confident she's truly safe in my embrace.

"I'm fine for now," she whispers. I note the uncertainty in her voice.

Adding some space between us, I gaze down at her and press a kiss to her forehead before releasing her and turning to my friend. "Cruz, thanks for coming."

"Always, brother. You would do the same for me."

"I would. Please join us for dinner."

Cruz shakes his head. "I can't, but thank you for the invite. I'll see you soon anyway."

I raise an eyebrow at him. "I was invited to the baby shower for Callie and Connor's twins. I assume you both will be there."

"Yes, we'll be there," Madeleine answers Cruz. Clearly, she wants Cruz to leave.

I would love to catch up more, but I would prefer to be alone with my woman. We need to talk. "I'll walk you out."

"Thank you, Cruz," Madeleine states.

"You're welcome. If you ever need assistance in the city again, please don't hesitate to call me. I'm always there for my brothers."

"I will."

I fully release her and follow Cruz to the elevator. "We'll catch up more at the shower. I appreciate your assistance."

"No problem. Hold on to her. Despite the circumstances, happy looks good on you."

We bro hug, and he steps onto the elevator. Once the doors close, I turn back to Madeleine. "Did I hear you right? Did you say *we* need you?"

A few tears fall down her face. "Yes, we're going to have baby."

With two large steps, I drop to my knees on the floor in front of her with my hands bracketing her hips. "Hi, baby. It's Daddy. I can't wait to meet you." I press a kiss to her belly and draw her against me.

"We never talked about kids." Her words barely are audible.

"No, we haven't, but I want a houseful of kids. Now it will be sooner than I thought."

"Even with having only Betty?" I hear the concern in her voice.

"Especially having only Betty. She's amazing and Gramps too while he was with us. It was lonely being an only child though."

She nods in agreement.

"What about you?"

"I've always wanted to be a mom, but my life didn't truly lend itself to finding a partner to share it with. I don't know about a houseful but at least two kids. I wanted to tell you in person, but I—"

"When did you find out?"

"Yesterday afternoon."

"I understand. I would have preferred to share my feelings in person as well." I rise from the floor and slide my hands around her face. I skim my lips over hers and pin my gaze on her. "I love you, Madeleine."

"I love you." She leans forward and presses her lips to mine. The flood gates of emotion open. Every ounce of desire, passion, and love I feel I give her in my kiss. She meets me in equal measure. We dance toward the couch, and I sink to the cushion with her in my lap. Unfortunately we're interrupted by the food delivery. Madeleine finds what we need in the kitchen while I set out the food.

After a few bites, she asks, "What happens now?"

"Right now, we're safe here and so is everyone else. I got word from Maia. She's with Estelle."

"I assume they started following me too."

I nod because my mouth is full of food. I didn't realize I was starving. She waits me out. "Jake will call when he has more information. Blaine has determined the private investigator has some high-level help protecting his servers. Not even Blaine can get in. He's reaching out to his friends for assistance."

"So we wait here for now."

"Yes. We have so much to talk about though. Did you have any idea you were pregnant?"

"Not until the doctor put all my recent ailments together. My appointment was for my yearly physical. The blood work showed my pregnancy. She gave me vitamins, and I made an appointment for Monday morning. Can I still go? Will you come?"

"Relax. We'll be at the appointment even if Jake must come here. How pregnant are you?"

A deep laugh erupts from her mouth.

I hang my head at my word choice.

"She estimates about ten weeks. The appointment includes an ultrasound."

"Did she give you any other information or tips?"

"The nausea may subside in a few weeks. Small meals will help in the interim. Breast tenderness and fatigue will also decrease."

"Is the baby the reason you fell asleep after the interviews with Callie."

"Most likely." She finishes her meal.

Soon thereafter I finish as well. "Does anyone else know about the baby?"

"No, only you and me. I want to wait until after the appointment at least to tell anyone else. Okay with you?"

"We can wait at least until then. Please know I want to tell anyone and everyone who will listen."

"Really?" Shock weaves through her tone.

"Absolutely. I'm over-the-top excited about having a baby with you."

"Me too."

I clean up the dishes while she clears the trash. We curl up on the couch and promptly fall asleep. Near midnight I gather her in my arms and carry her into the guest room and sleep the rest of the night more comfortably.

Bright and early, I wake and discover she's not beside me anymore. After a deep breath to remind myself she's safe here, I pad around until I find her on the terrace wrapped in a huge blanket.

"Morning, beautiful."

"Morning."

She stops scrolling on her laptop when I sit beside her.

"What are you reading?"

"Baby stuff. I found a site that provides weekly updates and some other information about changes during pregnancy."

"Cool. Anything I need to know?"

"Not really. If Dr. Sullivan is correct, our baby is about the size of a Polly Pocket doll."

"Polly Pocket?"

She smiles and googles it for me. A colorful doll and accessories appear on the screen. At most it's about two inches tall.

"Amazing! How are you feeling?"

"A little hungry, but otherwise fine. Did you guys order groceries too?"

"No, Cruz wasn't sure if we were staying here or not"

"No problem. I'm going to call Jake and see if he has an update. Then we can determine what to do next." I kiss the top of her head and find my phone. When I return to the terrace, Jake answers.

"Do you have an update?" I ask him.

"Blaine was able to get more information. His hacker friend indicated she's making it difficult for him to access the files. She did share the client is an attorney from Texas. Blaine is trying to broker a deal with her to find out what we need to know. So far she isn't budging. He's going to search for this attorney and see if he can find information some other way. Hopefully, the breadcrumb is enough for Blaine."

"What does it mean for us?" Madeleine asks.

I overhear, "Thanks, Nor. Yes, fine." Then I hear shuffling of papers. "Sorry about that. Right now, I would suggest limiting your movements as much as possible. You don't need to stay at the Morgan's. Her building has adequate security. More so with you there."

"Good. She needs to pack for her business trip."

"Please elaborate," Jake requests.

"After an appointment in the city on Monday morning, she's travelling to the DC office to do a site visit."

I see her attention shift to what I'm saying.

"She plans to be there for a week, and then she's on vacation for the two weeks after."

"Conveniently the same time you're off," Jake states.

"Purposefully the same time I'm off."

"There's no threat of physical harm to either of you. Like I said, limit your movements. I assume you plan to stay at your condo while you're in town."

"Yes. If you need me to sign a contract for Madeleine, Betty, and Estelle, I will."

"Not necessary. We take care of our own."

"Thanks, Jake. Please keep me updated."

"Please check in when you get to her apartment," Jake requests.

"I will." I end the call and return my gaze to the laptop screen. The article is titled: Sex during pregnancy. A first-timer's guide.

"Something you want to share, *anamchara*?"

She snaps the laptop closed. "Nope, nothing at all. Not right now anyway."

I stifle a laugh and draw her against me. "Did you hear Jake's recommendations?"

"Wasn't listening intently."

I share Jake's recommendations with her. "Let's get going. We can order breakfast, pick it up, and order whatever we need for your place until we leave for DC."

"Sounds good."

I tug her lower lip between my teeth. She groans as I release it.

"I saw the title of the article before you closed the laptop."

"Oh. Well, I was curious, and now I have information we will use tonight."

"I see." I kiss her. "I need coffee."

She frowns. "Only decaf for me."

"Decaf it is then."

With the scent of a delicious meal wafting from the bags in my hands, we ride up to her apartment. After eating, we get a head start on packing for our trip to DC and vacation.

"How does your family dress for holiday dinner?" she asks, standing amid her massive walk-in closet.

"I wear jeans and a collared shirt. Will something similar work for Estelle's?"

"Yes, it'll work. You need to keep the sleeves down though."

I raise an eyebrow and move behind her in the closet, my arms clasped over her abdomen. "What's wrong with my forearms?"

"Nothing, absolutely nothing. Yours drive me insane with desire."

I immediately push the sleeves of my Henley up to my elbows.

"That's dirty," she states.

"Well then, let's get dirty together."

She pulls her lower lip between her teeth and turns in my arms. "Yes, let's."

I drop a kiss on her head. "I need you to promise me one thing first."

"Anything."

"If you need me to stop or shift or… if you're uncomfortable at all, I need you to tell me immediately today or at any time in the future."

"Don't worry. We've been doing fine before we knew about the baby."

I press a kiss to her forehead. "Please, say the words."

"I promise."

"Now lose the clothes."

She presses a kiss to my left forearm and draws the sleeve back down, repeating the same thing on the right before pushing my shirt up and off. Piece by piece our clothes mark a path to her bed.

I hover over her. Her hair spread on the duvet around her head, her chest rising and falling in anticipation. Her belly isn't rounded yet, but knowing she's carrying our child sends panic through me again despite her promise.

She cups the side of my face, her eyes conveying confidence in me, in us. "Christoph, we are fine. Make love to me."

Her words sear into my brain. I lower onto my elbows and unleash my unflinching need to love and protect them through my lips. Despite the concerns outside of these walls, every worry falls away when we're together. Nothing else matters, and the outside noise quiets to a point where I can only hear her heart and mine beating as one.

I capture her hands and hold them above her head in one of mine as I skate my fingertips down her arm, along the side of her breast, down to her knee, leaving a trail of goose bumps in my wake. I follow the same path down her other side before nipping and sucking my way down to her core. She trembles beneath me with each deliberate stroke of my tongue on her soft skin.

"I need you to fill me," she demands.

I take in the sultry and intense look in her eyes. There's no room for me to mistake the ache and yearning staring back at me. She widens her thighs, inviting me to bury myself into her already pulsing core. Slowly I push my throbbing, hard length forward until she surrounds me. She wraps her legs around my hips, taking me inexplicably deeper.

We set our demanding rhythm and chase decadent pleasure as one. My mounting release makes my balls tighten and draw closer. Her fingernails score my back with half-moons as radiating sensations ripple through her sensual form. The moment she reaches the pinnacle of her release, I careen over the edge, bucking into her.

When the spikes of pleasure subside, I turn us onto our sides and tuck a few strands of stray hairs behind her ear. "*Anamchara*, open your eyes."

Her ocean-colored eyes meet mine. "That was intense."

"As crazy as this may sound, you feel tighter."

"It doesn't sound crazy to me. It felt intense too."

Not only are we going to have a baby, but the already spectacular sex gets better too. After a long, sexy shower, we finish packing except for last-minute items. With the newly delivered groceries, we prepare a big dinner and then stargaze on her terrace until she succumbs to the pull of dreamland in my arms.

CHAPTER NINETEEN

MADELEINE

Early on Monday morning, I snuggle deeper into Christoph's arms.

"Do we need to get up already?" he murmurs against my shoulder blade. "I love being here in the quiet with you."

"Afraid so. I love it too. The good news is we get to see our baby today."

Reluctantly, only because we were cozy, I rise and get ready for the day. Jack drives us to my appointment.

"This shouldn't take too long. Then we're headed to the airport," I inform Jack.

"No problem. I'll be right here when you're ready."

Christoph takes my hand in his. I tighten my fingers around his as we enter the office.

"Madeleine Wilton," I inform the receptionist.

"Please have a seat. Dr. Richardson will be right with you."

We take a seat near the back corner of the waiting room.

"Why are you shaking?" Christoph whispers.

"I'm nervous."

"We can handle anything together, including a gorgeous baby girl who looks like you."

A small smile cracks on my face and I nod.

"I love you. Both of you." He reaches over and swipes a single tear from my cheek.

"I might need to steal your gratitude for Callie's stalker."

"Steal away."

"I love you." I press a tender kiss to his lips as the nurse calls me in.

She instructs me to disrobe from the waist down and informs us the doctor will join us in a few minutes.

Dr. Richardson enters the room. "Madeleine, lovely to see you. You must be Dad." She extends her hand to Christoph. "Pleasure to meet you."

"We're going to take some information and get baby's first photo."

I'm answering all her questions, but my focus is on Christoph. He pulls the chair closer beside the bed and threads our fingers before kissing the back of my hand. I'm so enraptured in his gaze; I don't even acknowledge the wand for the ultrasound until Dr. Richardson directs us to the screen.

"There's baby."

We turn our eyes to the screen. I have no idea what I'm actually looking at except to say our baby is perfect. Christoph kisses me lightly. The doctor pushes buttons on the machine and makes notes in my chart. I'm staring at the screen mesmerized. I won't say it didn't feel real before, but now…. Dr. Richardson hands Christoph a strip of images she took from the ultrasound.

"You're measuring at almost eleven weeks. Your estimated due date is May 19th." She informs us. "On your way out, you'll make your next few appointments, and Sammie will provide you with a schedule of lab work and a bunch of information. I see in your chart your primary care prescribed prenatal vitamins for you. Please take them as required. As far as things to avoid, no shellfish or sushi, and one caffeinated coffee per day is fine. You can continue your normal exercise for the most part. The basic rule is if you're comfortable, your baby is too."

"Thank you."

"Please don't hesitate to call with questions. Congratulations!" she states as she leaves the room.

Sheer elation is coursing through me. I sit up, slide off the table to the floor, and redress. Christoph is staring at the strip of images in his hands. I have only seen that look on his face once before when we agreed to start dating. I'm confident in the depths of my soul no other woman has seen that look aimed at them. I set my hand on his forearm and squeeze.

"Ready?"

He nods. When he finally looks at me, I see the tears welled up in his eyes he's fighting to hold back. One escapes down his cheek, and I wipe it away with my fingertips. "I wouldn't want to do this with anyone else. I love you, Madeleine."

"I love you."

A few minutes later, he's composed and ready to leave. I make my next few appointments and stop at the restroom on the way out. We slide into the back seat of the car after I tuck the images in my handbag.

The flight to Dulles is blissfully calm. Only recently have I learned Christoph isn't a fan of flying, especially when it's bumpy. Eventually he'll share where his fear came from. Instead of settling at the condo, we head straight to the DC office in a rental from the airport.

The building is half the size of the New York office but has the same opulent fixtures and presence. Christoph ushers me inside before him and retakes my hand.

"Good afternoon. How can I help you?" The perky receptionist looks right past me to Christoph. Her eyes start at his knees and slowly wander up his body to his sexy-as-hell cleft chin and finally stop at his lips.

His gaze never strays away from me.

I glance at my watch. "I suppose it is afternoon. I'm Madeleine Wilton. Could you please direct me to an available office?"

"Oh." Her eyes snap to me once she hears my name. "Please excuse me for not recognizing you. It's a pleasure to meet you in person. I'll show you to an available office right away."

We follow her through the waiting room and down a long corridor to a sparsely furnished but large corner office.

"I'm Angie. Please let me know if you require anything while you're here, Miss Wilton."

"Thank you. We'll be fine."

She closes the door behind her. I can't suppress the laughter any longer.

"I assume that's never happened before."

I put up a finger and contain my laughter. "No, but having you beside me at work is a recent development. It also makes sense considering I'm the only female senior agent in the company. There's no reason for her to assume I was anything other than your arm candy—a fresh out of the NFL or NHL hotshot rookie agent."

He grins at me and draws me against him. "I'm not offended at all it's the other way around."

"I know. It's one of the reasons we fit so well. You aren't diminished by my successful, lucrative career in any way. It's rare, and I'm grateful."

"Good, because you're stuck with me."

"Not stuck at all." I kiss him and round the desk.

Christoph takes a seat in one of the chairs and pulls out his phone.

I set up everything I need on the desk and tackle my overfilled inbox while I call Simon.

"Hey there! How was your flight?"

"Smooth, exactly how I like them. Anything of note there?"

"I've got this, Mads. Let me know if you need anything from afar."

"Thanks, Si. I will."

I complete two contract reviews and a call with Mr. Stockton's new agent. I wish him well. Stefan is a handful of drama.

Near six we exit the lobby and head to his condo. The ride isn't riddled with traffic, which is a welcome departure from my expectations. Anything less than an hour would be perfect. I'm excited to see where Christoph lives.

He pulls into the driveway and parks outside the garage before rounding the car and opening my door. He unlocks the door, disengages the alarm, and follows me up the short staircase.

"You decorated this?"

"No, not at all. Connor hired someone. Why?"

"It's perfect from the colors to the balance of stereotypically feminine touches a man's home wouldn't have." She sets her hand on my arm and tugs off her heels.

"Why don't you sit, and I'll get our luggage."

"I can help." She tugs one of her shoes back on.

"No, you're going to sit. After I bring everything in, I'll cook something." He leads me to the couch.

"Are you going to let me do anything for the next seven months?"

He takes my shoe off my foot again and grabs the other. With a kiss, he replies, "Not if I can help it."

My head falls back, and I let the soft cushions absorb my weight. By the time he finishes bringing in our luggage, I'm lying on my back looking at the ceiling.

"You good?"

"Yup. It feels nice to relax though."

"Jake is on his way with the groceries and to take the rental back. Do you want to change now or later?"

"I'll change after Jake leaves. I don't want to do it twice, but I could unpack a bit."

"Sure, right this way."

I follow him into a huge master with a large bed with hunter green linens. "Is this your bed?"

A confused look materializes on his face. "Why wouldn't it be?"

"Didn't you say this was Connor's condo?"

"Oh, yeah. It's my bed. The dresser on the left is empty, and I'll make room for you in the closet."

"Thanks." I busy myself with items for the dresser.

"Can we talk about our actual vacation?"

"What about it?"

The doorbell chimes as he's about to answer me. He steals a quick kiss. "I'll be right back."

I finish putting my clothes in the dresser and move on to the garment bag. I hang my suits and organize the shoes I brought on the racks beneath my clothes. Connor's interior designer has serious skills. This closet is enormous and could easily hold my clothes, Christoph's, and still have plenty of room for my considerable number of shoes.

I zip my luggage and slide it beneath the bed. Then I empty his. I shouldn't be surprised his drawers are neat and orderly. It matches him perfectly. I add the clothes into the appropriate drawers and set the large bag on the couch near the fireplace. I consider lying down but decide against it.

I return to the kitchen to join Christoph and Jake.

CHAPTER TWENTY

CHRISTOPH

I greet Jake at the door and carry a few bags into the kitchen.

"Thanks, Jake. Here are the keys."

He laughs. "You're as bad as Connor and myself. You aren't getting rid of me that easily."

I would prefer not to dissect our relationship more. I'm confident Jake won't be able to tell we're about to be parents yet. Even if he could, he wouldn't. I start putting the groceries away while we talk. "Do you have an update?"

"Betty and Finn are getting along perfectly. In fact, I offered to replace him, and he declined."

"It isn't surprising. Betty is amazing, as you well know. She's probably putting him to work during the day and doting on him at night."

Jake grins. "I'm sure you're correct. Betty's blueberry pie is still the best I've ever tasted. Estelle isn't happy about Maia's presence but is heeding her nonetheless."

"Good. Blaine?"

"Blaine was able to speak to the attorney directly. The good news is his client isn't looking to harm you, but you won't like who it is."

Madeleine approaches from the hallway. "Hi, Jake."

"Madeleine. Nice to see you again." Jake lifts his head to ask if he should continue with Madeleine present.

"It's fine. I'm going to tell her anyway," I assure him.

The look on his face tells me he understands. Jake knows I will protect her if it's the last thing I do, exactly as he would for Norah and Connor will for Calliope. I will protect our child too. "We should sit then."

This can't be good. Jake takes a seat. I do as well after pulling out Madeleine's chair. Madeleine threads her fingers with mine under the table.

"There's no way to sugarcoat this. Weston Fairbanks represented your parents in the past. He has been searching for you for at least the last six months based on Blaine's research and the information he learned after speaking with him." Jake slides a file across the table. "Here is what Blaine learned about your parents since they left you with Betty."

Madeleine tightens her grip on my fingers.

"What does it mean for my family?" I don't need to include Madeleine and Estelle or my unborn child. Jake knows from the moment I asked him to monitor them and my offer to pay for Maia and Finn.

Jake exhales before speaking. "Security wise, we could likely remove Maia from Estelle. Blaine's report indicates they aren't following her. It also appears they only followed Madeleine to keep tabs on you."

I will not leave Madeleine alone even if there's no threat to her or our baby. "What do they want?"

"They haven't made any demands. According to Blaine, Attorney Fairbanks indicated he was gathering information only. A regular person wouldn't have any clue they were being watched."

"That's terrifying in itself."

"I agree. This contains all the information Blaine could uncover about your parents. I didn't read it in its entirety. However, from the synopsis he provided, prepare yourself for what you'll find between those covers if you choose to open it. Please discuss with Madeleine what you would like to do about Estelle and Betty's security and let me know." Jake rises from his chair.

"I will. Thanks, Jake."

"You're welcome. Bye, Madeleine."

"Goodbye, Jake."

I escort Jake to the door.

"Let me know if you need anything."

"Thanks. I will. Good night." I scrub my hands down my face and return to the kitchen. I'm getting hungrier by the minute, and I know Madeleine needs to eat soon to keep the nausea at bay. "What would you like for dinner?"

"Are we going to talk about it?" She points to the file in the center of the dining table.

"Yes, but not right now. You need food."

She moves beside me in the kitchen. "What are my choices?"

I list the options, and she chooses meatloaf with sweet potatoes and roasted asparagus.

"Will you let me help?"

"No, your only jobs are to slay as the CEO of Scala and protect our baby. I've got the rest."

A flicker of anger appears briefly before she acquiesces.

Maybe it isn't anger…. Discomfort from my refusal to let her do anything is more accurate. "I want to take care of you. Making sure you eat and don't do anything extra is something I can do. Please let me."

She presses a kiss to my lips and sits at the island. "Can we talk about our actual vacation until you're ready to talk about the file?"

"Sure."

"Is there somewhere you want to go?" she asks.

"Hadn't really thought about it. When I asked for the vacation time, I was a single guy with an amazing grandmother who I haven't seen enough in the last year. My plan was to spend a week with Betty and then a week with you. Now, I have a successful, smart, and drop-dead gorgeous woman to share my life with, a baby on the way, and so many things to figure out. What about you?" I get the pan with the meatloaf into the oven.

"You can't simply say you have so many things to figure out without sharing what they are."

I hang my head. I was hoping to process a bit more before I shared my thoughts. "While I was in Maine, I was considering what my options are for work."

"You don't want to work for Blackthorne anymore?" Concern is noted in her tone.

"Not exactly. I don't want to be away from you longer than necessary. I decided before I knew about our baby. Now, I'm sure of it. I'm considering a conversation with Jake and Connor about my options that don't require me to travel as much as I do."

"Why Connor? Is it a realistic option?"

"Connor and Jake are partners in Blackthorne. I won't know if it's a realistic option until I talk to them. Was I unclear about my intentions?"

"No, but I didn't think you would leave a job you have exceptional aptitude for either."

"It isn't possible for both of us to work long hours and travel frequently. I don't want to miss anything with you or our child. I refuse to miss a single moment if I have any control over it. My parents may have given up on me, but Betty showed me love and cared for me as if she were my mother. I want to be like Betty for my children."

Her body posture softens.

"What about you? When do you plan to make your decision about your home base?"

"I gave myself a deadline of when I return from vacation."

"What were your plans before?" I continue preparing dinner while we talk.

"I was going to spend some time with Estelle and some with you."

I set the potatoes in the sink and take the stool beside her. "What if we went to Estelle's for a few days, then we can visit Betty until Thanksgiving and go back to Estelle's for dinner?"

"It makes sense. Then we can go to the baby shower. What about the following week?"

I press a kiss to her lips and the tip of her nose before rounding the island again. "What kind of vacation person are you?" I mash the potatoes and plate them as the timer expires.

"I'm a relaxing vacation person. I don't want to hurry from one excursion to the next. As far as locale, it doesn't matter if it's in the mountains or on a beach."

"I don't know if I can handle you in a bikini on a beach for a week."

She blushes and waves off my compliment. "The feeling goes both ways, babe."

I lean across the island and kiss her. "We can go to Maine. There are beaches, but it certainly isn't bikini season there."

"It's a good idea."

"Can you get drinks?"

"Now you want help." She winks at me, pours two glasses of water, and retakes her seat.

I set our meal on the island and sit beside her. After eating, we clean up and change before tackling the file about my parents from Jake. I grab a hoodie and a blanket from the ottoman in the living room before taking her hand in mine and leading her upstairs to the rooftop patio. There are two sitting areas. One has a firepit and the other has a pergola with string lights.

"Wow, this is amazing!"

"It is. I think it's partly why Connor doesn't want to sell his condo. This space is almost as spectacular as yours." I start the firepit and settle into the corner of the couch and draw my family into my arms.

"I bet the stars are more visible here than at home."

"I'm sure they are. We can stay up here as long as you want."

"What do you know about your parents, Christoph?"

I take a sharp breath. "I only know what I've already shared with you. My mother showed up one afternoon with me in her arms. The next morning, she was gone. Gramps and Betty never heard from her again."

"How did she know your father's name?" Her question comes out guarded, as if she doesn't have the right to ask.

"My mother left two pieces of paper behind—my birth certificate and social security card. I never looked for them. Not even as an adult with the vast resources I have available to me with Blackthorne."

"Do you plan on reading the contents of your file?" Her question hangs between us for a solid minute.

"I don't know. I have no desire to know anything about my parents. They were truly clear in their opinion of parenthood when they left me. Not once have they ever reached out to me in thirty years. I don't owe them anything. Betty may not have given birth to me, but she's my mother."

"I understand completely. As far as I know, the last time Estelle talked to her estranged husband and my parents was near my sixth birthday. She basically gave them an ultimatum—come back now or don't come back at all. They opted for the latter. If I were in your position as far as having every detail I could possibly want at my fingertips, I don't know if I would have the courage or desire to open it either. Whichever option you choose, I support you."

"Thank you."

"Is your history why you're so adamant about being with me and the baby?" Madeleine asks.

I shift and lift her so were looking directly at one another. "I fell hard for you months ago but didn't want to break our agreement. After our date in the city, I needed to share my feelings or walk away. It's the reason I asked you about the following weekend. I need you to understand... having a family is the only thing I've ever wanted for my life. I loved my time in the military. It helped me provide for Betty against her wishes and save for my future. Working for Blackthorne did the same but with a much higher pay scale. Being a bodyguard was never going to be the sole focus of my life. I have been investing wisely since I started in the army and added to it when I went private with Blackthorne."

"What did you want to do?"

I have never shared this with anyone, not even Betty. I hesitate too long.

"You don't have to share."

Cupping her face with my hands, I lean in and kiss her deeply and deliberately. "Madeleine, I love you with everything I am. I want you to know everything. My hesitation has nothing to do with you, only me. I have never shared this with anyone before. The fact I'm sharing with you is huge for me, and the gravity of it hit me hard."

A tear streams down her cheek. I kiss it away.

"Damn hormones." She laughs softly.

I smile at her and kiss her lightly again. "I've always wanted to own a boxing gym."

"What was your timeline before us… before our family?"

She sees me, all of me. I set my hand on her belly. "I surpassed it. I planned to walk away from Blackthorne after four years. When the time came, I wasn't ready to walk away. Jake and Connor are great to work for, and I didn't have anyone in my life to create a family. Now I do."

"Do you know someone who can help you get started with the gym? Other than notifying Jake you want to leave, does he need to be involved? Did I miss a connection?"

"If I were to chase my dream, I have connections to make it happen. Cash Morgan was a venture capitalist. I'm sure he still has contacts at his old firm. Not necessarily. There's a gym at the farm, which you wouldn't know. A gym off property may not be something Jake or Connor ever considered as something Blackthorne needs or how it would fit into the long-term goals of the company."

"Maybe you should talk to them." She settles against my chest, and I wrap my arms around her.

"Maybe I should. Do you want to stargaze or go to bed?"

"I would love to stay up here and bask in starlight, but I need sleep more."

We head downstairs, I verify the locks, engage the alarm, and follow Madeleine to bed.

CHAPTER TWENTY-ONE

MADELEINE

It has been almost a week since Jake set a file containing information about Christoph's parents on the table. Other than moving it into the office, he hasn't opened it. I understand more than anyone his desire to ignore the contents. Making peace with the fact my parents didn't want me happened years ago. I have a suspicion he did too, but the opportunity to learn about where he came from might have a stronger pull than he imagined.

"Ready, gorgeous? Five or so hours sits between us and two glorious work-free weeks together." He takes our bags toward the front door.

"Absolutely." The ride to the office is basically traffic free today. It takes about thirty minutes.

We're greeted by Angie when we step into the office building. "Good morning, Miss Wilton. Mr. Anderson. This was delivered for you this morning." She attempts to hand me a large bouquet of flowers, but Christoph takes them instead.

"Thank you." We move into the office.

Christoph sets the flowers on the credenza and boots his laptop. Since our discussion, he has been researching the area for available real estate and working on a business plan.

"Can you hand me the card?" I empty my bag and boot my computer as well. I take it and read the message aloud. "Congratulations on your promotion. I'm excited for the next chapter in your life. Leanna."

"That was nice of her."

"Yes, it was."

"What are you working on first?" he asks me.

"A final review of the junior assistant candidates first. Then some changes to a contract or two."

He turns back to me. "Were there any front runners?"

"All four of the candidates were great, but one stood out. She's currently in New York, but Simon intentionally included potential relocation in the ad. I plan to meet her in person with Simon."

"It makes sense. He'll be working with her the most."

My phone indicates an incoming video call. "Speak of the devil. Good morning, Simon. How are you?"

"I'm well. You look gorgeous and glowy. Early vacation vibes are flowing through the screen. Hello, Christoph."

"Hi, Simon," he replies but doesn't turn toward my desk.

"Can you schedule an in-person appointment with Lucia Rinaldi as soon as possible when I return?"

"Ooooh! I liked her too. Will do, boss lady. What else?"

"Please schedule a meeting with Stavros midweek when I get back as well. I'll have decided by then regarding my base. Also, can you pull the HR regulations for new hires."

"On it. Have a wonderful holiday. Please enjoy yourself."

"Thank you. Enjoy your holiday with your family as well," I reply at once and end the call.

I finish changes to the Rodin contract and email them to Simon.

Angie buzzes me from reception. "Miss Wilton, there is a Mary Jane Wilton here to see you."

Immediately, Christoph's attention is on me. "Who is Mary Jane Wilton?" he whispers.

"I have no idea who she is or how she knows I'm here in this office. No one knows I'm here."

"Angie, I'm tied up with appointments today. Please have Ms. Wilton leave her contact information. Thank you."

Christoph is already on the phone with Jake by the time I dispatch Angie.

"Yes, please find out who Mary Jane Wilton is. She showed up here at the office. I'm putting you on speaker so Madeleine can answer you."

"Hi, Madeleine."

"Jake. Before you ask, I have no idea who she is. Like Christoph, I was raised by my grandmother, Estelle, which you probably already know."

"No, I didn't read your file. You aren't a client. The only thing I reviewed was your background check when we worked with Callie."

"I appreciate your discretion. Feel free to dig wherever you need to. I'll speak with Estelle when we arrive later today."

"Do you need assistance leaving the building safely?" Jake asks.

Christoph hangs his head. "I don't know yet. I'm going to talk to Angie to gather as much information as I can and do a sweep of the building. I'll call you back afterward."

"I'll call Blaine immediately. Talk to you later."

He closes his laptop and rises from his chair. "Come here please." His hand reaches toward me.

I slip mine into his and melt against him. In his arms, I feel safest.

He drops a kiss onto my head. "I'm going to speak with Angie and do a sweep of the property. I don't know who she is or what she wants, but until I know more, please do not under any circumstances leave this office until I get back here. Don't let anyone in either."

I nod against his chest.

"Madeleine, no one. I don't care if Simon magically teleports himself outside this door from New York. No one other than me."

"You're scaring me."

"Good, that's my intention. Please do as I ask. Stay here, lock the door behind me, and don't let anyone in other than me."

"Okay."

"Breathe, *anamchara*, this is what I do. I love you. I'll be back as soon as I can." With one more kiss, he's out the door.

I lock it behind him and sink onto the love seat in the office. I never truly considered his profession could be dangerous. Of course it is. Connor was shot on an assignment. I chastise myself. It isn't as if he's going up against an army alone. At most its one woman looking for me.

I can't even take an educated guess who Mary Jane Wilton might be. I need more information. What does she look like? Approximately how old is she? What can Jake learn from Blaine? The more I ponder her identity, the more questions come to mind. Instead, I shift my focus onto Estelle. What has she been withholding and when did it start? The more intriguing question is why.

About twenty minutes later, there's a strong knock on the door. "*Anamchara,* it's me."

I open the door and throw my arms around him. One arm clamps around my waist and he steps forward, closing the door with his foot. "Relax, gorgeous. Worrying can't be good for the baby. I'm fine. Are you really nervous about me talking to a single woman by myself?"

I shake my head. "When you put it that way, it sounds like I'm overreacting a tad."

"Thank you for loving me so fervently."

"I could say the same to you. Potentially putting yourself in harm's way for me."

"No harm will come to you or our family as long as I live." He draws me closer, eliminating the sliver of space between our bodies. *If I hadn't fallen for him already, his statement would have done it.*

"What did you learn?"

"According to Angie, she looks a lot like you. Blonde, light eyes, thin but not as tall. She left her number and email address but not why she wants to see you. I did a search of the building and found nothing. There is only one entrance where Angie is stationed and two exits."

"How old?"

"Meaning?"

"Aunt or sister? Could she be my aunt or my sister?"

"I don't know, but we'll find out. Angie wasn't really helpful regarding her age. However, Mary Jane is an older name. Like me, you truly have no idea about your family other than your parents and Estelle."

"No, once they left me with Estelle, it was only the two of us. I went to school, and Estelle limited my extracurricular activities," I mumble against his chest.

His phone rings.

I attempt to move away, but he refuses to release me.

"Yeah, Jake."

He relays all the information he shared with me. "The building is secure, but there isn't onsite security like New York." He pauses, then asks, "How long will it take?" After listening to Jake's answer, he states,

"We'll be in her office. She will inform Angie to expect them. Thanks, Jake."

"Who is coming and when will they be here?" I ask.

"Connor and Callen are more than halfway here already as a precaution. They will escort us to the car and tail us to Estelle's if necessary."

"Okay. Let me inform Angie. What about Estelle?"

He waits for me to call Angie and takes a seat with me in his arms on the love seat. "Maia is still with Estelle. Perhaps it will change after we arrive tonight. She's fine."

I forgot about Maia. After a possessive kiss, we pack up to leave. Less than five minutes later, I'm escorted out of the building after a brief introduction to Callen and we're on our way to Estelle's.

My childhood home is a family farm with two huge barns and a massive greenhouse. The closer we get to the house, the more agitated I become. I was looking forward to this visit, but now… I'm not so sure.

"What's on your mind?" He lifts my hand to his lips but never takes his eyes off the road.

"I was looking forward to this visit. Now, I want to go home with you."

"I'm sorry I didn't ask if you still wanted to visit. We can go home if you want."

I shake my head. "No, I need answers. I might as well get them today."

"There's my fiery woman. If you don't want to stay, we can find a hotel or go back to my place tonight."

"I'll keep it as an option. Thank you."

"I've got you. Always."

We pull through the unlocked gate at the bottom of the driveway and ride up the uneven road to the house. Connor and Callen have followed us the entire way here out of an abundance of caution. The moment we park, Estelle is crashing through the front door with Maia following closely behind.

"Oh my ladybug! You're here." Estelle tries to hug me, but I step backward against Christoph. "What is going on? Who are all these people? You must be Christoph." She extends her hand to him.

He doesn't take it.

"We need to talk inside," I inform her.

Nervously she leads everyone into the house with a large wrap around porch.

CHAPTER TWENTY-TWO

CHRISTOPH

"What is going on, Madeleine?" Estelle demands.

Madeleine glances around the room. Maia is behind Estelle off to the side. Callen and Connor are a step inside the kitchen but no more. I'm beside her, our fingers linked between us.

She looks over at me, and I nod tightly.

"Who is Mary Jane Wilton?"

Estelle's face is now ashen. "I have no idea. Why are you asking?"

"Of all people, please don't lie to me. A woman claiming to be Mary Jane Wilton showed up at my office today. According to the receptionist, she looks an awful lot like me. When is the last time you spoke to Gramps or my parents? How long have you been hiding things from me?"

I squeeze her hand in support and to settle her even a little bit.

Estelle attempts to speak a few times, but falters. "Can we speak privately?"

"Christoph stays. If the rest of you could excuse us, I would appreciate it." The others immediately leave the kitchen.

"I'm not speaking about my shortcomings with a stranger in the room," Estelle states forcefully.

"Take it or leave it. It seems you owe me a few explanations. He may be a stranger to you, but he isn't to me. I suspect I'm going to need his support after I hear what you need to share."

I love her immeasurably. I won't ever leave her side unless she asks me to. I thought we were going to deal with my family issues, not hers.

Estelle sits up straighter in her chair and then leaves the kitchen. I move to follow her, but Madeleine stops me.

"Estelle won't leave. I'm sure the exits are secured anyway."

"Agreed. Do you need anything? Crackers, water. It's been a while since you've eaten."

"Good idea. If you want to grab two waters, I'll find the crackers. Hopefully, they're in the same place." She rises from the chair toward the oak cabinetry. On the first try, she locates a box of Town House crackers.

With waters in hand, I take a seat beside her again and press a kiss to her temple. After Madeleine eats a few crackers, Estelle returns with a large box in her arms.

"Those have always been your favorite. Would you like peanut butter too?"

"No. Please answer my question." Anger is evident in Madeleine's tone.

I don't blame her. I'm angry with my parents and I don't know them at all—although I'm completely confident Betty hasn't lied to me my entire life.

"All the answers you're searching for are in this box. Mary Jane Wilton is your mother."

"No. I may not wish to see my parents or Gramps, but I distinctly recall their names. My mother's name is Marcea. You never forget those who abandon you."

I set my hand on her thigh beneath the table and squeeze lightly.

"Mary Jane is Marcea's sister. She's six years younger. When she learned she was pregnant, she begged Marcea to claim you as her own. Your aunt Marcea agreed."

"Is the man who I believe to be my father actually my father?"

Estelle hangs her head. "No. Your biological father was a boy she met at a party on summer vacation. She never saw him again. Marcea and Samuel were already engaged. They agreed to raise you as their own and eloped."

"Is this the first time?"

I understand her question, but Estelle doesn't.

"What do you mean?" Estelle asks.

"Is this the first time someone has come looking for me to share the truth?"

"No."

I would have thought my fierce woman would stop there, but she doesn't.

"My whole life is built on lies. You have been lying to me repeatedly. Were you ever going to tell me?"

"No. It wasn't my information to tell." Estelle is emphatic in her words. She truly believes it wasn't her place to share Madeleine's true parentage even though she has been raising her since she was six.

Tears well in Madeleine's eyes, but none fall. "Wait, why does my biological mother and her sister, who I thought was my mother, have the same last name?"

Damn! Her mind astounds me. Her biological mom married her sister's husband? What happened to Marcea?

"All the answers are in the box. What can I make you for dinner?"

Madeleine rises from the chair. "Are you out of your mind?"

I stand beside her and set my hand on the small of her back. She has every right to be angry, but I know she won't jeopardize our child's well-being all the same.

"Don't speak to me like that, ladybug."

With the increased volume of the conversation, Connor and Maia step into the kitchen. Connor moves to the other side of Madeleine. Maia remains in the threshold.

"Don't call me 'ladybug.' You don't get to tell me how to talk to you or how to feel. You lied to me each day for most of my life. When backed into a corner with your lies, you hand me a box with answers. It isn't acceptable." She turns to me. "I want to leave, right now."

I nod. "Estelle, I would have preferred to meet you under more pleasant circumstances."

"Don't walk away, Madeleine. We need to talk about this," Estelle bellows as best she can from her rail-thin frame.

"I can't be here right now. I can't even look at you. All I see are lies."

"If you leave now, don't ever come back," Estelle threatens. The moment the words leave Estelle's mouth, a sky-high wall is erected with precision between her and Madeleine.

"For the first time in my life, I know without question none of this is my fault. My insecurities about building a family of my own, my drive to be the best at everything, and my inability to let anyone in until very recently are your fault. Completely your fault. Somehow, I knew in my heart the bubble you built around me, like not allowing me to have friends over and limiting my school activities, was purposeful. It was meant to protect you, not me. Goodbye, Estelle." Madeleine turns on her heel and walks through the door Maia vacated not a moment too soon.

Madeleine walks directly to my truck and whips open the passenger door before I have chance.

I kneel on the driveway and take her hands in mine. "You're even more incredible than I already believed." Wiping the fallen tears, I press a kiss to the back of her hand. "I love you, anamchara." I lower my hand to her abdomen and whisper to our child, "I love you, baby." Standing, I press a kiss to her forehead. "I need to update Connor. Do you want me to send Maia over?"

She shakes her head. I feel like my heart was ripped out of my chest. It's possible the pain she's experiencing could feasibly happen to me, but not to the same degree. It's heartbreaking. Callen and Maia move to the driver's side of my truck and block any view of Madeleine from Estelle who is peering out the front window.

"Damn, brother. What does she need?" Connor asks as I approach him.

"Nothing aside from leaving here as soon as possible, a stiff drink or three, and a good cleansing cry." A drink she can't have, but I don't share with Connor.

"Understood. There's a luxury hotel about twenty minutes from here, or does she want to go home?"

"I'll ask her. She will likely opt for home."

Connor acknowledges my response. "What about Maia?"

"I don't see any reason for Maia to stay here at this point. Do you? I'm angry and a bit too close to think clearly."

"I agree. Monitoring Estelle was precautionary. Madeleine's biological mother showing up at her office wasn't connected to your concerns in any way, but the timing is atrocious."

"Okay. You can pull Maia, but please leave Finn with Betty for now. We may have eliminated Estelle as a pawn but not Betty or Madeleine, at least not yet."

"Roger. Let me know what she decides. Do you want us to follow if she opts for the hotel?"

I nod. "Yes, but I'm fairly certain she'll choose home. I'll send Maia over." Rounding the car, I send Maia to Connor and kneel beside Madeleine again. Her breathing is jagged, and her face is blotchy. "Home or hotel?"

"Home, please, even though it's further."

I text Connor her decision and request he order some food to be delivered as well. Shortly thereafter, we're pulling away from Madeleine's childhood home, her heart crushed and everything she believed about her family obliterated. Her eyes remain pinned out the windshield, unwavering, and her body completely still with shock. Not one word falls from her lips until we're about ten minutes from home.

"Is there somewhere we can pick up food?" Her voice is barely audible.

"I already took care of it. If you're starving, there's probably a protein bar in the glove box."

She turns her gaze to me. "I would be falling apart right now if it weren't for you. I don't know what I would do without you."

"The same is true for me. If you need to fall apart, I'll hold you until the last tear falls from your eyes and the final sob wracks your flawless frame and every moment afterward as long as you'll have me."

I pull straight into the garage and thank Connor via text. Our dinner is on the porch. Connor doesn't pull away until the garage door closes completely. Wordlessly, I lead Madeleine inside and leave her on the couch. Two trips later with the remainder of our belongings, I find her seat empty. Even though I know with every fiber of my being she's safe, I know she's hurting. I drop silverware and two waters into the takeout bag and search for her.

It doesn't surprise me to find the door to the patio ajar. I climb the stairs and find her staring up at the stars with a blanket draped over her shoulders.

"I thought I might find you up here."

"I didn't mean to worry you."

I set the bag down, arrange the food, and start the firepit. "Please eat."

Within minutes, half of her meal is gone. She sits back and leans against me.

"Do you want to talk?"

"No." Her response comes out harsh and terse. "Sorry, I'm not angry with you."

"I know. I can take it. I'm here when you're ready."

She nods against my arm. I finish eating my meal, lean back against the rattan couch, and draw her against me. Madeleine shifts so her head is on my chest but she's facing skyward. With each passing moment, she relaxes a bit more. Her eyes flutter closed, and her breathing slows. Unfortunately, we can't sleep up here.

I reach down and set my hand on her abdomen and talk to our baby. "Hi there. Daddy here. Your mommy is an amazing woman. She has me beat by miles. Together though, we're a fantastic team. Please know, we promise to be here for you every single day. If you need us, we'll be there to support you. I can't wait to meet you."

I doze off myself. Sometime later, I wake with a start. "*Anamchara*, wake up. We need to go to bed."

Slowly she registers my words and sits up. I clean up the food and lead her downstairs. I remove her jacket, blouse, skirt, and bra before tucking her into my bed. Expeditiously I gather our trash, lock up, and draw her against me for the night.

CHAPTER TWENTY-THREE

MADELEINE

I've been awake for the last hour. I refuse to wake him. His arms are tightly wrapped around me, but he's still sound asleep. I feel safe, loved, and protected even though my family life crashed down around me last night. I have so many questions, but I'm not sure I want the answers at this point. How many times did any of them look for me? What happened to Marcea? Did my bio mom really marry her sister's husband? Did Estelle thwart them, or did they fail to find me? I wasn't hiding per se. My name has been listed in the Scala directory for the last nine plus years. I've lived in the same apartment for the last six. How could the woman who raised me be so callous? She said, "The answers are in here," shoved a box across the table where I learned to write, and then asked me what I wanted for dinner.

"Breathe, beautiful." He presses a kiss to my shoulder blade. "How you handle the contents of the box is completely up to you, like the unopened file Jake provided to me."

I turn in his embrace. *Good god, my man is gorgeous.* Stubble running along his jaw, mussed hair, and sleepy eyes. "How have you not opened it yet?"

"The contents of the file has no bearing on my life today. It contains history. My parents' alleged attorney has been trying to locate me. At this point, he's been successful. Yet I haven't heard from him. He's known my rough whereabouts for approximately six months. Yet he hasn't reached out. Not one call or letter has been initiated. I could've had Jake secure the information through Blaine at any time since I started working for Blackthorne. I didn't want to know before, and I don't believe I want to know now. My focus is us and our family. I have no desire to look backward, only forward with you. If you want to dig into the box, I'll stand beside you and support you."

"It's terrifying and heartening at the same time how well you understand me."

"The same is true for me, gorgeous."

"Before we move on, I want to ask you something. Please don't answer right away; think about it. What if you learn something you would want to know? That's where I'm stuck. What if I could learn something that could impact our future, our family?"

He's silent. I suppose it's what I asked for, silent contemplation of my question. "I never really thought about it that way. I'll consider it. My concern is there's no going back. I can't unlearn anything either."

"Thank you for considering it. Now, no more talk about files and boxes, at least for today. What can we do around here today?" I push him onto his back, straddling his hips. Clearly, I didn't think it through beforehand. The sheet falls away, leaving me exposed, and his impressive morning wood is perfectly notched against my folds. I couldn't stop my arousal from pooling between my thighs even if I willed it to happen.

"We can go into town and check out Norah's store, the candy shop, or walk to the point at Jake's."

"Can we do everything you listed?"

"Anything you want. First though, come closer." His hands slide to grip my ass.

I obey his demand and lower myself so my bare breasts are against him and our lips are a mere inch away from each other.

"I want to make love to you until you scream with pleasure before we leave." His words send tingles down my spine and straight to my core.

A desire-laden sigh falls from my lips before I kiss him. He opens to me, and our tongues twist and tangle in an exquisite dance. Kissing Christoph alone makes my heart race. The sheer bliss of cresting the edge of bliss is beyond anything I've ever felt before. I rock against him as his hand slides around my hip and seeks access. Lifting my hips, his fingers spear my core. Leaning up onto his elbow, he draws one of my nipples into his mouth before biting down.

"Chris…."

His mouth and fingers move in unison until my body convulses and tightens around him.

Before the ripples subside, I push his boxer briefs down to his hips. "Now… you. All of you." My voice sounds desperate, and I don't care even the slightest bit. I want to shatter around the man I love with every fiber of my being. I lift as he withdraws and aligns himself with my dripping core. With excruciating precision, I impale myself with his rock-hard shaft. I take a few moments to revel in the fullness of him inside me.

"*Anamchara*, I need you to move."

I lift and plunge right back down, taking him deeply inside me. I'm sure we've been in this position before, but I didn't feel this suffused. He meets me thrust for thrust in an intoxicating rhythm. I lean forward and slide my hips back, taking him inexplicably deeper in order to eliminate every sliver of space between us.

"Don't stop, gorgeous. You feel incredible."

Goose bumps skitter over my skin from his words. Radiating pleasure climbs up my spine. As I savor the intense spikes cascading through me, he explodes beneath me. The force of his release makes my inner muscles tense in ecstasy, and I splinter moments later.

I meld my lips to his and kiss his perfect lips. Bringing my mouth near his ear, I ask, "How does it keep becoming more each time?"

"It has ever since we've shared our feelings with one another. I imagine it will continue exceeding the time before into the future."

"I don't know if I can handle more. It's exceptional as is."

"Yes, we are, and we're going to be a family."

Oh my heart. "You fill in each part of my soul my upbringing destroyed. I didn't know it was missing until I fell for you. I love you."

"I was content until I met you. I didn't realize there was a stratosphere of levels beyond where I was. I love you, *anamchara*."

"Let's clean up and get moving. Baby needs to eat." Her smile lights up every room she's in.

"Walk first, then into town. What do you think?"

"Sure." She walks into the bathroom and turns on the water.

I send a quick text to Jake to let him know we'll be by later and join her for a sexy shower. Armed with breakfast and coffee, we ride to Jake's. When we pull in front of the house, Maia and Norah are leaving the gym.

"Morning, ladies," I state while rounding the car to open her door.

"Morning, Christoph. Hi, Madeleine," Maia says.

"Morning," Madeleine replies to them.

"Christoph, Jake is in his office. We'll keep Madeleine company while you get an update," Norah informs me.

"Good?" he murmurs near my ear.

Controlling my physical responses to him is difficult. All I can do is nod and work to push the ideas in my mind away for now.

"How are you this morning, Madeleine?" Maia asks.

"Torn between digging into the box and burning it without checking the contents. I realize those are extremes, but it's where I am. Part of me is fine with leaving the past in the past, but what if there's something in there that could affect our future? I need to know, but as Christoph succinctly stated last night, we can't forget the bad we learn either."

"It doesn't surprise me he sees all sides. It's one of the many tactical things he's exceptional at," Norah adds. "Would you like some coffee or a water?"

"A water would be great." I follow Norah and Maia into a gorgeous colonial with a wraparound porch. The wide plank flooring and modern fixtures are perfectly appointed, as is the structured sectional bracketing a fireplace. When we step inside, two dogs come barreling toward me and halt at my feet.

"*Freund*," Norah commands. "This is Tank." She points to the taller, thinner dog. "That's Sabre."

I reach down and set one hand in front of each dog. Both lick my hand and I pet them. "Your home is beautiful, Norah."

"I can't take any credit. Jacob did this himself before we were a couple." She hands me a water. "I understand you're on vacation for a little bit."

"Yes, this week and next. Then I'll go back to New York."

"Will Christoph be joining you?" Maia asks.

As I consider my response, the guys join us in the kitchen. Jake slides his arm around Norah and kisses her temple while Christoph tucks me against his side.

"Will I be joining her?" Christoph asks.

"In New York," I supply.

"Actually, I scheduled a meeting with Jake and Connor to discuss my home base and a few other matters after our vacation. Jake indicated they wanted to discuss my assignments after vacation anyway."

I nod and tighten my fingers in his.

"Ready to hike?"

"Sure."

"Please take the dogs with you. They need some exercise," Jake instructs Christoph.

"Sure. Maybe we'll see you later." He leads me to the French doors and into a spacious backyard.

"This is gorgeous."

"It is. I think they have about a hundred acres."

"Where do you want to live? Does it look like this?" I question him.

We step through an iron gate, and he links our hands again. Tank and Sabre are running ahead of us about a hundred yards or so. "In North Carolina, we had a large farm. If I recall correctly, it was maybe fifty acres. Where Betty lives now, which is where I grew up for the most part, is twenty acres with a large stable to board horses, a massive personal garden for vegetables and one for flowers, and a dog."

We continue walking up a decent-size hill. As we reach the top, the view of the mountains is exquisite. "This is majestic."

"Yeah. What about you? Are you a city girl or a country girl?"

Deep down I know the answer, but now I'm afraid to voice it. Well, I would be to anyone but him. "Before last night, I would've answered a country girl without hesitation. Now I don't know if I can go back there."

We take a seat at a picnic table beneath a massive oak tree. "You don't have to go back to Estelle's to decide where your ideal home would be."

"True. Then, I would say country, but I need to be close enough to a metropolitan area for work."

"Makes sense."

"What is your appointment with Jake about?"

"Our future. Before you get nervous, I didn't tell him about the baby yet."

I lean closer and kiss him softly. "What about our future?"

"I asked to make an appointment to discuss the boxing/training gym option and if where I sleep matters when taking assignments. He answered the latter part already with an emphatic no."

"Good, but it doesn't handle your disinterest in travelling so much."

"Not yet, but I will when we have the meeting. My plan is almost complete."

"I know you only shared your dream with me recently, but I'm crazy proud of you."

"Not remotely as proud as I am of you, Miss President and CEO of Scala Talent Agency."

I take a deep breath. "Until last night, I was leaning toward choosing DC. Now I'm not so sure."

He turns so he's facing me on the picnic bench. "Please know if you still want to choose DC, I will secure our home and your office, so you have complete control over access. The building security needs to be upgraded anyway. It should be equal to what is currently in the office in New York in my opinion. If you choose it, please make sure you tell Stavros it's necessary. There are a few areas of concern."

"You can secure our home and the office?"

"With Jake's help I can. Do you see the short, white pillar over there?" He points toward the shoreline.

"Yeah."

"It's a perimeter alarm. It'll go off if someone enters the property from the water or the forest over there. There's a lock at the gate. At most, eight people know the code."

"Including you?"

"Yes, including me."

"It does make me feel a bit better about it. Yet even if I decide to go through the contents of the box, I may not ever want to see Estelle again."

"I assure you I can secure our home and your office."

"Can I ask you something? Well, a few things."

"Of course."

"First, are you going to share the file with Betty?"

His face falls. "I hadn't considered she might want to know or should be given the choice either. Maybe I should."

I shrug. "Is it possible for Blaine to make a file for me about my family?"

"Yes, but why would you want a file if you have the box?"

I take a deep breath. "The box is Estelle's version of my life. I'm sure it paints her as the victim when in fact I am. A dossier from Blaine would be cold, hard facts without emotion."

"We can have Jake request one if you want it."

I consider for a moment. "I think I do. At a minimum, I'll have it if I choose to learn without Estelle's hand impacting the info."

His assurance adds more confidence in my choice. We enjoy the quiet for a while before heading back to the house. Tank and Sabre run circles around us. When we arrive, the house is empty. We let the dogs inside and lock up.

"Where to next, milady?"

I laugh. "Book store and then candy. Is there good pizza around here?"

"Yes, we have delicious pizza. What is your no-go topping?"

I wrinkle my nose. "Anchovies and pineapple. You?"

"I agree about the anchovies, but pineapple isn't a deal breaker. I will eat it if I have no other choice. My favorite is sausage and peppers. You?"

"Big, floppy, New York Style cheese for me if we're in the city. I could get behind sausage and peppers as well."

We take the short ride through the quaint village of Crescent Bay. "Tell me more about this town. It's super cute."

He grins at me. His smiles get me every time. "Crescent Bay is a small town. Main Street is exactly as you would picture it. There's a hardware store owned by the same family for generations, a general store also family owned, a florist, and a candy store. There's a Blackthorne office, and the newest addition is Norah's bookstore. I'm not sure it's a bookstore exactly. The Nook is a store where you can grab a cup of coffee, browse shelves of books, and actually read them. You can purchase books too, but she wanted everyone to be able to enjoy the space regardless of their ability to pay."

"Now I want to go even more."

"We're almost there."

We park in a small lot beside a stately brick building. As we round the corner, a petite young woman runs straight into Christoph. He's hard to miss given his height, but her nose was in her phone.

"Easy, Gemma."

"Sorry, Christoph. My mom is driving me nuts. You must be Madeleine." Gemma extends her hand to me.

"I am. Pleasure to meet you."

"I would love to chat more, but I need to deal with this." Gemma hurries around us and continues into the parking lot.

"She's the one who sent your clothes?" I ask.

"Yeah. Her father was our commanding officer. According to him, her teen years were tough. She's exceptional at running the office." He opens the door to Norah's store and ushers me inside.

I'm speechless. This is fantastic! Of course, there is shelf after shelf of books, but Norah included cozy reading areas and even a coffee bar. I could stay in here for hours.

Norah comes over and hugs us both. "Hey there! I didn't know you were stopping in. Let me know if you're looking for something specific."

"Thanks, Norah."

I meander around the store and pick up a few books for myself. Then I find some in the children's section. "Which one? *Velveteen Rabbit* or *Goodnight Moon*."

"Both," Christoph answers with a kiss to my head.

After checking out, we wave to Norah and head to the candy store where we make quick work shopping and spend too much money on chocolates. Our cart includes truffles, caramels, and even some peanut butter cups.

I'm officially spent. "Can we go home?" *Home, his home. More accurately our home. If he can control access to wherever we live, I want to stay here.*

"Yes."

Under thirty minutes later, I'm sitting on the couch snuggled with Christoph. We share a pizza and curl into bed and watch movies until the wee hours of the morning.

CHAPTER TWENTY-FOUR

CHRISTOPH

I have been looking forward to spending time with Betty. This visit seems more significant since I invited Madeleine. Her hand is linked with mine on the console.

"Why are you shaking, beautiful?"

Her eyes lift to mine. I've seen that look one other time, right before she asked me to have a drink with her.

"I've seen that look before. There's no reason for you to be nervous. Betty is amazing. I love you; she will too."

"Promise?"

"Promise."

I park alongside the house and open Madeleine's door. Huck scampers over, and we greet him.

"Oh my, I can't take it. You're here!" Betty is average height with blonde hair with gray streaks and blue eyes like mine. She throws her arms around me and then hugs Madeleine to her.

"You left out the fact she's stunning, Christoph. You're the one who stole his heart all those months ago."

I've never seen Madeleine speechless. She knows Betty's words are accurate, yet acknowledging them is something else. "Thank you. Yes, I did."

"Thank you. In love looks good on him."

Madeleine smiles, and we follow Betty toward the house. The ladies head inside.

Finn is standing on the porch watching Betty gush. "Good to see you."

"Hey, man. Thanks for staying until I arrived. We'll be here until Friday morning. You're officially off until then."

"Your grandmother is a hoot. Dude, how were you not as big as a house with the amazing meals she cooks?"

I laugh. "I did a lot of extra running when I lived with Grams. Thank you for hanging with her."

"I have been on some high-profile assignments with the rich and famous. It hits differently protecting a regular person when you know who you're protecting them for."

"Thanks."

Finn steps inside and says farewell to Betty. After he leaves, I join Madeleine and Betty in the kitchen. They're sitting at the table chatting over a plate of banana bread muffins. I grab a water and join them.

"Will Finn be returning?" Betty asks me.

"Probably for a bit longer. Do you want an update?"

Betty sits up straighter in her chair. "Yes, please. Whatever it is, we can handle it."

"Our team has determined an attorney connected to my parents has been looking for me for six months. Recently, the searches expanded to include you and Madeleine. The attorney hasn't made any effort to contact me. I have no idea why he's interested in my whereabouts. Blaine created a file for me at Jake's request. I haven't opened it, but Madeleine suggested I should offer you the chance to read it or not."

Madeleine covers my hand on the table. I flatten my palm, and she curls her fingers around mine.

"What do you believe is in the file?" Betty's tone is contemplative but even.

"Knowing Blaine, it's a comprehensive point-by-point timeline of my parents' life from the moment they left me with you."

"What are your reservations about reading it?"

I have no reason not to share with Betty. I'm confident she isn't like Estelle. Betty would have informed me if my family came looking for me after she laid into my mother. "The past is in the past. You're my family. I've lived my entire life until now with you as my sole guide. I don't need to know specifics why I wasn't enough for my mother to stay or where she's been the last thirty years. Truthfully, I don't have any idea who my father is. The information has no bearing on my life, except if it could impact our future. The tradeoff of learning something I didn't want to know and protecting our future is heavy."

"I see your point. I never expected Carolyn to leave the next morning. When she arrived with you in her arms, I was overjoyed but nervous at the same time. When I woke the next morning and she was gone, my worst fear was confirmed. She wasn't ready to be a parent."

"When was the last time you saw her before she left me?"

Betty covers my other hand with hers. "After graduating high school, Carolyn travelled around Europe for a few years. When I suggested she return and attend college, her calls and letters decreased. Her contact dwindled to a card on my birthday and our anniversary. Gramps told me to let her find her way. I heard from her again about six months before the night she left you with me. I assured her she would always have a soft place to land if she would come home. The next time I saw her was with you bundled tightly in a secondhand, green blanket. As you already know, I never searched for her. Perhaps my choice was unfair to you, but I felt it was the right thing at the time."

"I'm not angry, Grams. You and Gramps gave me everything I needed and raised me well. I have you, my green family, and my Blackthorne family. Now I have Madeleine too."

A few tears fall down Betty's face. "I understand your concern with not being able to unlearn the facts about her life." She turns to Madeleine. "I appreciate your consideration of me in this circumstance. If it's all the same to you, I would like to think about it a bit before answering."

"Of course," I reply.

Madeleine breaks the silence after a few minutes. "Will you give me a tour, Betty?"

"A tour sounds like a lovely idea. I suggest a sweater though, dear."

"I'll get our bags from my truck."

After we settle into my old bedroom room, which clearly hasn't been touched since I lived here, we step off the porch and follow Betty on a tour. She walks us through the barns with Huck hot on my heel. He's a good dog. Betty shares the basics on most of the horses in the stable. Next we step into one of the largest greenhouses I've ever seen. This one houses her vegetable garden. Betty truly lights up when we step into her flower greenhouse.

"These are lovely," Madeleine gushes.

"Thank you, dear. I love being in here. Aside from cooking, this is my favorite way to pass the time."

"Do you sell these to local florists?"

Betty shakes her head. "I hadn't really thought about it. I use them in the house, or I give them to the church when there's a funeral or wedding in need of floral arrangements."

"That's kind of you," Madeleine offers.

"I have a good life here. I don't need anything else except more visits from a certain someone who shall remain nameless."

I scowl at them. "I'm right here, Grams."

"I know, but it's fun to irritate you. I know you visit when you can. What does a talent agent do exactly?"

My gorgeous woman beams and shares the ins and outs of her career with Grams. Both women are smiling and laughing as we finish walking through the floral greenhouse.

"Grams, what is ready to pick for veggies?"

"Green beans, cherry tomatoes, and most of the spices. Why?"

I grin at her. "I'm figuring out what to cook for my ladies for dinner."

Both Grams and Madeleine shake their heads. I gather ingredients with Grams while Madeleine heads back into the house.

"She's wonderful, Christoph."

A huge smile beams on my face. "I never thought I would find someone like her."

A wistful look comes over Grams. "You look at her like my Harold looked at me."

"I know. I remember." *It's how I know she's the one.*

"She's highly successful. I'm proud her success doesn't bother you."

"Not even a little. She's the fiercest negotiator I've ever met, but there's another side of her she only allows me to see."

"I gather something recently went down with her family."

I tilt my head her direction. Clearly my observation skills came from Grams. "How did you see that?"

"She was markedly uncomfortable when we were talking about your mother leaving you here."

"If she wants to tell you, she can. I will share a little bit. She was raised by her grandmother as well. However, recently it took a turn, and she's working through whether she can forgive her grandmother's huge missteps."

"Thank you. I won't push her. Are you moving to New York?" Leave it to Grams to lay out her concerns.

"I don't think so. She earned a huge promotion. Along with it comes the ability to choose where she wants to be based. She's deciding between the big apple and DC."

"Her grandmother lives near here too, so it put a wrench in her decision," Betty surmises.

"Exactly. I will know for sure by the end of next week. She needs to tell her boss by then."

"I'm happy for you, Christoph. Now let's get to work on some great-grandbabies. I'm not getting any younger."

I busy myself picking the rest of the veggies so Grams can't read my face. It'll be a dead giveaway. Composing myself, I reply, "I'll see what I can do."

We return to the house. I get to work in the kitchen while Grams embarrasses me with photos from my childhood.

Grams sets the table while Madeleine assists me in the kitchen with plating and finishing dinner. I pull her into my arms and hold her close.

"She's amazing. I see where you get it from."

"Thanks. She said the same thing about you while we were in greenhouse."

I pull out their chairs, and we eat dinner. We chat about the horses, and Grams shares a bit too much information about Lucy, my not really girlfriend in high school. I didn't realize she knew so much about the two of us.

"How are you at Yahtzee, Madeleine?" Grams asks.

She shrugs. "I've never played before."

"No, no way. She'll crush us both," I object to Gram's suggestion.

"All the more reason to play."

Reluctantly, I fetch the game from the guest bedroom and explain the rules to Madeleine.

"No problem. Poker with dice. Game on."

After her challenge, I knew we were going down hard. Three games later and Madeleine has wiped the floor with both of us handily.

"I'm going to turn in. I'll see you both in the morning," Betty states when we finish our games.

"Good night," we reply at once.

I finish putting the game away and sneak into my bag to grab a gift for Madeleine. When I return, I lead Madeleine outside. We take a walk through the stables where I grab a spare blanket. I lay the blanket on the grass about three hundred yards to the right. This knoll is the best spot on the property for stargazing if you also want to keep an eye on the house.

I take her hands in mine and lower her to the blanket before taking a seat beside her. Lying back, I tuck her against me with her head resting on my upper arm facing the star-filled night sky.

"Thank you," she whispers.

"I'll do anything for you, both of you." I lean over and press a kiss to her temple. "I have a gift for you." I slide my hand into my back pocket and pull out the box.

"It isn't my birthday or Christmas."

"I don't need a day set aside for everyone to get you something, do I?"

A spark of joy dances across her face as she moves to straddle my hips. She opens the box, and her gift falls onto my chest.

"It's perfect! You got me both!"

"Did you truly think I wouldn't let you choose both?"

"Honestly, not then. It's why I chose one. Now, I know you would find a way to give me a penguin enclosure and family of penguins if I truly wanted one." She drags her fingers over the platinum charm bracelet. I added a penguin, a snow leopard, a sailboat, and a taco... for now.

"I would." I fasten the bracelet on her wrist and draw her closer to kiss her breathless. Resettling on the blanket, we gaze up at the stars until the cold is too much. We wander slowly back to the house. I spend a solid hour walking down memory lane with Madeleine with the memorabilia in my bedroom. I shared stories about my football days and summers on the farms with Grams.

"What was her name?" Madeleine lifts her eyes to mine.

"Who?"

"The girl you spent your summer nights with under the stars."

I drop a kiss on the top of her head and haul her into my lap. "I was more likely hanging out with the Kramer boys who lived down the road. There was no girl. I have never shared my stargazing spot with anyone but you."

"I feel honored."

"You're the only woman for me, Miss Wilton. Well, it might be a tie next year, but I'm sure you understand."

"Yes, I will." She burrows deeper into my arms, and I lean against the headboard. "How does it work here for Thanksgiving? What time are we getting up to cook?"

"The turkey is defrosting in the spare fridge. Betty will start baking at six. Once the pies are in the oven, she'll make the stuffing and then cook."

"You allow her to cook?"

I laugh and nuzzle her neck. "Holiday meals with Betty are beyond compare. I will follow instructions, and so will you."

"Cooking is not my specialty. You've seen my fridge. It's full of takeout leftovers and delivery."

"True, and I love cooking for you, but it's tradition."

"I'm in as long as Betty is patient."

I grin at her. "She raised me, and I wasn't an easy kid. You'll be fine. You're not hopeless in the kitchen."

The next morning it would appear I was dead wrong. Madeleine is hopeless in the kitchen. She smashed the egg so hard against the edge of the bowl, Grams started the batter over instead of searching for all the little pieces. After she turned the mixer on and splattered the mixture everywhere, she bowed out gracefully and watched from the table.

Once Grams has the meal cooking, we take seats in the living room and watch the pregame show.

"You like football, Betty?"

Grams shakes her head. "Not at all, but it's where I can spend time with you two."

"Awww, she loves you, Christoph."

I laugh and lean closer to her. "She will love you too soon enough."

Near the end of the first game, Betty calls us into the dining room for one of her most magnificent holiday meals to date.

I'm certifiably stuffed, and I haven't had her famous blueberry pie yet.

"Grams, everything was perfect as usual."

"Thank you."

Madeleine rises from her chair and extends her hand to me. "Come on, we've got the dishes. I can certainly handle washing dishes."

"As you wish."

We finished cleaning and watch the second game before digging deep into Gram's prize-winning pie. Soon after dessert, Betty turns in for the night. After a short walk, we climb into bed as well.

After breakfast, which I'll cook for Grams and Madeleine, we're heading home to Connor and Calliope's baby shower. We need to make a stop at the condo to pick up the huge gifts we bought for the twins. *All the things we'll need as well.*

CHAPTER TWENTY-FIVE

MADELEINE

The aroma of a huge breakfast wakes me from a sound sleep. If I were at home, I wouldn't think twice about wearing my pajamas to the kitchen. I pull Christoph's shirt off the chair and tie it at my waist and tug on a pair of my yoga pants.

"Morning, gorgeous," Christoph greets me when I enter the kitchen.

"Morning. Betty still sleeping?"

He flips the pancakes. "No, she's in the barn making her morning rounds."

"Perfect." I round the island and kiss him hard. "It's peaceful here."

"Yeah, it is. Growing up here was amazing."

"Would you want to move somewhere like this for us?"

He sets down the spatula and wraps his arms around me. "I'll be happy anywhere with you beside me. Aside from the recent developments, it's fair to say our childhoods in the country were pretty fantastic."

"Yeah, it was. Can we look for a similar property close enough to DC?"

"You made your decision? Own it, gorgeous. Be decisive."

"Let's find a farm where we can raise our family near here."

"There's my girl. I'm so proud of you!" He lifts me in his arms and spins me around. After setting me on the floor, his lips meld to mine in a searing and possessive kiss that makes my knees buckle.

"What are we celebrating?" Betty returns from the barn.

"Go ahead," Christoph urges me to share the news.

"I'm going to be based in DC!"

"Oh my old lady heart! You'll be closer!" Betty throws her arms around both of us. "Let's eat and discuss more."

Christoph finishes our breakfast while I make coffee for everyone. I take my time with the cup; it's the only one I get today. Aside from the initial nausea and breast tenderness, I'm feeling much better. Not a fan of the fact I only get one cup of coffee a day though.

Unfortunately, our time with Betty is up for now. Leaving is harder than I anticipated. Betty is amazing and reminds me of the Estelle I knew growing up. I refuse to allow Estelle's choices to impact my life with Christoph and our child. After breakfast we pack up and return to his condo.

The baby shower is being held in the barn at Jake's. I suppose this is more of a celebration of the babies pending arrival rather than a shower. Even though Callie and Connor didn't create a registry, we purchased two car seats for the twins. The barn is gorgeous inside. The walls are decorated in blue and pink flowers. There are mixed centerpieces on the ivory linen tablecloths.

After we set our gifts on the designated table, we're greeted by Norah and her in-laws.

"Hi, Christoph. Madeleine."

"Hey, Norah. Mrs. B., Mr. B, pleasure to see you. Madeleine, these are Jake's parents, Connie and Ben Blackthorne."

"Pleasure to meet you."

"Where have you been hiding her, young man?" Connie asks.

"Not hiding her, but we haven't been free to visit when a family party is happening."

Connie glances over at Norah for confirmation. Norah nods.

"Well then, welcome. We're happy to have you join our family," Ben states before they move on to the next arriving guests.

Christoph wasn't kidding about the Blackthorne's being family to him. I chose to walk away from Estelle after her betrayal, but I may have gained a bigger family than I could have imagined. The next hour is a whirlwind of introductions, including Jake's brother, Cameron, and Alex, one of the newer members of Blackthorne. We chat quickly with Maia, Nolan, and Callen.

Then I realize Callie and Connor aren't here for their own party. "Hey, where are Callie and Connor?"

"Let's go find out." Christoph takes my hand and leads me over to Jake's house. "Jake," he calls out.

"In the office," Jake replies. "Hey. Hi, Madeleine."

I nod in greeting.

"Can you have Blaine create a file on Madeleine's family?" Christoph immediately asks, jumping right in.

Jake looks over at me with questions in his eyes.

I push out a breath I didn't know I was holding. "I recently learned my parents have been looking for me more than my grandmother let on. She gave me a box with all the information, but I would prefer facts rather than Estelle's version. We'll bring the box in from the car before we leave."

"I understand. I will request it from Blaine," Jake replies and scribbles on a notepad to his right.

"Where are the guests of honor? Is everything okay?" Christoph asks. "Come to think of it, where are Connor's parents as well?"

"Everyone is fine. Great, even. I've been sworn to secrecy."

I see Christoph's brain working. "Is it a boy or a girl?"

Jake raises an eyebrow. "Connor didn't give me those details. All I know is they're going to be late to their own party because they needed to meet someone."

My heart squeezes and tears threaten. *Damn hormones.* Joyce was able to facilitate an adoption for Connor and Callie. It takes immense restraint not to set my hand on my belly.

"Is that why you're hiding out? Worried you'll betray their confidence?"

Jake gives him the side-eye but agrees, "Yes."

We laugh and leave his office.

"How are you?" Christoph asks as we leave the house.

"I'm happy for them."

"I meant you. How are you feeling?"

I smile. "I'm fine. Overall, most of the ailments have subsided."

"Good. Let's get some food while we wait."

We meander over to the barn again. Cruz arrives at the same time.

"Hey, man! Good to see you so soon." Christoph bro hugs him.

"Hey, C-top. Madeleine, pleasure to see you again." He kisses both my cheeks.

Christoph doesn't make a big deal about it, but I'll ask later. Perhaps it's a habit.

"How are things with you?" Christoph asks.

Cruz shrugs noncommittally. "I was passed over for captain, and I'm pissed. I have been busting my tail at the department, and it wasn't enough."

"I'm sorry, man. Are you going to make a change?"

Cruz clearly has what it takes to be part of Blackthorne. He has the qualifications, and the team clearly trusts him if they sent him to my office.

"It's a possibility. I need to get over my anger first and then make decisions."

"I get it. Taking some time isn't a bad idea, but we're here if you're ready."

"Thanks, bro. I need to greet Mr. and Mrs. Blackthorne. Talk later?"

Christoph nods tightly.

"Bye, Madeleine."

"Bye, Cruz." I watch him as he walks away. His gaze trips on Jill as she sets up some food at the buffet. Then he approaches Jake's parents and kisses Mrs. Blackthorne like he kissed me. It explains why Christoph didn't freak out about it. Some Hollywood types kiss on both cheeks, but it's typically reserved for red carpet events or televised things, not everyday life.

We approach the buffet as Jill finishes setting it up. "Hi, Jill."

"Hi, Christoph. Madeleine, right? Callie's agent."

"Yes, nice to see you again, Jill." I don't miss her gaze zipping down to our clasped hands. Does she have a thing for Christoph? Interesting, considering she spent the entire wedding reception with Cruz. I push my thoughts away. "I need something to eat."

"Okay. I'll be right there." Christoph kisses me softly and releases my hand.

I walk past the buffet over to the appetizers near the outer edge of the barn. With a plate of hors d'oeuvres, I move back to Christoph who is chatting with another older couple. If I had to guess, it's Connor's parents. I join them and hand him a water.

"Thanks. Madeleine, please meet Connor's parents, Ed and Joyce Michelson."

"Nice to meet you."

Joyce gives me the once-over. Christoph has all types of family looking out for him in addition to Betty. I appreciate it on his behalf. "How did you two meet?"

"We met at Callie's final concert in Atlanta. I'm Callie's agent," I reply.

"Lovely."

"You're very good at keeping secrets, Joyce."

Her face turns bright red. "I have no idea what you're referring to, Christoph."

"When will they be here?"

I can tell he's excited for his friend, and so am I.

Joyce glances at her watch. "It should be soon. They wanted to take some time at our house before coming here. That's all you're getting out of me, young man. Jake stinks at secrets too apparently."

"Yes, he does." As Christoph answers Joyce, a round of applause erupts in the barn.

Connor and Callie appear in the doorway with a baby wrapped in pink. A throng of people rush toward them. We stay in our place until the crowd thins out before moving to meet the newest member of our extended family.

"Congrats, guys!" Christoph accepts the tiny infant Callie sets in his arms.

"Thanks. This is Amara. She's three months old," Callie informs us.

I can't take my eyes off Christoph with a baby in his muscled arms. She looks so small. *How will I feel when it's our baby?* My chest tightens and I take her tiny hand in mine with the other wrapped around Christoph's waist.

"If her name isn't serendipity, I don't know what is," Christoph adds.

Connor tears up, "I know."

I'm not sure what he means about her name, but I'll ask later as well as about Jill's reaction to the two of us. I'm downright mesmerized by the look on Christoph's face. So much so, I need to look away to keep our news a secret a bit longer.

"Wow, what a sight!" Norah exclaims as she joins our little group with Jake in tow. "Can't wait for that to be you, Jacob." Her hand flies to her mouth. "Oh no! I wanted to give—"

"No worries. We didn't know we would be picking her up today. Congrats to you too! When are you due, Norah?" Callie asks.

"May."

I dig my fingers into Christoph's flank. I don't plan on sharing our news today. I only decided to move my base here this morning. More well-wishers join our small group. Christoph hands Amara to Connie and escorts me outside.

"You look insanely hot holding a baby in your arms," I whisper.

"It felt amazing. I can only imagine when it's our child." He stops near the corral fence and leans on the post. He curls his arm around me and pulls me against him.

"Me too."

He kisses me tenderly at first before taking it up a few notches to barely appropriate for our surroundings.

A few moments after we break apart, I finally catch my breath. This man is mine, and I'm still floored. "Can I ask you a few things?"

"Anything."

"Why is the baby's name serendipity?"

A flicker of sadness crosses his features. "Connor had a twin sister who died about seven years ago. Her name was Mara, and she was Jake's first wife."

"How sweet and terrible at the same time. Why was Jill taken aback about our relationship?"

He exhales sharply. "At one time, I thought Jill and I could be a couple. Before we met, I was Jill's first call when something would go wrong, even though Connor and Jake live equally as close. I've fixed flats, her dryer, and even her garage door opener."

"Okay, but isn't she into Cruz?"

A look of surprise crosses his face. "Yeah, I saw the sparks too. I don't think they've acted on it though, at least not recently."

"Meaning?"

"When Jake and Connor were injured on their deployment, Cruz and I were on a different mission. It hit Cruz harder than me because he was switched out the morning of the mission, whereas I was never assigned to it at all. The moment we returned stateside, he spent every waking moment at the hospital and physical therapy with Jake and Connor. Jill was there frequently too. I got the impression they grew close but didn't pursue anything because Cruz took the job in New York."

"Well, the looks they're throwing at one another clearly indicate some feelings are still there."

"I agree. Ready to return to the party?"

I set my head on his shoulder and press a kiss to his neck. "Almost."

"What else, *anamchara?*"

"When do you want to share our news?"

"We can do it right now, if you want."

I shake my head and lift my gaze to his.

"How about I share with Jake and Connor when I meet with them at the end of our vacation?"

"Perfect. What are we going to do?"

His face lights up. "I've been working on it. Given our desire to move here, I found a nice lake house we can get away to starting tomorrow."

"Really? When?"

He grins at me. "I have been looking since we left New York, but I was torn between a beach and the mountains. I opted for the mountains a few days ago."

"Perfect. Let's go celebrate Amara and the twins so we can run away together."

"I'm in." We return to the party and rejoin my rapidly growing family. Soon enough everyone will know our family is gaining a new little person too.

A few hours later, after consuming a few too many of Jill's desserts, we head to the condo to pack for our lake house vacation.

CHAPTER TWENTY-SIX

CHRISTOPH

The lake house I found is perfect with its rustic décor, exposed beam ceilings, and stunning view of the lake. It is the perfect escape for us. We haven't discussed the contents of my file on my parents, nor her box from Estelle. Ideally, Blaine's report on her family will be complete when we return.

We've spent the week hiking in the morning and relaxing in bed most afternoons, whether reading or tangling up the sheets. Madeleine has only spoken with Simon once since we arrived. He wanted to confirm she would in fact be returning on Monday and to clear the changes he made to her schedule, including adding a client meeting with two of Stavros's current clients who want to interview her before they agree to extend with Scala. I reached out to Jake to confirm our meeting later today and spoke with Finn to check on Betty. I talked to Betty as well, but she wouldn't share if anything has gone awry so I won't worry.

"Ready, beautiful? New books and old books await your credit card."

Madeleine hurries to my side, and we leave for my meeting. She plans to browse more at Norah's store while I meet with Jake and Connor. I'm sure the nursery for our child will have a few more books by the end of my meeting, even though it doesn't exist yet.

I escort Madeleine into the store and introduce her to Jessa, Norah's store manager.

"Pleasure to meet you. Norah is in the back."

"You as well. I'm going to browse." With a kiss, she walks away to find a buried treasure in Norah's shelves.

I step outside and into the office next door. "Hi, Gemma."

"Hi, Christoph. Something to drink?"

"A water would be great."

She reaches into the mini fridge behind her desk and hands it to me. "They're ready for you."

"Thanks." I clutch my plan, take a deep breath, and step into the small conference room.

"Hey!"

"Take a seat," Connor points to one of the chairs across from them.

Jake speaks next. "We know you asked for this meeting to discuss your plans to expand into a training facility and self-defense mecca where we can assist our clients to protect themselves if they ever need to. Your plan is exceptional and includes some aspects we hadn't thought of before."

I nod. *I don't like where this is going at all.*

"We looked at an off-site gym as an option when we added Alex to the team. She has a background in training women in Krav Maga and Aikido, as does Norah. The idea itself is promising. However, the infrastructure we would need to pull it off extends far beyond a state-of-the-art facility. To bring our high-profile clients here to train, we would need somewhere secure to house them for the duration of their training."

I didn't think of those aspects at all. "I see."

"We have a different proposal for you."

"Our client list has increased more rapidly than Connor and I expected over the last year. We don't want to continue to pass off clients to other firms, especially ones that in our opinion are inferior."

"Come on, Jake. Spill it already. I'm anxious, and I know what you're going to offer." Leave it to Connor to break the tension in the room. I grin and shake my head.

"We want to offer you a stake in Blackthorne and for you to head up a third team."

I'm speechless. This will be perfect for my family. "Thank you. I'm floored."

Jake slides a stack of paperwork across the table. "This binder includes the proposed buy-in agreement, an updated partnership agreement with the three of us, and a compensation plan. Take some time and review it."

I nod slowly. "What is your proposed timeline?"

"We want to add the new team members by the end of the year to have the team in the field by the end of January," Connor answers.

"Understood."

Jake shares more information. "We have taken the liberty of posting new team positions in the last month. Here are the top eight resumés. We're looking to hire four team members for your team."

"This is not how I saw this going. I was prepared to walk away for Madeleine and our child, but now you've given me—"

"Child?" Connor asks.

I shake my head. "I know exactly how Norah felt blurting it out at the shower. Yes, we're having a baby in May as well."

"Congrats, man!" they say in unison.

"Wait, you were going to resign?" Jake inquires.

"No. Maybe. It was an option. Both of us can't travel for work and have a family at the same time. As you both know, Madeleine is a sought-after agent and highly successful. Recently, she earned a promotion and will be the president and CEO of Scala Talent on the first of the year. Her base will be in the DC office—although the information isn't public knowledge yet."

"Crazy changes happening for everyone," Jake adds.

"Seriously. How is Amara adjusting?" I ask Connor.

"Once we switch her internal clock, things will be wonderful."

"I'm afraid to ask. What does that mean?"

Connor laughs. "She's awake most of the night because she sleeps all day."

"Gotcha! Good luck, and make sure you write down any tips in case we need them." I motion between Jake and myself.

"Will do."

Jake slides another file across the table. "I almost forgot. Here is the file you requested for Madeleine's family. Like yours, I didn't read it."

"Thanks, Jake."

"Have you delved into your file?"

I shake my head. "No. I talked to Betty about it over the holiday. I have two reservations." I explain my reservations to Jake and Connor, and both are quiet when I finish.

"Both concerns are legitimate. If you want a review of your file or Madeleine's beforehand, I would be willing to do it. I understand your fears wholeheartedly," Jake says.

"I appreciate your offer. I'll suggest it to Madeleine and Betty and get back to you on both."

Gemma knocks on the glass of the conference room. Jake waves her in. "Mrs. Blackthorne and Miss Wilton are here."

"Which one?" Jake asks with a smirk.

"Your wife, not your mom."

The ladies join us in the conference room. Norah rounds the table and kisses Jake. Madeleine leans down and kisses me as well before settling in the chair beside me.

"Congratulations, Christoph," Norah states with a smile.

"For?"

Madeleine sighs and leans closer to me. "I'm sorry. I cracked. She noticed all the books were for children."

The guys and I laugh. "It's fine. I did too. In fact, I blurted it out like Norah did at the shower."

"When are you headed back to New York?" Connor asks.

"Our flight is tomorrow midmorning. Beyond that, I don't know."

"The teams are finishing their current assignments, and we'll be assignment free for the last two weeks of the year except for Finn. For now, you're on call. I don't expect any issues."

I nod. "Thanks, Jake. I'll look this over and get back to you soon."

Norah and Madeleine hug, and we make our way back to the condo. My brain is spinning to the point where I haven't said a word since closing Madeleine's door.

Her hand covers mine on the center console. "Christoph?"

"Yeah."

"What's wrong?" Her hand grips mine tighter, and her tone is laced with concern.

"Our meeting went very differently than I anticipated. I'm processing. It isn't bad."

"Will you share with me?"

"Of course, it impacts both of us. I need to sort through their offer and the other forthcoming changes."

She relaxes visibly. For the rest of the ride to the condo, she gives me the time to think. I have every intention of sharing the offer with her and the numerous other things we need to handle. The list simply keeps growing from securing and furnishing the DC office, where to live, and when she plans to leave New York to name a few.

When we get to the condo, we take drinks and blankets upstairs to the patio despite the brisk temperature. Once the firepit is roaring, we snuggle into our spot in the corner of the couch.

"You're making me nervous, babe, and it isn't an easy feat," she murmurs against my chest.

"No reason to be nervous. Let's start with the easiest decision first. When do you want to be in this area permanently?"

"Timing our move is worrying you?"

"*Anamchara*, I'm not worried per se. There are a substantial number of changes happening in the near future. Right now, I feel unprepared, and it's unsettling for me."

"I have a month until Stavros's farewell celebration. I have meetings with two of his clients on Monday and then a meeting with Lucia Rinaldi for the junior assistant position on Tuesday and then a meeting with Stavros on Wednesday. Simon will be handling furnishing the office as soon as I tell him my decision. Can Blackthorne work with the NY company and secure the DC building?"

I press a kiss to the top of her head. "I'll talk to Jake about securing the building. Do you need to clear the security plan with Stavros first?"

She wrinkles her nose at me. "Why? It's my building, and I'll oversee it. One of the reports he gave me was for security at all three locations."

Damn, her work mode is sexy! "Yes, ma'am."

She giggles. "To answer your question, next weekend if possible. I can work from here until the building is furnished and secure. I'll need to go back to New York for the party though."

Her answer is as expected, at least the party part. Moving by next weekend will be fast, but I'm sure I can pull it off. "What is your plan for your apartment? Are you keeping it?"

She shakes her head. "No, I don't need it. I plan to list it and sell it furnished, except for the...." Her face falls.

"What piece is from Estelle?" I ask, tugging her even closer.

"The bedroom set in the guest room, which you may not have ever noticed, is mine from when I was a little girl. I'm still working through whether I want to see Estelle ever again, but I may still want to keep my furniture."

"We can do whatever you want. Do you want to stay here for a while, or do you want to look for a farm property immediately?"

"Do you mind putting it off a bit?" she asks quietly.

"Whatever you want is fine. If you're comfortable here, we can hold off."

"I think waiting makes the most sense."

I exhale before moving onto the next topic we need to discuss. It isn't an easy one. "Back to Estelle, sort of. Jake offered to read the files Blaine compiled before we do. Would you be interested in having Jake preview the file for you?"

"What would that accomplish?"

"Jake would be able to tell us if there is anything that could impact our future. If there isn't, we can still choose not to read the contents. If there may be, we would have to consider reviewing it ourselves."

She shifts around so she's sitting facing me, tugging the blanket around her shoulders and shoving her feet beneath mine. I draw her legs around me and wrap her in my embrace.

"I hadn't really thought about it that way. I'll consider it. What about you?"

"I trust Jake. If he tells me there's nothing I need to know, I'm fine with it. The reverse is true as well. If he tells me there's info I should know, I have the option of having him tell me rather than reading the entire file and learning things I don't want or need to know. I'm leaning toward having him read it. I will be offering this to Betty too."

"How much longer are you going to keep me in the dark?"

I lean forward and kiss her thoroughly, almost to the point of making love to her on this couch before I share the huge offer Jake and Connor presented to me. She listens intently while I lay out their offer from this morning and how it would work, including little-to-no travel, increased responsibilities, more administrative duties, and I assume more pay.

After thinking a moment, she asks, "Did you have any idea they were going to offer you a partnership?"

"No, not even close. I was prepared to walk away and pursue the gym on my own. Now, I'm considering grabbing a partnership I never fathomed as a possibility."

"Is there any instance in which you would turn them down?" Her question is the very one I'm wrestling with.

"There's only one reason to turn them down, but it doesn't make sense. I won't be able to pursue a boxing gym, now or perhaps ever."

She tilts her head in contemplation. "If you take the partnership, I assume there's a buy-out or sell provision. Suppose you hate the job; you could always move on later. You may love it though. It isn't as if you're old. You have plenty of time."

"Aren't you older than me?"

Shock materializes on her face. "Not *that* much! Eight months doesn't put me in cougar territory."

I laugh heartily and kiss her breathless. "I love you, a*namchara.*"

"I love you. Let's finish packing and get some sleep. We're going to need it."

CHAPTER TWENTY-SEVEN

MADELEINE

Thankfully, the fatigue of my first trimester has dissipated. My energy levels are good. I'm going to need it.

I breeze into the office on Monday morning. "Good morning, Simon."

"Morning, Mads! No escort today? You look gorgeous!"

"Christoph has a boatload of things to do. He didn't ride up. Thanks. What time is my first meeting?"

Simon taps on his tablet. "It's at ten."

"Perfect. Please give me fifteen minutes and we can start on the things you need to handle."

He has been my assistant for almost five years. The giddiness and glee infused with his demeanor tells me he can read between the lines perfectly. When he joins me in my office, he's ready to tackle this huge undertaking with me from the office side.

"Ready, Si?"

"I've got you, boss lady. What do you need?"

I list all the things I need him to handle, from furnishing the office for me, himself and, ideally, Lucia. We discuss my timelines and his. I grant him the ability to work remotely as much as he needs to during the transition to the new office. I provide him with Christoph's contact information so they can interface about the security as needed.

"I'm stupidly happy for you, Mads!"

"Thank you. I'm so glad you're able to join me. I couldn't pull this off as effectively without you."

"You're welcome. Do you need lunch?" he asks.

I sift through my bag and find a lunch already inside. "No, I'm set."

"He's special, Mads."

"Yeah, he is." Discreetly, I set my hand on my belly and smile as Simon leaves.

I tackle my inbox and scan my texts from this morning.

CA: Dinner out tonight?

Me: Sure. Thank you for lunch.

CA: I like taking care of you.

Me: I know. I'm still getting used to it. Love you.

CA: It won't change. Love you.

I consider not opening the next few messages from Estelle.

Estelle: Ladybug, we need to talk.

Estelle: I can't believe you're ignoring me.

Estelle: I will not stand for this disrespect.

The last one does it.

Me: I heeded your ultimatum and walked way. You can't take it back.

Me: You made your choice. I made mine. Goodbye, Estelle.

Surprisingly, standing up for myself feels better than I thought it would. After a few deep breaths, I walk to the conference room and meet with Cecily Jones about taking over for Stavros.

Simon is finishing delivering drinks and small plates of petit fours to her as I step into the conference room. "Good morning, Miss Jones. Thank you for coming." Cecily Jones is a few years into the movie business. Some industry types call her the next Julia Roberts. Her projects are mostly romantic comedies and indie films.

"Thank you for taking the meeting. I simply wanted to meet you in person and discuss what type of agent you are."

"Meaning?" I thought this was simply a formality.

"I'm a busy woman, and I'm booked through the next two years with projects courtesy of Stavros's management. How do you differ from him?"

A flicker of relief passes through me. "If you sign with me, I will manage the incoming project requests and seek projects based on the parameters you set. For example, if you want to branch out into the theatre to showcase your singing talent, I will seek those types of roles for you."

She shifts in her chair. Miss Jones wasn't prepared for my knowledge of her career. I know one of her earlier dreams was to star in a Broadway production.

"If you want to expand on the dramatic side of your talent, I will search for opportunities to meet your goal. Once I understand your career plans, which we will discuss should you retain me, the transition will be seamless."

A small smile graces her face. "Perfect, Miss Wilton. Please forward your agency contract to my attorney and we can schedule a time to meet once it's signed." She rises from her chair and extends her hand to me.

We shake hands, and she scurries out the door. I exhale, pleased with the outcome of the meeting, and return to my office. After my delicious lunch, I sign two more of Stavros's clients and wrap up for the day. When I reach the lobby, Christoph is waiting for me.

"Hi, sweetheart. How was the rest of your day?"

"Good. You?" I take his arm and walk to my car.

"Evening, Jack."

"Good evening." We settle into the seat, and he whisks us away to our dinner date.

Wherever we are, I'm clearly overdressed and so is Christoph. I look at him with questions in my eyes.

He smiles. "Don't let the exterior fool you."

We enter the dilapidated-looking building and ride an elevator to the roof. When we step off, I'm shocked. The rooftop is elegantly decorated with a dinner for two complete with heaters and blankets.

"You know I don't need all this, right?"

"Yes. Doesn't mean I don't want to give it to you."

I can feel my body flush with heat from his words. No one has ever put me first. As painful as it is to admit, not even Estelle. I mentally shake the painful thought away. I won't let her ruin his desire to romance me. "You never answered my question. How was your day?"

He serves me a drink from the low table nearby and a large charcuterie board without too many deli meats. It has mostly fruit, cheese, and crackers. "Productive. I talked to Betty and shared Jake's offer about reading the file. I finished reading and dissecting the partnership agreement. I scanned the resumés for the new team members. I disassembled your childhood bedroom set and packed the contents of the closet."

"In one day?"

"It wasn't too much work; plus, you aren't doing more than necessary. Speaking of which, do you plan your work clothes in advance?"

"Sort of. Why?"

"I want to get started with the master bedroom tomorrow after my call with Jake about his offers."

"I can choose for the rest of the week when we get home. What did you decide?" I'm almost afraid to hear his response. I don't want him to forgo his dream completely, but clearly there are holes if Jake considered it and dismissed it, at least in its current form.

"I'm going to ask Jake to review the file from Blaine." He takes a sip of his water and pops a cracker with cheese and salami into his mouth.

"You realize I'm a savvy negotiator and a critical listener, right?"

He grins at me. "Yes, it's one of your best qualities. I was hungry."

I shake my head and raise my hand to inform him I'm waiting for him to continue.

"Irritating you by making you wait is fun for me. I'm probably the only person in your life who makes you wait for anything."

True. I roll my eyes and wait.

"I'm going to buy into Blackthorne."

A huge smile grows on my face. I lean forward and kiss him hard. "I'm so happy for you and proud of you at the same time."

"Thanks. How did it go with Stavros's clients today?"

"I signed all three."

His head drops. "I would expect nothing less. How did Simon take the news?"

"Like his normal sunshiny self. He'll have a plan by Wednesday for the furniture and office equipment, and he's starting to look for somewhere to live as well. What else do you have over there?" I point to the covered plates.

He shifts and produces a heaping plate of pancakes and crisp bacon.

"How on earth?"

One of his signature dashing grins graces his gorgeous face. "I heard you debating between eggs and pancakes for breakfast. You had eggs earlier, now you have pancakes for dinner."

"You're amazing." More than I ever imagined. Finding someone comfortable with everything around me didn't seem possible, especially given gender norms and how Estelle raised me.

"So are you, gorgeous. Eat."

We finish our amazing dinner and head home. After selecting some outfits for the rest of the week, we watch a movie in bed.

Bright and early, I roll over and find his side of the bed empty. Slowly, I sit up and find a glass of orange juice and a note beside the bed.

I went to the gym downstairs. I'll be back soon. Love you, C

I smile and sip the juice. We found a bit of juice wards off the morning unsteadiness. Once I finish the glass, I step into the shower and dress for work. When I move into the kitchen to prepare breakfast, I find Christoph shirtless and still dripping with sweat.

"Morning, gorgeous."

"Morning." I bend at the waist to kiss him since I'm already dressed for work. It isn't ideal but necessary. I consider reminding him I can make my own breakfast, but truthfully, I love that he wants to do it. "What time is your meeting with Jake? Did you find anything wrong with the agreement?"

"Ten. Wrong, no. I think we need another Gemma, if you will though. She's stretched handling Jake and Connor's teams."

"Makes sense."

"What else do you need packed other than your closet and your drawers?"

"The linen closet and the kitchen. Maybe tonight or tomorrow, I can decide what décor to keep and what to leave. I can store it with the bedroom set until we find a property to purchase. Calling my relator is on my to-do list today."

"Okay." He sets a plate with a spinach and pepper quiche and fruit in front of me and one beside me.

After I take a bite, I inquire, "Is Betty a trained chef?"

He laughs. "No, but she liked to find fancy recipes for me that weren't difficult to make."

"She succeeded."

"Thanks."

We finish eating, and I rush into the office.

"Thank goodness you're here!" Simon is already flustered this morning. His demeanor so early in the morning can't be good.

"I'm not late, Si."

"Didn't say you were, Mads. There are a bunch of things happening right now. Drop off your bag; we need to go for a ride." He follows me into my office and closes the door.

"Mads, Leanna had a stroke last night. Stavros wants to move up your meeting to ten minutes ago. He sent a fresh copy of your new contract over."

"Oh, Simon, how awful. I gather from your demeanor the prognosis isn't good."

Simon shakes his head. Within minutes I'm back in the car headed to the hospital with Simon.

Me: Today is already off the rails. Good luck with Jake and Connor.

CA: Thank you. Are you okay?

Me: We're fine. Leanna isn't. Love you.

CA: That's awful. Love you.

Jack pulls to the visitor entrance of the hospital and indicates he'll wait for us.

We meet Stavros in a small meeting room outside the ICU. "Thank you for coming so quickly, Madeleine." In the almost ten years I've worked for Stavros, I've never seen him this distraught.

"No problem."

"I gather Simon has filled you in."

"Yes. Has there been any change?"

"Yes and no. The doctors feel the damage isn't as significant as originally expected, but it'll take substantial effort to regain her strength."

"If anyone can do it, it's Leanna. What can I do for you?" I have no reservations about offering something so open-ended to him. Stavros has been nothing short of an exemplary mentor and boss in this cutthroat industry. Leanna is like a wise older sister to me.

"I need you to assume your new position today. Regina will be available until you've completed hiring your new assistant."

Sheer glee and panic course through me at once. "Of course."

"Simon, do you have the contract?"

Simon reaches into his messenger bag and pulls out a file containing my new contract. "Here you are, sir."

Stavros nods, flips to the last page, and signs it. Then he hands me the pen. I dutifully sign my name above my new titles. "Congratulations, Madeleine. You're officially the president and CEO of Scala Talent Agency."

"Thank you. May I visit Leanna?"

Stavros frowns. "Unfortunately, they are limiting her visitors. I'll be sure to tell her you were here and asking for her."

"I understand. Be with Leanna. We can handle this for you."

"I know you can. It's why I chose you." Stavros turns on his heel and reenters the ICU.

Shocked and elated, I walk toward the elevator. Once I take a seat in the car, I plan to call Christoph, but I can't. He's in his meeting with Jake and Connor. "Si, please call Regina. I need a meeting set up for four this afternoon in the large conference room for everyone present. I would like video conference invitations to anyone travelling or in the LA or DC offices."

"Got it. What else?" Simon is scribbling furiously.

"My interview with Lucia is set for one, right?"

"Yes."

"Okay. I need to maintain the appointment as scheduled. Also, please contact PR and have them draft a press release and internal memo regarding the change in leadership. I also need to schedule meetings with the head of each department starting on Thursday. I'll be travelling, so the meetings will need to be video conference."

"Consider it done."

"Si, don't worry about the timing. Please aim to be in DC by the beginning of the year as originally planned. I'll indicate as much to Lucia if she accepts as well. I would like her to start as soon as possible to lighten your workload too."

"Thanks, Mads."

"We've got this, Si." I breathe deeply.

Jack parks in front of the office. "Congratulations, Miss Wilton. It's well-deserved."

"Thanks, Jack." I'm going to miss him when I move. We ride upstairs, and I head straight into my office.

Me: Please call me when your meeting is over. I'm fine.

Me: I repeat, we are fine. Love you.

I leave my office and grab a water and some fruit from the break room. When I get back, Regina is waiting for me.

"Miss Wilton, sorry for barging in, but I wanted to verify what Mr. Dumont shared."

"Please have a seat. I understand this seems sudden, but Mr. Scala asked me to replace him two months ago. The announcement was set to happen at the end of this week, and I was to take over at the beginning of the year. Due to Leanna's illness, Stavros pushed it up today."

"I understand. I'll take care of your request for a meeting."

I nod. "Regina, if you would like to discuss your position with the company later this week, please let me know."

"Thank you, Miss Wilton." As she rises, Simon buzzes me.

"Mads, Mr. Anderson on line one."

"Thanks, Si." I stand and round my desk. "I appreciate your assistance, Regina."

"Of course. Mr. Scala was a great boss."

Once she leaves, I retake my seat and explain my morning to Christoph and ask him to be here for the announcement later today. Next, I scan my email again and send off the final points for the Rodin contract. Before I can blink, Simon is showing Lucia into my office and indicates the conference is set and PR will have a draft for me by three.

Lucia is tall with dark hair and hazel eyes, and her fashion sense is... original. She's wearing a plaid skirt with a white blouse and a floral jacket. "Miss Rinaldi, I'm Madeleine Wilton. Pleasure to meet you."

"Likewise."

"Your resumé was impressive. Please share what a typical day was like as the assistant to the head of the fashion house."

Lucia takes a moment to gather her thoughts and expounds on a typical day at her current position. Honestly, she's a glorified gopher and secretary. I don't have Si, nor will I have her, get my dry cleaning or schedule personal appointments for me. Blocking my schedule, sure. Actually making the appointments, no. Along with Simon's input, we will create a flow of work for the two of them.

"Thank you. Your work for me will lean less on my personal needs and more on office needs. Will it be an issue?"

"No, not at all. I would prefer it actually. Please don't misunderstand, I'm not above ordering your lunch if you ask or you forget it at home. However, I would prefer not to drive to Connecticut to get a specific salad from a certain establishment on a whim."

"It isn't your job to spend hours tracking down a salad."

A tight smile appears on her lips. "I appreciate it."

"Are you willing to relocate to the DC metro area?"

"Without question."

At her response, my shoulders relax a bit more. "Wonderful. When would you be able to start? I'll be here in this office until Friday and then working from home until the DC office is complete."

"Does right now work?"

I knew I liked her. "Certainly. I'm confident Simon has plenty for you to assist him with." I extend my hand to her, and she takes it. "Welcome to Scala Talent." I buzz Simon on the intercom. "Si, could you join us in here?" Moments later, he knocks and enters.

"Hello again, Miss Rinaldi."

"Hi, Simon."

I address Simon. "Lucia is ready to hit the ground running. Please escort her to HR. Afterward, could you set her up as close to you as possible and use her to get through this afternoon's conference? We can discuss separating my tasks first thing tomorrow."

"Of course. Mr. Anderson called and asked if you wanted different shoes for the conference."

I smile. "Thanks. I'll call him back."

CHAPTER TWENTY-EIGHT

CHRISTOPH

I answer on the first ring. "Hey, beautiful! How are you holding up?"

"Hi. Ecstatic, nervous, and a bit tired. I don't need different shoes, but thank you for thinking I might."

"I want you to be comfortable. It's something small I can do for you."

All those little things add up. "I appreciate it. How was your meeting?"

"Fine. We can talk about the details later. I'll leave soon for your announcement. I'm crazy proud of you, *anamchara.*"

"Thank you. See you soon."

I end the call and ride down to the lobby and wave to Theo who is on a call. The weather is downright cold today. I'm glad I grabbed her coat. The ride to her office takes longer than I would like. When I arrive, I find Simon's desk occupied by a brunette with colorful clothes.

"Can I help you?" she asks.

"Yes, I'm here to see Miss Wilton."

"She's—"

"Mr. Anderson, nice to see you again. Sorry to interrupt, Lucia. This is Madeleine's beau," Simon informs her.

"Pleasure to meet you, Lucia. Hi, Simon."

Simon acknowledges my greeting. "She's with Regina in Stavros's office. Would you like to wait or seek her out?"

"I'll wait in her office. Thank you."

Madeleine steps into her office, closes the door, and leans against it before she sees me.

"Sweetheart, are you okay?"

"You're already here!" Joy is clear in her voice as she throws herself into my arms. "I'm freaking out and proud at the same time. It makes absolutely no sense."

I kiss her temple and then her lips while softly cupping her face. "It does. It's a lot to handle and celebration worthy all at once. Plus, we have another reason to celebrate, which you haven't shared yet."

"You're right."

A devilish grin marks my face. "Say that again?"

"You're right. Not repeating it again."

I kiss her thoroughly until a knock on the door interrupts us. I release her, and she opens the door.

"Miss Wilton, your mail has arrived," Lucia states.

"Thank you, Lucia. Please bring it back to Simon, and he'll share our process for my mail."

She frowns. "He did explain it to me. This one is personal."

"Oh, I apologize. I didn't realize how much he has gone through already. Thank you." She takes the letter from Lucia as she leaves. Without a second glance, Madeleine drops the letter into her handbag.

"She seems like a go-getter."

"She is. Her last boss was a real bitch based on the details she shared in her interview. It isn't her job to make sure my water is full or fetch a salad from Connecticut on a whim."

"That's terrible. There are CEOs like that?"

"Apparently her old boss was. It gives the rest of us a bad name."

I guide her to the edge of her desk. "There are always women who mistreat people when they obtain power because they feel like they can or they have to maintain the aura."

"Who mistreated you? I need to teach her a lesson."

This woman slays me. "Easy, my sexy, feisty defender. It was a client. Jake released her when I shared her behavior."

"I still want to know who."

I shake my head. "I can't tell you. I signed an NDA."

"Fine, but if we ever come across her at an event or she wants to be a client of Scala, you say 'purple gremlin,' and I'll refuse to take her on. Deal?"

"Deal. Ready to charm all of Scala Talent?"

"Terrified but excited at the same time."

I draw her closer and assure her, "You earned this promotion with years of tenacious, demanding work and grit. While it isn't the way you planned as far as the pace or certainly how Stavros wanted to announce it, but you are the head of this company and everyone out there should know it."

"Thank you for truly seeing me, all of me, especially the parts I hide from the rest of the world."

"You're welcome. Those parts are my favorite. Let's go, beautiful."

With fingers linked, we walk to the large conference room. I stand off to the side with Simon and Lucia. My gorgeous woman and mother of my unborn child takes a settling breath.

"Ladies and gentlemen, thank you for joining me here this afternoon on short notice. I appreciate those of you listening in from LA, DC, or your travel locations. A few months ago, Mr. Scala indicated his intention to retire at the end of this year. He planned to announce his replacement companywide at the end of this week. However, Mrs. Scala took ill last evening, and he has expedited both his announcement and retirement. Earlier today, Stavros Scala retired as the president and CEO and named me as his replacement."

Hushed whispers wave through the crowd.

She takes a deep breath and continues, "I'm sure Mr. Scala's sudden departure is jarring. I understand. It was for me as well. I intend to speak with all department heads beginning on Thursday. I have no intention of making any significant staffing or policy changes in the next six months. However, I will be based in DC not NY. Thank you."

A low round of applause fills the room, and the video participants sign off one by one. She rounds the table and shakes hands with those who remain. From the little bit I can overhear, their overall concern is more for Leanna than Madeleine taking the helm of this multibillion-dollar company. Lucia and Simon maneuvered their way out of the conference room immediately when Madeleine finished speaking. My eyes are trained on her, and I see she's growing unsteady with the limits on her personal space. It could be she's not used to this amount of attention or with her pregnancy her personal space requirement from strangers has increased. Either way, it needs to be addressed.

I approach from her right, cup the back of her elbow, and slide one arm around her. "You okay?" I whisper.

Her head shifts the slightest bit to indicate she needs space.

I raise my hand above my head and say, "Excuse me, if I could have your attention. Miss Wilton will gladly speak with each of you. However, if we could all take a few steps backward to add some space."

Slowly the group of agents and support staff back away from Madeleine, and she takes a step backward herself. After half a water, she returns to speaking with the assembled staff. Most of the remaining statements are well wishes and congratulatory messages. When the last person leaves, I escort her back to her office and into a chair.

"Thank you. The press conference was more exhausting than I anticipated."

"You're welcome. Are you ready to leave, or do you have more work to do here?"

She wrinkles her nose. "I wanted to go out for a double celebratory dinner, but I don't have it in me today. Can we order dinner from Romano's and celebrate at home?"

"A quiet evening at home would be my preference too. You gather what you need here; I'll order and check in with Simon about calling Jack."

"Sounds good."

I speak with Simon first. "Could you call Jack for Madeleine?"

"Sure can. Is she heading out?" Simon asks.

"Yes, she's packing up now. Is there something I need to give her?"

Simon places a large box of files in my arms.

"What is this?"

"She requested these files from Regina. These are Stavros's clients whose contracts expire in the next ninety days."

"Thanks." I walk back to her office and set the files on the edge of her desk.

"The files I requested from Regina?" she asks.

"Yeah. Ready to go?"

"Sure. How did my coat get here?"

I grin at her. "I brought it when I came. It was colder than this morning when you left."

A grateful smile graces her gorgeous but tired face. "Thank you. Let's go home."

I grab the box of files, and we ride back to her apartment.

Her head leans against the leather headrest, and her eyes close briefly. "Crap!" Her eyes fly open.

"What's wrong?" I take her hands in mine.

She purses her lips and shakes her head. "I'm sorry. Aside from being tired, I'm physically fine, but I didn't call the realtor today."

"There's no rush. Today absolutely didn't go as planned."

"No, not at all." I usher her into the lobby with the box of files.

Theo is all smiles when we near the concierge desk. "Good evening, Miss Wilton. Congratulations!"

She looks at me. I shrug.

"Thank you."

"I have a few deliveries for you. I'll bring them up shortly."

"Thank you, Theo. Our dinner should be arriving soon as well."

She leans against me as the elevator doors close.

"Almost there, sweetheart." When the doors open, I set the box on the floor and guide her near the couch.

She unbuttons her coat, sits, and removes her shoes.

"Need anything right now?"

She shakes her head and closes her eyes as she rests against the back of the structured couch. I move the box to the island and admit Theo with the first round of deliveries. The cart has two large bouquets of flowers and a fruit arrangement. Neither are the one I ordered.

"I'll be back, Mr. Anderson."

"Thank you."

I grab these three cards and bring them over to Madeleine along with a small glass of juice. "What is the last thing you ate?"

"My intentions were good, but the day got away from me. I haven't eaten since some fruit when I returned from the hospital."

Now her condition makes sense. "Drink this please. Perhaps you should consider telling Simon about our child. He'll make sure you eat when I'm not around."

"I will. Forgetting to eat isn't ideal for the baby."

"Not you either."

Theo returns with two more floral deliveries and our dinner. "Thank you, Theo. Have a nice evening."

"You too."

I grab the card from the flowers and hand it to Madeleine. "Do you want to eat there or the island?"

"Island works. I'll be right over."

"Who are the flowers from?"

She reads off the names. "One is from Callie, the second is from Simon, and the third is from Mary... my biological mother."

"How?"

"The only person who knows where I live who could tell her is Estelle."

I leave our food on the island half open and kneel on the floor in front of her. "What does the card say?"

"She would like to meet and talk."

"Have you heard from Estelle?"

She nods. "She texted a few times with anger and disrespect, and I responded. I doubt she'll reach out again. She threw down the ultimatum without considering I might need to process what I thought was true and the actual truth. She was disrespectful, and I walked away. Even now, without reading the file or searching through her box, I'm still angry and don't want to see her again. I may never want to, even if I decide to read Blaine's file."

"I understand." I rise and offer her my hand. "Did you read the letter Lucia gave you earlier?"

I shake my head. "No, I completely forgot about it."

Once she's sitting, I return to plating our dinner and take the stool next to her. Before I even take a bite, I grab her handbag and set it beside her. "You should at least see who it's from."

She shrugs and rifles through her purse. She pulls the letter out and notes the return address is from M.J.W at an address in South Carolina. What was she doing in DC last week?

"It's from Mary Jane." She sets the letter aside and digs into her food. "Did you decide what to do about your file from Blaine?"

"Betty wants to have Jake read it and determine if we should. If Betty wants to know, the choice is up to her. I don't need to be present when Jake shares the information she needs to know."

We talk while we eat.

"Feel any better?"

"Much. Thank you."

"Please promise me you'll tell Simon tomorrow. I have his number; I can check."

"You wouldn't dare!"

"Yes, I would. I love you both. If I can't be there to remind you to eat, Simon will."

"I'll tell him tomorrow. When are we going to tell Betty?"

She may have asked the question, but I see the pain behind it. I don't know what she'll decide about Estelle, but deep down despite her anger, she wants to share she's going to be a mom. "Maybe we can visit her this weekend. What do you think?"

"Sure."

"Madeleine, you're rightfully upset with Estelle. I would be too. If you want to tell her anyway, we'll visit her too."

"Yes. No. Maybe. Part of me is thinking hell no, I'm not sharing one of the most important parts of my life after what she did to me. Yet another part of me feels guilty for withholding our news out of anger. It doesn't make sense."

"It does to me. You're angry and betrayed. Yet she raised you and you can't reconcile the woman who raised you being the same one who kept your true parentage and your family away from you all these years. I support whatever you decide."

"Thank you." She finishes her meal and waits for me. While waiting, she asks, "What did Jake and Connor say when you accepted their offer?"

"They were happy for us, even though I suggested hiring another staff member for the office."

"Gemma is going to need help with the three of you," Madeleine states.

"Yes, she will. They agree but have been putting it off because it means the office will need to expand upstairs in the building and it'll cost more money. For each of us to have an office and appropriate meeting space, we need to renovate the second floor of the building so Gemma, our new employee, and the conferences can happen in the first-floor space."

"Jake and Connor have some construction skills. Do you?"

I lift my eyebrow in question before asking, "How do you know about Jake's house?"

"Norah told me Jake and Connor renovated the house when I complimented her."

"Oh. Yeah, they did the house. I helped with the exterior stuff like shoveling, raking, seeding, and mowing. They did the interior stuff."

She points to the bouquet from me. "Those roses are stunning. Thank you."

"You're welcome."

I clean up from dinner and convince Madeleine she needs to soak in her jetted tub.

"I will if you join me."

What man in their right mind would say no to joining their gorgeous girlfriend—a term that isn't sufficient for what we are—in a huge whirlpool tub? None. "There's nowhere I would rather be."

The water is scalding hot when we first dip into the tub. When it's time for us to get out, the water level is substantially lower and there are puddles on the tiled floor.

"I'll clean this and be right in."

She skins a sweet kiss on my lips and pads to the bedroom. She's sound asleep beneath the ultrasoft sheets when I finish drying the floor.

CHAPTER TWENTY-NINE

CHRISTOPH

"Morning, sweetheart. Feeling better today?"

She smiles at me. I may not have said it in so many words, but I plan to spend the rest of my life making this gorgeous woman and our children happy. "Morning. Much better. I'll tell Simon this morning. I promise."

"Thank you." I set some oatmeal with fruit and her only cup of caffeinated coffee for the day in front of her. "What's your schedule for today?"

"Office transition and hopefully visiting Leanna near the end of the day. Would you like to come with me?"

"Yes. Let me know when I need to meet you at the hospital or the office."

"I will."

Less than an hour later, I'm returning to the apartment after escorting her to her office.

Me: Are you free for lunch?

Cruz: Yeah, I'm off today. Everything okay?

Me: Yup. All good here. I'll meet you at the corner deli on 6th at 1.

Cruz: See you then.

I spend the majority of the morning packing the master bedroom and the linen closet. Thankfully, she has narrowed down the shoes she needs for this week. I've been in her closet numerous times, but I vastly underestimated the sheer number of luxury heels and handbags my woman owns. I ride down to her storage area in the basement and procure three more totes to pack. Her holiday decorations and the other items in storage are neatly packed and labelled.

I hurry through the shower and dress to meet Cruz for lunch. I take a table near the rear of the deli and wait for him to arrive.

He greets the host and the manager as he walks in.

"Hey, bro!" I rise and hug him.

"Hey. Not following the missus today?"

I drop my head. "We aren't married."

"Not yet. I give you three months before you ask."

"I think we're going to have our baby first."

"Dude! Congrats!"

"Thanks. There's a serious influx of babies for our team. Jake and Connor are going to be dads too!"

"Damn! I knew about Connor but not you or Jake." Buried in his tone is a hint of longing. As long as I've known Cruz, becoming a dad was a top priority. At one point, he thought he found his lifelong partner. She crumbled under the pressure of the army and deployments.

"Yeah, there are a lot of changes. How are you doing?"

Our server approaches our table. "Lt. Cruz, good to see you."

"You too, Nancy."

She takes our order and walks behind the counter.

"To answer your question, I'm still pissed, but there isn't anything I can do about it. The position was the only open slot in the department city-wide, and I didn't earn it."

I nod. "I understand. I invited you here to offer you a spot on my team."

Surprise registers on his face. I explain, with Madeleine's promotion and the baby, both of us can't travel and, with my newly minted status as a partner in Blackthorne, I'm building a team. He was my first thought when Jake handed me the stack of resumés. I briefly explain his duties and what the starting salary would be. "What do you think?"

"Wow, C-top! Congrats!"

"Thanks, like I said, I was prepared to resign."

Nancy returns with our lunch. Cruz takes a huge bite. I can see the gears in his head spinning. After years in the army together and three deployments, you know when your brother is thinking and needs to process things.

"How much time do I have to think about it?"

At least he didn't shut me down completely. "Jake wants to fill the team by the end of the year so the team will be fully trained thirty days later. However, you probably don't need the full training given your experience. I would say three weeks at most."

"Thank you for offering me a spot."

This doesn't sound good.

"I'll give it some serious thought." His expression is pensive but matches his words.

"Is there a woman to consider?"

He pauses a bit too long for my liking. "Not here."

I can read between the lines. Maybe Madeleine was right about Jill and Cruz. "Fair enough."

We finish our lunch and go our separate ways after Cruz assures me he'll reach out soon. Satisfied with today's progress, I return to her apartment and start packing much of her kitchen.

Anamchara: *Can you meet me at the hospital at five?*

Me: Sure.

I continue packing until I need to leave for the hospital. I'm pleased with my progress. I have a portion of the kitchen remaining, and she needs to decide on the décor. Otherwise, I simply need to pack it into the moving truck on Friday morning. Best-case scenario the truck will arrive on Saturday afternoon. Monday morning is more realistic.

I arrive at the hospital before Madeleine and take a seat on a bench outside the entrance. A sleek, black car pulls up to my right. Jack parks and hops out to open Madeleine's door.

"Good afternoon, Mr. Anderson."

"Hi, Jack."

I offer Madeleine my arm and kiss her cheek.

"I'll wait here to bring you home," Jack states after closing the rear door.

"Thanks, Jack," Madeleine replies.

"Hi, gorgeous. How was your day?"

"Busy, but not like yesterday. I had a few people pop their heads into my office, but other than the workload being heavier and some parts different, it was normal. Before you ask, I ate the lunch you made and had a snack before I left today."

"Thank you."

"What about you?"

We sign in and ride to Leanna's private suite.

"I finished your clothes and shoes and most of the kitchen. I met Cruz for lunch and offered him a spot on my team."

"What was his response?"

The nurse has us wait in a small room for Stavros to escort us.

"He said he was still angry, but he would seriously consider my offer."

"What do you think is holding him back?"

"Honestly, his family and a glimmer of hope he may get the promotion the next time around."

She gazes out the window and turns to face me again. "What is the likelihood of the position reopening within the next year?"

"Slim, and Cruz knows it. He has to accept it and talk to Mama Cruz and his sisters." Something else is holding him back too. I'm not sure who or what it is though.

Stavros steps into the doorway. I've only seen him at most three times, and he looks awful. I wasn't expecting anything different, but it's something else when it's worse than anticipated.

"Thank you so much for coming, Madeleine and Christoph. Right this way, Leanna is awake now."

Seeing the vibrant Leanna Scala in a hospital bed is heart-wrenching. Madeleine's grip on my hand tightens as we step into her room.

"Than... kkk... you." Leanna tries to speak.

"Of course." We spend almost an hour sitting with Leanna, mostly listening to Stavros talk with her before the nurses kick us out. Once we arrive at home, I cook some dinner and follow her around, noting which items she wants to pack for storage. We curl up on the couch and talk more about her day, how Lucia is doing, and how well she and Simon are meshing.

"Do you want some help packing your office?"

She lifts her head and kisses me lightly. "Simon and Lucia are going to do it tomorrow. If you could meet me to bring it here, I would appreciate it though?"

"Absolutely. Do you want to leave on Friday after work or wait until early Saturday?"

"Actually, I'm aiming for midafternoon."

"Sweet. I love your boss."

She yawns deeply before mumbling, "Me too."

"Time for bed, sweetheart." I follow her to the bedroom, and within minutes, she's sound asleep with her head in the crook of my arm.

After she eats a hearty breakfast, Madeleine heads to the office. I spend the morning packing the rest of her apartment and stacking the boxes near the doorway for the movers tomorrow.

Jake: When would you like to schedule a meeting about your files and interviewees?

Me: Does Monday late afternoon work? I'm sure Betty is available too.

We can meet him at the office or at the farm.

Jake: Three at the office work?

Me: We'll see you then.

I shower, dress, and head to Madeleine's office building.

Simon greets me upon my arrival. "Good afternoon, Christoph."

"Hi, Simon. How's our girl?"

Simon chuckles. "Congratulations! She ate her lunch, by the way."

"Thank you. I know a lot has gone awry, but she needs to take care of herself too."

"And what will likely be the most gorgeous child ever," Simon posits.

"I'm not your type, Simon."

He blushes. "A man as good looking as you is eye candy for men and women alike."

I shake my head, thank him, and knock on Madeleine's office door. She waves me in because she's on a call.

"Bea, honestly, the producers are overreacting yet again. Mikhail has done nothing to violate his contract. There are four days of shooting left. Urge the film company to get it done, and then we can worry about the promotion tour." Madeleine shakes her head as Bea responds. "He toed the line, and you know it. Finish the damn movie, Bea!" She listens again and ends the call.

"Hi, gorgeous." I lean over her desk and kiss her lightly.

"Hi."

"What did Mikhail do this time?"

She laughs. "He played beer pong with his costars on set between their trailers. The producers are only angry with Mikhail not the other A-list cast members who did the same. For the second time, they're blowing it way out of proportion."

"What can I start with?"

"Lucia moved everything into the small conference room off the lobby. It'll probably take you two trips from there."

"No problem. I'll start my review of proposed candidates for my team while I wait for you. I want to give the names to Jake at our next meeting. Are you free Monday afternoon at three to meet with Jake about the files?"

She wakes her laptop and clicks a few times. "Sure, I can be done by then. Is Betty joining us?"

"I plan to ask her to join us on Saturday. If you want, she can stay with Gemma or Norah while we discuss your family."

"I'll consider it. However, Betty was nothing but warm and welcoming to me. Eventually, she'll know about Estelle and the rest of my dysfunctional family."

I nod and return to scanning candidates' information on my phone. I'm halfway through the second potential candidate I want to propose when Simon buzzes Madeleine. A true southern guy named Barrett Beaumont. He's a marine veteran and is looking to leave the police force in Albany.

"Mads, Regina would like a few minutes to talk."

"Sure."

She looks up at me as if she shouldn't kick me out of her office. "Can you hang out with Simon or in the break room while I talk to Regina?"

I rise and round her desk. "I'll get you a snack while you meet with her." With a soft kiss to her lips, I'm out the door. I stop by Simon's desk. "Could you direct me to the break room?"

I follow his directions and find it easily. I return to working after taking a seat on the hard, cold, and stiff chairs. Honestly, they're probably purposefully uncomfortable so no one stays in the break room too long. About thirty minutes later, Simon texts.

Simon Dumont: She's finished with Regina.

Me: Thanks, Simon.

I grab some graham crackers and a water for her and meander back to her office. She accepts them gratefully and continues working. I retake my seat on the couch and busy myself with a cursory search for real estate in Maryland. Other than wanting land, we haven't truly discussed specifics. I close the search and return to my potential team members since I can't narrow the search enough to get viable options.

The next proposed candidate is Lane Hawkins. He was attached to our unit for our second tour. He's former army and has been working at his family farm in Oklahoma since retiring from the army two years ago. Wesley Hamilton is a member of the Charlotte PD. He's looking to move into the private sector. The remaining candidates are Garner Warren, Patton Daley, and Hughes Delaware. They all need to be reviewed by Monday.

Generally, my gut doesn't steer me wrong. I believed Cruz when he indicated he would seriously consider my offer. He would be an asset to our team and would fit in well considering our history.

"Christoph?" Madeleine calling me breaks my musing.

I look up at her and see she has a huge smile on her face. "What's the grin for?"

"Two more of Stavros's clients have signed with me based solely on his recommendation."

"Congratulations! Do you need another assistant already?"

She laughs heartily. Keeping this woman and our family safe and happy is all I truly need. If pressed, I'm confident Madeleine would say she only needs me and a few basics despite her wealth.

"What do you say to big slices of floppy New York style pizza for dinner?"

Her eyes light up. "Yes, but at home please."

"Sounds good to me. Did Simon already call Jack?"

She picks up the receiver and asks Simon to call Jack. After Madeleine packs her laptop and planner, Lucia shows me the other items from her office to pack in the car.

After a long ride home, I make two trips inside with the contents of her office while she orders our dinner. We change and cuddle up with pizza and a movie for our last night in her apartment.

CHAPTER THIRTY

MADELEINE

I'm beyond excited and nostalgic at the same time as I walk through the doors of the New York office for the last time. At some point, I'll be in this office again, but it won't be daily.

"Morning, Mads."

"Hi, Simon. Any updates since our chat on the way here?"

"Only one. Becky from payroll needs you to give her a call or stop by. She needs to discuss how you want certain aspects of your new contract will be handled. Otherwise, your day only includes a meeting with the department head from PR."

"Perfect. Thanks. Actually, can you and Lucia stop by for a few minutes when you have a chance?"

"Of course. As soon as she gets back from the mail run."

I settle into my chair and take a deep breath before calling Becky. "Hi, Becky. This is Madeleine Wilton. You asked me to give you a call."

"Hi. Yes, Miss Wilton. Thank you." Her demeanor seems nervous and a little concerned.

"No reason to be nervous or so formal. Madeleine is fine."

I hear her exhale. "Sorry. Mr. Scala wasn't as personable." She isn't wrong. Stavros always seemed unapproachable to the staff. It's one of the consistent notes from each department head.

"No problem. What do you need for my new compensation plan?"

"We need to make choices on how frequently you want your commissions paid out and the manner. For example, do you want your personal commissions separated from the company commission? Would you like monthly or quarterly payments?"

I answer her questions and then prepare to meet with the head of PR before heading to DC. After my productive meeting, I send a text to Christoph.

> *Me: Do you need more time there?*
>
> *CA: Nope, just finished loading the truck.*
>
> *Me: I'll be ready in about an hour. Can you pick me up?*
>
> *CA: Always. Love you.*
>
> *Me: Love you.*

Simon and Lucia join me in my office. As Lucia has gotten more comfortable with Simon and me, her demeanor has shifted to more joyful and her clothes less runway and a bit more classic. It seems her old boss was particular about more things than where her salads came from.

"Hi, guys. I wanted to check on your progress for DC before I start my drive there."

Simon offers Lucia the chance to go first. "Both of you have been so welcoming. Simon has been so patient, and your systems are much clearer than where I worked before. I appreciate it immensely. I've uploaded your office computer files as instructed by IT to a cloud drive until they can be moved onto your new computer in DC. The paper files from all your clients have been packed and will be transferred securely to the DC office. I'm up to date, including those you gained from Mr. Scala. Regina has agreed to forward them as necessary. I'm scheduled to check out two apartments virtually on Saturday afternoon. If all goes well, I can move next weekend."

"Sounds like you have a solid start. Si?"

Simon smiles. "I had a preliminary call with Mr. Blackthorne and Mr. Michelson, as well as a conference call with the building security here. The plan is to have the new measures in place by the end of the year. I'm negotiating with the DC office of your current transportation company. The furnishings are expected to be delivered after the holiday and assembled by the first of the year. The office equipment will arrive sooner. IT intends to have the servers up and running as soon as possible and will install our offices once the furnishings are in place. I'm flying down to check out a few apartment options this weekend. I also could be moving next weekend if one of them pans out."

"Perfect. I'll be driving down this afternoon. I'll be available again on Monday morning. Is there anything scheduled first thing, Si?"

"No, your next scheduled meeting is Monday at 1:00."

"Okay, please block off a two-hour meeting at the end of the day."

"Will do," he replies. "Safe travels, Mads."

"Same to you." As I finish speaking, I look up and see Christoph step off the elevator. I can't help the smile creeping onto my face.

"Our time is up for now, Luce." Simon rises from his chair and hugs me.

Lucia looks at Simon, unsure of what is happening. I don't know what I would do without Simon. Lucia nods and smiles before she leaves.

Christoph joins me in my office. "Hey, beautiful. Ready to go?"

Excitement courses through me. "Yes. I meant to ask sooner, and it slipped my mind. I want to ask before I forget again. Do you get a real Christmas tree or a fake one?"

He takes my bag from me and links our fingers. "We have hours to talk about holiday traditions, including the best type of tree. Let's get moving out of the city first."

"Yes, let's."

I slide into the passenger seat and slip off my shoes. After he settles into the driver's seat, he sets the radio on a low volume and eases into traffic.

Once we hit the thruway, he answers my question. "When I lived with Betty, we always had a real tree. I haven't put one up since I moved into the bunkhouse. We celebrated at Jake's, so I didn't see the need. What about you?"

Even though I asked the question, the sadness still filters in. He covers my hand with his. "We had a real tree when I was young. As Estelle got older, she switched to a fake one for maintenance. I've had a fake one every year, but only because there aren't any real tree farms in the city and I had no one to share it with."

"*Anamchara*, will you traipse through a huge tree farm with me on Sunday so we can pick our first real fir tree together?"

"Absolutely."

We chat as we cruise down the turnpike.

"I know we only talked about it loosely and I know we are holding off, but… what do you want in our home?" Christoph asks.

"The parts I've seen of Jake and Norah's house is almost perfect. I don't think we need or can handle 100 acres."

"Did you leave the main rooms?"

"No."

Christoph nods. "They have four bedrooms. The master has two walk-in closets with an en suite bathroom. The room off to the right is a guest room with a private bath. There's a large office with built-in bookcases around a large window seat. The lower level has a large family room, a small bathroom, and a wine cellar."

"I take it back. Their home sounds more than perfect. What do you think about the land part?"

"I agree. We don't need as many acres. What else would you include? A stable? A greenhouse?"

"I rode a lot as a little girl, but I haven't since I moved to the city. A few horses would be pretty awesome."

"If you want to ride, we can borrow Norah or Callie's horses at any time." He sets his hand on my belly. "I think we should wait until after the baby is born though."

I smile. "Do you think Betty could teach me to cultivate flowers?"

"I'm sure she can and would if you ask her. How about on Saturday I show you the size of Betty's land and we can figure out what we want from there?"

"Sounds good to me."

About fifteen minutes later, he pulls off at a rest area. I hurry to the restroom, and when I exit, I find Christoph walking around the convenience store like a kid who has never seen an abundance of candy before. The counter is loaded down with numerous types of chocolate, gummy candies, and bottled water.

"Do you plan on opening a candy store?"

He grins at me. "I wasn't sure which gas station candy you prefer, so I got them all."

I can't help but sigh. "Oh how I love you." I slide my arm around him.

He leans down and kisses my lips. After paying, we skip to my car.

"I know you prefer fudge truffles and caramels from Millie's in town. What is your favorite gas station candy?" Christoph asks.

I tap my finger on my lip. "If I have to choose only one with chocolate… Baby Ruth. One non-chocolate candy… sour gummy candy. The shape doesn't truly matter, but if it isn't sour, there's no point. What about you?"

"I'm more of a Caramello guy for chocolate. I agree about the non-chocolate. Sour gummy candy is the way to go."

With our spoils sorted, we continue toward home. At some point, I nod off until Christoph nudges me.

"Hey, sleepyhead. Could you put these on? I want to show you something?"

"Sure. Where are we?" I take a pair of my tennis shoes and tug them on. I reach back for my coat and bring it into my lap.

"Almost home, but I wanted to show you a secret spot only the team knows about first."

I throw my coat on after I step out of the car. We walk down a narrow, overgrown, snow-dusted path. It opens to a stunning view of a river. There's a small sitting area over to the right beneath a massive evergreen tree with a metal box at the foot.

With our hands linked, he leads me beside the box. He pulls out two heavy blankets. He sets one on top of the platform and he sits near the back edge.

"Come here." He opens his arm and guides me between his muscular thighs facing the river.

I settle in close, and he covers us with the other blanket. "It's peaceful."

"It is."

Never before him could I simply be with a man. The silence isn't troublesome; it's comforting. The steady brush of his breath on the nape of my neck and the beat of his heart against my back not only makes me feel safe but turned on. Then again, I'm in a perpetual state of desire when he's close enough to touch or to touch me.

A shooting star streaks across the sky. "Did you see it?" he whispers against my skin.

"Yes."

"What did you wish for?"

I crane my neck so I can look into his eyes. I want for nothing. I have a stable, lucrative career, an amazing man, and a baby on the way. The only thing I might add is a legal commitment, but I don't need it. We're in this together, paperwork or not. "I can't share. Then it won't come true."

"Understood. I wished for the same thing."

"There's no way you know what I wished for."

His dimpled grin weakens me. "Yes, I do. I know you, all of you. I assure you, when you least expect it, I will make your wish come true."

My chest tightens in anticipation for something possibly months away, but I don't care one bit. I shouldn't be surprised. Together we can handle anything.

"Ready to go home?"

Home. I realized it when he went to Maine. "I am home. Right here with you." Twisting in his arms is more difficult while trying to stay under the blanket. I tuck my legs beneath me and kneel between his thighs. "I love you. I'm glad you asked for more time after our day out around the city."

"I am too. I love you, *anamchara.*"

Sliding my hand up his chest, I thread my fingers into his hair, which is longer than normal. Our breath mingles together in the chilly air between us. I draw my tongue along his lower lip before tugging it between my teeth. A low groan echoes in my ears. He opens for me, and I dip my tongue into his mouth. Our kisses make me melt into a puddle since the very first brush of his lips on mine.

He's fighting between keeping the blanket wrapped around me and his desire to touch me properly. "How private is this spot?"

He raises an eyebrow in my direction. "Not private enough, and did you not notice the cold?"

"I'm never cold with you. Let's christen my car then, right now."

An unsure look crosses his face momentarily. The instant it passes, I'm on my feet. He's folding the blankets and securing them in the box. The walk back to my car is exponentially quicker. As we walk, I unbutton my coat and untuck my blouse from my pants.

"Into the back seat," he directs me.

I shuck my coat and throw it onto the floorboards of the passenger seat before climbing in. He follows me and sits in the middle of the back seat. His legs widened, and his knees press against the back of each seat. I finish opening my blouse and cast it forward. As I shimmy out of my shoes and pants, Christoph lifts his shirt and tee over his head. Then he wrestles his jeans and boxer briefs down to his ankles. The sight of him isn't new to me, but each time my mouth goes dry knowing the depths of pleasure awaiting me. I straddle his thighs and kiss him deeply. His hard length perfectly aligned with my sensitive nub. Each tiny movement sends slivers of heat deep into my core. My bra joins the growing pile of clothing. As soon as it floats to the carpet, he latches onto my nipple.

"We feel—"

He swallows my words with a hard kiss and tugs my satin panties to the side, filling me in one deep thrust upward. Every nerve ending in my entire body is on fire. I hook my feet behind his calves and dig my fingers into his shoulders. His hands bracket my hips, and we find our intoxicating rhythm. I plunge downward as he pushes upward.

"Go over with me, *anamchara*."

Each time he refers to me as his soul mate, I fall deeper for him. Never did I think there was more beyond deciding to be together. The commitment to building a life is knowing you will never be alone. Knowing without a doubt we will always have each other's back. I shatter around him as he explodes into me. I collapse forward, and his arms hold me against his rock-hard chest until our breathing calms to almost normal levels.

"Now, I'm regretting not using the semi-private cabana in LA. What other semi-illicit places can we make love before the baby arrives?"

The look in his piercing blue eyes shows me he's completely on board. "I'll create a list as soon as possible."

"I look forward to checking off each one with you. If we need to wait until after the baby is born, fine."

I lean back to grab some of our clothes, and Christoph hardens inside me.

"Can you handle round two?"

"Absolutely."

Furiously, we chase another round of explosive orgasms to the point the inside of my windows are steamed and my handprints mark the rear window. Once our panting subsides again, we dress and drive the rest of the way to our home.

CHAPTER THIRTY-ONE

CHRISTOPH

After a long drive yesterday and fulfilling my promise to christen her car, we left our luggage unopened and fell asleep. Near seven, I slip out of bed and start breakfast. While my first cup of coffee is brewing, I scan through the pile of mail on the island. Gemma has been bringing it in and checking on my condo since my LA assignment.

Only one piece stands out. It's an ivory envelope with embossed lettering. The letter is from Attorney Fairbanks. As much as I would like to ignore it, I don't. I slice open the envelope and scan the contents. Despite my stomach in knots, there's nothing other than a request for a video conference with him to talk about a personal matter. *No thanks*. I have no desire to dredge up the past. I set the letter aside and sort through the rest. If—a small word with huge implications—Jake feels I should reach out to the attorney, I'll reconsider. Right now, I have no intention of doing so.

As I finish cooking breakfast, my gorgeous woman shuffles into the kitchen. "Morning."

"Morning."

She savors the first sip of her coffee, and I set a plate in front of her. "Thank you."

"I love taking care of you and the baby."

She digs into the huge stack of pancakes and bacon. If I hadn't heard her moan similarly from my mouth or hands on her body, I would be offended.

"Seriously? It's pancakes."

She giggles. "Don't you worry, this one is different from the moans you draw from me, like yesterday in my car. I still can't believe we christened my car—*twice*."

"Why not?"

"Sex with you is never boring, but it was a bit more thrilling knowing we could get caught."

"It's part of the allure of it. Wasn't it worth it?"

Her skin blushes profusely.

"I'll take your blushing silence as a yes." We finish eating and dress to visit Grams.

The ride to Grams never gets old. Long, open road with trees on all sides. Only the occasional driveway interrupts the green stretches. The light snow cover adds a bit more to the peacefulness of the scene. We've been on the road for about fifteen minutes.

"Are you nervous?"

I glance over at Madeleine. Her hands are resting on her barely visible belly. Her second trimester has been much easier on her. The nausea subsided, and she's getting enough sleep now.

"No. I'm excited to share with Betty. Aren't you?"

I grin at her. "Grams already has us married. I've never introduced any woman to her. Bringing you to meet her was all she needs to know about how committed I am to you. She told me to hurry up with the great-grandbabies when I introduced you to her."

"Why didn't you tell me?"

"Which part? The introduction part or the baby part?"

"Both?" Her voice sounds unsure.

I lift her hand to my lips and then place it over hers on her belly. "I didn't want you to feel any pressure. I love you. I knew Betty would too."

I turn off the main road onto Betty's gravel driveway. When we pull up, Betty is leaving the barn with Finn closely behind her.

Betty hurriedly opens Madeleine's door before I can get around the car. "You're here! Is everything okay?"

Once she's standing, Betty throws her arms around her. "Hi, sweet girl! It's great to see you again so soon."

Tears well in Madeleine's eyes. She pushes out a breath slowly. As much as she would like to blame her hormones, she's still upset about Estelle and what the letter from Mary Jane may contain. Betty's hugs can soothe almost anything ailing a person.

Finn nods, a universal signal amongst our team indicating all is quiet since his last update to Jake. I had Finn updating Jake simply because I was travelling and he was closer if something went wrong.

"Hi, Christoph. Thank you for visiting." Betty releases Madeleine and hugs me as well.

"We have some news."

Betty's face lights up. "Well, let's get inside and warm up."

I slide my arm around Madeleine, and we follow Betty into the house. As usual there's a plate of banana bread on the table and some muffins cooling on a rack in the bay window.

I pull out Madeleine's chair and take a seat beside her. I set my hand on her thigh palm up, and she threads her fingers around mine. Finn is leaning in the doorway. Betty brings the muffins to the table and sits as well.

"What's this news?"

I shake my head. "Jake is finished with his review of the file on our family. We have an appointment to meet with him on Monday afternoon."

"Okay. I'll be there. You didn't come to visit for an appointment with Jake, what else?"

"Jake and Connor offered me a stake in Blackthorne, and I accepted."

"Wonderful. Would less traveling be involved?"

"It means almost no traveling. Both of us can't travel when the baby is born."

Madeleine's fingers tighten around mine.

Finn says, "Congrats!" from his spot.

I nod in acknowledgement.

Betty inhales sharply and tears fall from her eyes. "Oh my goodness! I was joking around, but I'm overjoyed! When?"

"May," Madeleine replies.

"You look fabulous, dear! How are you feeling?"

Madeleine blushes. "Thank you. Much better actually. The first few months were tough, but most of the joys of early pregnancy have subsided."

"Wonderful! He is waiting on you, right?"

Madeleine nods. "Yes. Admittedly, more than I believe necessary. You raised him well, Betty."

"Thank you. Along with Harold, he's the light of my life. Now I have you and, soon enough, a little baby to dote on." She takes one of my hands and one of Madeleine's in hers and squeezes.

We catch up about her flowers. Betty reached out to the local florist after Madeleine's suggestion to sell her excess flowers. Betty has a meeting to discuss a contract the first week of January.

Betty informs us her neighbor, Mr. Stillman, died last week. The Stillman farm abuts Betty's. I believe they have about fifteen acres of land with one large stable and one greenhouse.

"Are the kids going to take over the farm?" I ask Betty.

"Lacey indicated they were going to sell it."

Madeleine tightens her grip on my hand.

It could be perfect. We would be close to Betty and still have the farm Madeleine wants. "Could you give me her phone number?"

Betty stands and goes to the drawer beneath the phone. She flips through her address book and jots down a number. "Here's her number. Her name is Lacey Nash now."

As Betty retakes her seat, I hear a car travelling up the gravel drive. "Stay here."

I give Finn a pointed look and move to the front porch. A nondescript, dark sedan pulls to a stop behind my truck, and a young guy steps out of the car. He can't be much more than twenty. He's tall, lanky, and looks eerily like me.

"Can I help you?"

"I'm looking for Elizabeth and Christoph Anderson."

Fear courses through me. Nothing about this kid is threatening to me physically. Yet he's looking for Betty and me. "Finn!"

Within seconds, Finn is beside me.

"Please keep Betty and Madeleine in the dining room until I sort this out." The dining room is literally in the middle of the house and has no windows. Overreaction—probably—but my whole world is in the house.

"Will do." Finn turns back into the house.

I decide to start with the basics. "What's your name?"

"Collin Murphy Davenport." There's no agitation or aggravation in his response.

His middle name in addition to his appearance gives me pause. "Do you have ID?"

He hands me his license and military ID he fished out of his wallet.

"Thank you."

"I understand this is abrupt, but I need to report to Fort Meade soon. My parents' attorney has been trying to reach you."

All the air leaves my lungs. "You're claiming to be my younger brother?"

"Yes."

"Can you give me a moment?"

He nods and shifts onto his other foot. I pull out my phone and dial Jake.

"Hey, Christoph."

"Does one of the facts in my family file include me having a younger brother?"

"Why?"

"A young man who looks a lot like premilitary me is at Betty's."

Jakes replies, "Yes. Give me a second."

I have a brother. I have no reason to doubt Blaine's research. Is he the only sibling I don't know about? I hear footsteps and then papers shuffling.

"His name is Collin Murphy Davenport. He's almost twenty-two. Do you want me and Connor to come out there?"

"No, thanks. Finn and I can handle it. Given what you've read, does Finn need to stay here?"

"No. Your family is perfectly secure."

I let his words simmer a bit. The relief I feel is only partial. Knowing everyone I care for is safe removes a heavy burden from my shoulders. Reading the file will be something else. "Thanks, Jake."

I end the call and take a few steps closer to my brother. "I apologize for being rude. It's a lot to take in. It's nice to meet you." I extend my hand to him. He takes it. "Betty, I mean Elizabeth is inside. I'm sure she would like to meet you. Please give me a moment to ask her."

I send a quick text to Finn and ask him to switch places with me. Once Finn steps onto the porch. I move into the dining room.

"Who is it?" Betty asks.

"His name is Collin, and he's your grandson."

Tears plunge down Betty's cheeks.

"Would you like me to invite him in?"

All she can do is nod. Madeleine holds Betty's hand in hers. I retreat to the front and escort my younger brother into the kitchen. Betty is already on her feet.

"Hello, it's nice to meet you," Betty offers.

"I'm sure this is unsettling, but my parents' attorney has reached out to Christoph by phone and by letter. I realize the letter was recently, but I'm due to report for duty in a few days. Plus, your address is nearby."

"This is my—*everything*—Madeleine." They shake hands. "As indelicate as this may sound, where are our parents?" I demand.

He shakes his head. "They died in a car accident about a year ago."

Betty grabs my forearm and slowly lowers herself into the chair she just vacated.

"I'm sorry, Mrs. Anderson. I should've considered my audience."

She shakes her head profusely. "Grams, please call me Grams. If it's too soon for you, Betty will be fine. Please sit, Collin. I assumed they passed when you said 'my parents' attorney,' but hearing it aloud solidifies the pain of knowing I survived my only child and never had the opportunity to meet the father of my grandsons."

"I understand. I was overseas at the time, so the notification took a little longer. Once Attorney Fairbanks contacted me after he learned of their passing, I informed him about you. You were the only thing my parents told me about their life before. They drilled into me when it was safe or something happened to them, I needed to find you. You didn't make it easy. There are more layers to our family history, but that's the brief version."

I'm not sure I want to know, but I ask anyway, "What do you mean 'before'?"

"Our parents were in witness protection. From the information provided by Attorney Fairbanks, our father was a stockbroker vacationing in Europe when he met our mother. There was a small age gap between them, but Dad didn't care. When she learned she was pregnant with you, they came back to the United States. Back then, they lived in Chicago. Soon after you were born, they came to North Carolina near Betty. Dad uncovered fraud in his firm. When he brought it to the president of the company, they threatened him. Instructed him to keep his mouth shut and everything would be fine. Together our parents decided you weren't going to be safe. Soon after you were born, our mother brought you to Betty."

She left me with Betty to protect me. Choosing to leave me had to be one of the hardest decisions of her life. I have so many questions but decide not to interrupt Collin. Madeleine threads her fingers into mine but doesn't let go of Betty either.

"They married a few days later. When they returned to Chicago, their home was destroyed. Luckily, our father had the evidence stored in a bank safe-deposit box. After retrieving the evidence, they drove to the FBI office in Ohio. Within a few days, they were in witness protection until the trial. Once it ended, our parents were assured they would be able to come back for you. However, new threats were levied from jail by the fallen CEO and president of the firm. The marshal service determined they couldn't leave witness protection."

I ask the only question that will quell my building anger. "Were you born in witness protection? Do we have other siblings?"

"Yes. No."

His response pushes some of my anger away. I was almost an adult when he was born. "Was the car accident an accident?"

Collin hangs his head. "I don't know."

Betty pushes to her feet. "Do you have anywhere to be, young man?" Her question directed at Collin.

"Not until Monday morning."

"Please join us for an early dinner."

Collin nods.

"You too." She points to Finn, Madeleine, and me.

"Did you really think we were going to leave before dinner?" Finn grins at Betty.

Betty shakes her head. "Christoph and Madeleine, please go get some vegetables to serve with my famous meatloaf."

"Yes, ma'am." I draw Madeleine to her feet. We leave the dining room and walk to the greenhouse in silence.

Once we step inside, she stops in front of me and slides her hands up my chest and cups my face. "He could be your twin if it weren't for all these muscles."

I can't stop the smile overtaking my face. "I looked exactly like him at his age. Even though I called Jake to verify, I knew the second he stepped out of the car. More so when he shared his middle name is the same as mine—Murphy."

"Isn't Fort Meade nearby?"

I nod as I walk down the rows of vegetables. I gather enough green beans for the five of us.

"Christoph, come here," Madeleine calls from a few rows over.

Fear slices through me despite the lack of urgency in her voice. As I approach, she grabs my hands and sets them on her abdomen beneath her shirt. I'm about to ask what is going on when I feel her belly roll beneath my hands.

"Incredible."

She kisses the fallen tear on my cheek. "Stay still," she whispers.

Our child continues to push against my hands, and then I feel a harder kick under my fingertips.

"Does the baby moving hurt?"

"Not yet, but my reading indicates it may later on."

I'm mesmerized, and we stand there longer than necessary to pick vegetables. So long Grams comes to look for us. The feeling of our child moving has my guard lowered; I didn't hear her approach.

"First time?" she asks me.

"Yeah. It's indescribable."

She smiles. "Take your time." Grams takes the basket of green beans and leaves the greenhouse.

Later we rejoin Grams and the others in the kitchen for dinner.

"What unit are you with, Collin?" I ask about midway through our meal.

"I'm with the 308th MI Battalion."

He's active duty in military intelligence. Kid's smart. It tells me a few things as well. Blaine is better than I thought at protecting Blackthorne. If

Collin is in military intelligence, he likely has some serious computer and analytical skills. Our identities and locations are secure.

"Nice. You're stationed at Meade?"

"I am now. I have three years left on my contract."

His duty station gives me hope we can forge a relationship going forward. "I would like to get to know you better. Will you have any leave around Christmas?"

"I would like to get to know you as well. I'm on duty on the holiday this year, but we can set up a time to get together when it works for both of us."

We talk about numerous topics over dinner and exchange numbers to stay connected. I escort him out.

"I was nervous to come here. I've known about you my entire life. Knowing I had a brother who didn't know I existed was difficult. Once they passed, the marshals released me because everything was before I was born. Thank you for hearing me out." Collin extends his hand to me.

I take it and bro hug him. "Thank you for coming all this way. I wrestled with learning about my mother's life. Her motivations for leaving were not what we initially thought. I'm grateful I was wrong. Let's talk soon."

He starts the sedan and pulls down the driveway. Madeleine and Finn are standing on the porch.

"I hear I'm free to go," Finn states.

"Yeah, you are. Thank you for taking care of Betty."

"Anything for family." We hug and Finn retreats into the house.

I draw Madeleine into my arms. "Ready to go home?"

"Yes. How are you?"

After I press a kiss to her forehead, I reply, "Better than I thought I would be."

We take some of Betty's pie and head home. Once inside, I set the pie on the counter and follow Madeleine to bed.

CHAPTER THIRTY-TWO

MADELEINE

"Did you sleep at all?"

He tightens his arms around me. "Enough." He inhales sharply and exhales slowly. "While I haven't read the file yet, the small amount of information from Collin leads me to believe my mother was doing what she thought best for me. It's difficult to reconcile those facts with the notions I've been carrying my entire life to this point."

"Your feelings are completely understandable. There's no way you could've known. Even if you had Blaine search for your mother when you started at Blackthorne, would he have been able to find her in witness protection?"

"Not necessarily. Blaine probably could have surmised based on the timing of my mother leaving me here, the fraud at the firm, the whistleblower, and them dropping off the face of the earth."

"Even so, you wouldn't have been able to form a relationship with them," I state. Once the words leave my lips, I want to pull them back.

He pushes out a harsh breath. "You're right. The thought hadn't crossed my mind."

I turn in his arms and press soft kisses to his face and lips. "Are you still up for picking a tree with me?"

"Definitely. We can grab some breakfast on the way. They open at ten."

Armed with coffee and donuts, we take a short drive to Wilson's Tree Farm. It isn't markedly cold today, which I'm thankful for.

We're greeted by a cheerful young woman wearing a Santa hat. "Welcome to Wilson's. What type of tree are you looking for?"

"One without prickly branches," I reply.

She nods. Apparently, my request isn't odd. "You will want to select from aisles four through twelve. There are saws on the wooden chest beside the row of buggies to cart your tree back over there." She indicates the large red barn.

"Thank you."

We walk down each aisle three times before Christoph narrows our choices down to three. "What about this one?" It's tall, narrow, and has a good overall shape.

"Where are we putting this tree?" I ask.

"In the living room."

"Too tall."

He nods. "Onto the next."

The second two are near one another. Christoph glides between the two like one of the prize presenters on *The Price is Right*, waving his arms and jumping up and down.

I can't contain my laughter. "The one on the right is perfect!"

"Great. Take off your glove and grasp the trunk while I cut it down."

"Why would I do that?"

He grins at me. "So it doesn't fall on me after I cut through."

I giggle. "Okay. We definitely don't want you to be crushed by our first Christmas tree."

"No, we don't." He lies on his belly and saws through the trunk with relative ease.

After he heaves the tree onto the buggy, we hurry home and get to work. Within an hour filled with laughs and suggestions of traditions we want to start, like Christmas pajamas for everyone and watching *It's a Wonderful Life*, the tree is beautifully decorated.

"Can you promise me one thing?"

I gaze up at him. His face looks serious.

"What?"

"Can we limit our gifts to one for each other and the rest to things the baby needs?"

"Yes. We should pick out some furniture for the nursery soon."

"Agreed."

"Will you reach out to Leslie on Monday?"

His face scrunches up in confusion. "Lacey? Sure."

"What do you recall about the house, if anything?"

Christoph shakes his head. "Nothing at all. I would bet it needs work. Mr. Stillman hasn't lived on the property for about five years at this point."

"We can stay here while we make it a home."

We spend the afternoon relaxing and making plans for the holidays with Betty and Jake. While Christoph works out details with Betty. I text with Norah.

Me: What time are you getting together?

Norah: We meet near the end of the day.

Me: We're having dinner with Betty on Christmas Eve. We'll be there.

Me: Where can I shop?

Norah: We can go into DC or Baltimore. Is there a specific item you're looking for?

Me: Yes. I need a high-end jewelry store.

Norah: Both locations will work. Can we go Wednesday around lunch?

Me: Works for me. Will we need bodyguards? LOL

Norah: No, but if the guys make a fuss, I'll invite Maia or Alex.

Me: Sounds good. We can't shop for them if they're with us.

Norah: Exactly.

"What are you scheming over there with Norah?" Christoph asks.

I shake my head. "How do you know its Norah?"

He turns his phone in my direction. "Jake is asking if I want someone to shop with you on Wednesday afternoon."

"We'll be fine. There's no threat anymore, right?"

He draws me into his arms. "No, there's no threat to you. Would you be offended if I preferred Maia or Alex go with you?"

I shake my head. "No, but they're sworn to secrecy about what we buy and for whom."

He types a message to Jake. "Jake said 'Deal.'"

I laugh.

We spend the rest of the day unpacking and getting settled in our home for the foreseeable future.

The next morning after a quick breakfast, I work in the office fielding calls from the department heads and changing my information at most of my banking institutions. I also instructed Becky set up an automatic transfer of the funds for the company commission for our child.

My realtor forwarded a proposed contract for a full-price cash offer with occupancy as soon as possible. Ideally, we can close before the end of the year as well.

Before I know it, Christoph and I are driving into town for our meeting with Jake. Given the information Collin provided, Betty decided to delve into the file herself. She feels nothing could be worse than her guilt for outliving her altruistic daughter.

"Hey, guys!" Gemma greets us and hands Madeleine a small gift bag.

"It's for the baby."

I smile at her. "Thank you. You didn't have to."

"I got one for everyone. Amara, Connor's twins, and Jake's child too." Gemma beams.

Christoph shrugs. I dig into the package and pull out a onesie. The front has the words *Protected by Daddy* and the back has the Blackthorne Security logo.

"Gemma, this is perfect!" I hug her.

Jake and Connor break up the party and wave us into the conference room. "Hey. How are you doing after meeting your brother?" Jake asks.

"Surprisingly well. There was no way I could deny the resemblance and our middle name. I don't have to list everything about him, you already know."

"True. You likely don't need me to give you a rundown of what the file says. He shared the main points. There's nothing else of concern."

"Thank you for handling this for us."

"You would do it for us, if we asked," Connor adds.

Christoph nods and takes my hand in his.

Jake opens the file in front of him. "Madeleine, the information Estelle shared with you included some of the low points. There is more. At any time, we can stop."

Madeleine's chin drops slightly, and Jake continues, "Mary Jane Wilton is in fact your biological mother. No father is listed on your birth certificate. Marcea and Samuel never officially adopted you. Marcea, Samuel, and your grandfather left you with Estelle when you were six.

As you already know, the plan was to send for you when they struck it rich in real estate. They went out west near Las Vegas. They failed to get rich. Over the years, they contacted Estelle and asked her to allow visits. Estelle refused. From what Blaine could gather, there were at least two attempts each year."

Jake looks pointedly at Christoph, and his hold on me tightens. "Fifteen years ago, Marcea mixed alcohol and her depression medication and drove head-on into a tree."

I exhale sharply. *I need to know.* Our little person is busy right now reminding me this is my history. It won't affect our future if I don't allow it to. I move our hands to my belly.

Christoph sets his fingers under my chin and forces my eyes to meet his. Comfortable I'm handling this information well enough, he urges Jake to continue.

"Soon thereafter, Samuel and your grandfather travelled to visit you. Estelle refused to allow them to see you. At this point, Mary Jane comes back into the picture. She reaches out to Estelle requesting to take you back. You would have been about fifteen. Estelle refused, insisting you were doing well in school and she shouldn't disturb your life."

Connor sets a water beside me. "Thanks." I take a sip. "Please keep going. So far, you've only solidified I made the right choice about Estelle. Mary Jane is still up in the air."

"You're a strong woman, Madeleine," Jake states.

"Thank you."

Jake continues, "Mary Jane married Byron Wilton, who is Samuel's younger brother, about twenty years ago. They started sending support payments to Estelle around the same time."

My blood was simmering; now it's boiling. More lies Estelle told me during my lifetime. Why did we live in destitution then? Why wasn't there enough food or money for me to get a new dress for school dances?

"Breathe, sweetheart."

I heed Christoph's request and take a few deep breaths. I didn't even know I was holding it in. "I'm fine. Let me make sure I understand one thing before you continue, Marcea is my aunt and married Samuel. Mary Jane is my biological mother and married Byron, Samuel's brother."

"You're correct," Jake replies.

"Please finish so I know the extent of Estelle's lies," I urge Jake.

Jake eyes Christoph.

"I appreciate your finely-honed-over-the-years, silent guy speak, but I need to know all the facts so we can move forward.

Christoph drops his head. "Please continue, Jake."

"Every month since then, Mary Jane has reached out to Estelle by letter. Each one is in the box in the order Estelle received them. Only very recently did Estelle give her your contact information at Scala and your address in New York. I only read a few here and there, some from the beginning and the last two."

"Why now?" I mumble, slightly afraid to hear the answer.

"Estelle is ill."

On her death bed, my grandmother decides to share the truth in the worst conceivable way. *Lovely.* My head is spinning with anger, some joy, and more anger. I note three sets of eyes staring at me.

I turn my gaze to Christoph. "Stop worrying, guys. I can handle this like everything else life has thrown at me." The fact all three men have children on the way likely increases their concern. "Is there more?"

"Yes," Jake replies softly.

"Such as?"

"Estelle's prognosis and Mary Jane's contact information."

I shake my head. "I don't want to hear anything more about Estelle right now. She lied to me my entire life. She led me to believe my parents didn't want me." A deep breath in and then out. "Mary Jane provided her contact information when she sent flowers to my apartment in New York and in her letter."

"I understand."

"Thank you for agreeing to do this for us, but especially for me. You don't owe me anything."

Jake looks from Connor to Christoph and then back to me. I notice a slight nod of Christoph's head. "You're wrong. You're found family. Bonds of family don't require blood. Ours were forged in dusty barracks. When Christoph chose you, you became family."

"I appreciate it. Your huge family is amazing."

"They all said similar things about you, including you're too good for him." Jake smirks before laughing heartily.

Christoph lifts my hand to his lips. "They're absolutely right."

I shake my head.

"When are both of you available tomorrow to discuss my team member suggestions for interviews?"

"Nine work for you, C?" Jake asks.

Connor checks his phone. "Yup, video though. Callie has a session at the house at ten."

"Nine it is. I'll have the names for your review and for Gemma to schedule."

"Sounds good. If you have more questions, let me know, Madeleine."

Christoph squeezes my hand. "Madeleine?"

"Yeah, sorry. What?"

"Let us know if you have more questions," Jake repeats.

"I will."

We leave the office and ride silently home. I don't say much else until we sit at the table to eat.

His hand covers mine, drawing my attention away from my food. "Are you ready to talk about it?"

"I'm stuck again. Now I know my mother wasn't equipped to care for me given her young age. I also know she tried to come back into my life when she was able, and Estelle refused her. Truthfully, I'm not angry with Mary Jane. From Jake's synopsis, she did everything she could to reunite with me."

"I agree. Are you going to contact her?"

I shrug. "I'm seriously considering it. I wouldn't want our child to miss out on having a second grandparent." The moment I say the words, I regret it. "I'm sorry."

Immediately, he shifts his chair beside mine and takes my face in his hands. "Nothing for you to be sorry for. True, the news my parents died was difficult to hear. In every sense of the word, Betty is my mother. Our baby will have an amazing great-grandmother in Betty, and a set of grandparents in Mary Jane and Byron if you're so inclined to reach out and start a relationship with them, and an uncle in Collin."

"Okay. I'm sure that the Blackthorne and the Michelson families will dote on them in equal measure given their welcome to me too."

"Oh, they absolutely will. And Estelle?"

I exhale sharply. "I was already angry with her. The fact she kept my family away despite their attempts to reconnect only increased it. I need to let the information simmer some more before I consider my options. However, I'm fairly certain I'm done with Estelle."

"I understand. Can we move on to actually eating and lighter topics?"

"Sure, like what?"

"Christmas is in a few days. What are our plans? We need to shop for baby furniture and talk about names. Did your doctor give you a referral for someone down here?"

"I'm shopping on Wednesday for your gift. I thought we talked about spending Christmas Eve with Betty and then at Jake's Christmas Day in the evening."

"Okay. You're right, we did."

"As far as the doctor, Norah gave me the information for her doctor, and it was the same name I received from mine."

"Good. Then I don't have to run a check on him."

"Her."

"Even better."

I laugh and take the last bite of dinner. Exhausted both mentally and physically, I make my way to bed soon after the kitchen is clean.

CHAPTER THIRTY-THREE

CHRISTOPH

While I'm on assignment, I could be working from a hotel lobby, a fancy suite, or a nondescript conference room at any given hotel. Here at home with Madeleine is a completely distinct experience. First, we get to sleep in a bit more. The lack of a commute is amazing, especially for her. We're both in the office. I've taken the couch and the ottoman, and my paperwork is sorted around me. Madeleine is set up at the desk and already talking to Lucia. I ignore their conversation and focus on her.

She hasn't said anything, but I know her suits aren't fitting well anymore. My woman dresses comfortably working from home. Today she chose black leggings with mesh panels wrapping around her legs and one of my V-neck tees. Madeleine wearing anything of mine is a sight, but her pregnant with my child is beyond description. Being a dad is one of the goals of my life I never shared with anyone except Madeleine. My excitement grows each day we get closer to being parents. I know it's months away, but I can't wait.

"Stop staring and get back to work," she urges when Lucia signs offs.

"I'm doing both. Staring and working. I can't help it; you're glowing."

Her posture softens at the compliment. "Thank you."

I cross the space between us and kiss her softly. "I'm going to call Lacey while you have your call with Regina."

"Okay."

I leave the door ajar and walk toward the bedroom. Conference calls are not Regina's forte.

"Hello," Lacey answers.

"Hi, Lacey, this is Christoph Anderson."

She pauses a moment too long for my liking. "Betty's grandson. Nice to hear from you."

"Please accept my condolences on the loss of your father."

"Thank you."

"Betty indicated you plan to sell your father's farm. My...." *"Everything" isn't something I plan to share with Lacey.* "We would be interested in looking before you list it. We relocated recently but need a permanent home soon."

I hear some commotion in the background. "Sorry about the noise. My kids always need something when I take a call. I'll be frank, the house needs a roof and is completely outdated. If I recall, Betty taught you to cook as well as she can; the kitchen will need a serious upgrade."

"Understood. We're still interested."

"Great! I plan to list it at the beginning of the year. Feel free to take a look the next time you're in the area and let me know before then. Do you remember where the key is?"

It's under the flowerpot on the stump. "Yes, as long as it hasn't moved."

"It's still there. Let me know what you think, Christoph."

"I will. Thanks, Lacey."

I end the call and wander through the kitchen. With two waters, I return to the office.

"No, that isn't what I requested. I don't care about setbacks regardless of whose fault they are. Locate the contract requirements in a timely manner." She pauses for their response. "I expect you to fix this today." After a few moments, she ends the call. "Thank you." She takes the water.

I lean forward and kiss her hard. "I love it when you're feisty and take charge."

A fierce blush creeps onto her cheeks.

"Since when does that make you blush?"

"Not sure. Did you talk to Simon yet today?"

"Not yet. I planned to catch up with him after my meeting with Jake and Connor. I can go into the kitchen if you need me to."

She shakes her head and pulls out a set of wireless earbuds. "I'm good. I have to review a few contracts for the facilities and audit the annual review protocol because the process starts in three weeks."

I steal another kiss and plop down on the couch as Connor joins the virtual meeting.

"Hey."

"Hey. How's Amara? How is Callie feeling?"

"Amara is amazing. She's making progress on her sleeping, which makes me very happy. Callie is doing great. She says she feels like a beached whale, but I don't see it. She looks gorgeous to me."

Same for me and Madeleine. I grin and sneak a look at Madeleine. She's focused on the stack of papers in front of her with her pen poised to obliterate clauses and subsections. It's hot as hell. Her gaze lifts to mine. When I smile, she shakes her head and turns back to the contract in her lap.

"Hey, guys," Jake says, joining the meeting.

"Hey. How's Norah feeling?" I ask.

"So far so good," Jake replies. "You guys?" We repeat our conversation and get down to business.

"I want to interview Lane Hawkins, Barrett Beaumont, Patton Daley and Javier Cruz. The last one is going to take a bit more convincing," I inform them.

"Our Javier Cruz?" Jake questions me.

I shake my head. "Yes. We met up in New York after the shower for the twins. He was passed over for captain and indicated he might be looking to move on. I informed him about my team. He's seriously considering it."

"Nice, it would be great to have him here," Connor states.

"It sucks he didn't get the promotion, but I would love to bring him on board here," Jake adds.

"I don't have any objections to any of the others, do you?" Jake asks Connor.

"Nope, all good."

"Perfect, Christoph. Email the names to Gemma, and she can set up interviews for early next week," Jake instructs me.

"No problem. What is the status of the security for the building in DC?"

Connor answers, "The security locks and entrance and exit cameras are set for installation and initial testing early next week."

"Perfect. Madeleine plans to exercise a little-used portion of the employment contract for all employees at Scala which allows updated background checks each year. Will Blaine be able to handle a significant number of background checks, or should we find another avenue?"

"I'm sure she doesn't plan on submitting them all at once, correct?" Jake asks.

"No, she plans to do it as their contracts renew, except for Angie at the DC office. Madeleine wants hers done now given her position profile has increased with Madeleine's presence when the building is secure."

"Understood. Have Simon or Lucia send over her contract face sheet. It contains plenty of information for Blaine to start with. Also, I need Madeleine's revisions, if any, to the security contract for the building before year end."

"Got it. I'll talk to Simon and Madeleine when we're done."

"I'm done," Connor chimes in again.

"Same. I'll see you for the holiday." Jake signs off.

I send an email to Gemma and Simon before planning a quick exit. I need to pick up her gift and the stockings I ordered and some chocolates in town. When I close my laptop, Madeleine looks up from the papers.

"Jake asked for the revisions, if any, for the security contract."

"None needed. I'll send the executed one to him today."

"Do you need anything in town?"

She shakes her head but replies anyway. "No, don't think so."

I move beside her and kiss her thoroughly. "I'll be back in an hour or so. I need to pick up a few things for dinner, our stocking order, and your gift."

"Okay. Tonight, we can browse for some nursery furniture. Love you."

"Be back soon. I love you." I kiss her again.

A short while later, I park near the Blackthorne office and make quick work at the grocery store. After putting my items into the trunk, I recross the street and step into the candy shop. The aroma of the chocolate puts my senses on high alert.

I'm browsing the case when I come upon a friendly face. "Hi, Jill."

She comes closer and hugs me. "Hey. How are you?"

"I'm well. You?"

"Same. Congrats by the way." Her tone always gives her away. She's surprised.

"Thanks. Why the surprise, Jill?"

She looks up at me. Jill is short and curvy, but not overly so, with long blonde hair and bright blue eyes. Her profession as a teacher affords her the patience of a saint. "I didn't know you were dating anyone."

I'm not sure where she's going with this. "We've been seeing each other for over a year at this point. You and I were never a couple, Jill."

"True, but at one point I thought we could have been."

I scrub my hand down my face. At one time, so did I. Until I saw her with Cruz at Connor's wedding. The undertones of desire they were throwing at each other were unmistakable. "Maybe, but I always got the impression you were holding out for someone else."

Jill's face falls.

Nailed that one.

"You're not completely off base. The someone else and I have never been in the same place long enough to try to make it work. We likely never will."

"I understand how you feel completely. If you want to make it work with the mystery guy, tell him. Figure it out. You deserve to be happy."

"Are you? I don't recall fatherhood being high on your list of things to do."

"You don't really know me, Jill. If you think about it, you know I'm willing to drop everything to fix your sink, your tire, and your garage door. I served with your brother and Connor, but otherwise we only talked about surface things. We never went on a date or hung out alone outside of me fixing something at your house. Being a dad was always at the top of my priority list."

Her gaze drills through me. "I suppose you're right."

"You deserve the same happiness your brother, Connor, and I've found. If you need to put your feelings out there, do it. Once you do, you'll know for sure if he's invested too."

"Thanks, Christoph. I'll think about it."

"You're welcome. I'll see you in a few days."

She hugs me again and walks away. I don't know if she'll follow through. However, I made my feelings for Madeleine truly clear despite her opinion otherwise.

I check out with Madeleine's favorites. Then I stop by the office and pick up Madeleine's gift from the safe. When I arrive home, I find Madeleine in the middle of our bed with the contents of the box from Estelle strewn around her. Her face is blotchy, her cheeks puffy, and a small pile of tissues litters the bed beside her.

I toe off my shoes and maneuver myself behind her and haul her against my chest. "Why didn't you wait for me to be here, *anamchara?*"

"I thought I could handle it," she forces out before fresh tears fall and sobs wrack her body again.

I will never hurt Madeleine. Her pain and tears bring out a new side of me. This side of me never existed before her. I want to have a pointed discussion with Estelle and forbid her from ever contacting my Madeleine. *My everything.* Ever. Again. Frankly, if Estelle were a man who hurt her, I would think of more persuasive ways to get my point across. I'm not opposed to learning where to hide evidence if it protects what's mine.

"Do you want to share?"

Her head moves side to side against my chest and the sobs continue. A few minutes later, she taps the top of my intertwined hands. I release her, and she turns, burrowing into me as deeply as she can. Her head against my chest soaks my shirt with even more tears as my hands clasp around her back.

Slowly, the heaves lessen and her fingernails unembed themselves from my shoulder blades. Her ocean-colored eyes lift to mine. "I need you to promise me something."

"Anything." There's nothing she could ask for I wouldn't find a way to give to her, our child, or our future children.

"No matter what happens with us, our child deserves a stable home."

Instantly, there's a knot in my stomach and it twists tighter and tighter. Whatever she saw or read in the box rocked her to the core.

"You are everything I never knew would make me whole. We would be here, together, a couple making promises of a future even if we weren't going to have a baby."

She adds a sliver of space between us. Her eyes are filled with unshed tears. Although, these are different, these are for us. "How do you know?"

"Each moment I spend with you makes me a better man. You smooth out my rough edges. I didn't know it was happening until Emme... I didn't plan on having a family before pledging forever to you, but he or she wasn't willing to wait for my timeline." I set my hands on her belly and hers cup my jaw. "I love you more each day. I'm never going anywhere without you beside me."

"The privilege is mine. I love you." She shifts onto her knees and sets her lips on mine, and it's better than we've ever shared. It's as if all her concerns and fears are washed away with one toe-curling, passionate kiss.

She's wrong, but I will never correct her. If anyone is privileged, it's me. I lead her to the couch near the fireplace, expeditiously stripping her clothes as we cross the room.

She stacks two throw pillows and sets her hands on the arm of the couch. "Fill me now... please."

The last stitch of my clothes falls to the gleaming hardwood. My hands caress the curve of her hips, and I sink into her to the root. Making love to Madeleine will never be boring. Her core clenches around me. I draw back and plunge into her until she quakes around me. It isn't until her third climax that I allow her inner muscles to milk me dry.

After we clean up, she tugs on one of my shirts and moves to clear our bed.

"I'll do it."

Surprisingly, she walks away from the reminders of Estelle's betrayal each day of her life. I don't know what I would do in her position. Not true, I would never speak to Estelle again. Betrayal of such a magnitude can never be ignored. There is absolutely no appropriate justification. Whether she decides to let Estelle back into her life or not is completely her choice.

Once I finish clearing the bed, we curl up and narrow down nursery furniture options.

"Do you want to learn the gender from the doctor or when the baby is born?" I ask as we scroll through the options.

"I kind of want to know."

"Own it, gorgeous."

"I want to find out if we need pink or blue clothes."

I lean over and kiss her breathless. "Okay. Perhaps we should narrow this down to a set for a boy and one for a girl. Once we know the answer, we can order the appropriate one."

We cull the list a bit more and narrow it down to three. One set is white, one oak, and one cherry. I set the laptop aside and tuck Madeleine against me for the night.

CHAPTER THIRTY-FOUR

MADELEINE

My plan is to wrap work up this morning. So far, it's holding. "Hi, Si. What's the latest update?"

"You look extra glowy this morning."

"Thanks, Si. Update please."

Even through the screen his smile is contagious. "I'm finishing the small items to pack for my drive to DC. I'll be moving into my new digs this weekend. Lucia is already there. The IT people are done with the servers, and the office computers are on site as of last night. By Tuesday, they should be able to finish after the furnishings are delivered and assembled. The security upgrades will be in place by the end of next week."

"Perfect. Please have a wonderful holiday and safe travels here, Si."

Christoph leans against the doorframe. Post-workout him is almost as delicious as fresh-out-of-bed him.

"You too. See you soon, boss lady."

"Bye, Si."

Christoph rounds the desk and kisses me lightly. "How is your perpetual ray of sunshine?"

"He's good. Excited to be moving this weekend."

"What time are you leaving to go shopping?"

I glance at the clock. I'm still not dressed. I wanted to get my call with Simon done so he could take off for his holiday. "Norah plans to pick me up at eleven. Don't worry, Alex and Maia are coming with us."

I see his relief.

"I know there's no threat, but a little backup is never a bad thing."

"I'm not offended. Maia is awesome. I'm sure Alex is as well." We only chatted briefly at the shower.

He urges me to my feet and wraps his arms around me. "Without sharing too much, Alex didn't have it easy before she came here."

"Understood. I need to get ready. What are your plans?"

He shrugs, and there's a twinkle in his eye. "Nothing big. Why?"

"Curious."

"I meant to ask. How early do we need to leave for Betty's?"

"I thought we were going late morning so we could look at the Stillman farm."

He nods. "You're right. I forgot."

"We're only looking. We don't necessarily have to buy this property. However, there are a lot of pros to it."

"I know. You better hurry. Norah is never late."

I steal a quick kiss and hustle through the shower. As I'm getting dressed for shopping, I overhear Christoph ushering Norah inside.

"Hey, Norah. I'll get Madeleine for you."

I tug on my tennis shoe and grab my sweater.

Christoph is in the bedroom before I get into the hall. He seizes my gaze and lays a deep, possessive, ardent kiss on my lips. *Damn! He's nervous about this even with Alex and Maia joining us.*

As I catch my breath, I compose my thoughts. "We're going to be fine."

He scrubs his hand down his face. "I know in my head, but now having you out of arm's reach messes with the pesky organ in my chest."

This man. "We know what we're up against, and physically there's no harm, right?"

He drops his head. "Yes. I love you both."

"I love you."

He escorts me to the door and watches until we pull away.

"Is he okay?" Norah asks.

I shake my head. "No, he's freaking out."

Alex and Maia chuckle in the back seat.

"Don't worry, Jacob pulled the same thing on me last month. Have you been apart at all since you told him about the baby?" Norah asks.

I think about it and realize we've been attached at the hip since my appointment. "Nope, we haven't."

"He may blow up your phone all afternoon, but he'll handle it. I can't imagine both after the babies arrive," Norah states.

Me either. "Sorry, ladies. It was rude of me not to say hi first."

"No worries. Christoph is sending me instructions, and Jake is sending them to Maia," Alex informs me.

We laugh and chat about everything other than our overprotective significant others for the remainder of the ride. Once we arrive at the shopping area, Norah shifts into a super shopper. She clearly has a plan, and we're along for the ride. While she shops for gifts for her nieces and nephews, I browse the store for baby clothes. I won't have the ability to travel much given my new responsibilities and the baby. Tunics, long sweaters, and leggings will be a staple for me soon. Most of my dresses are too snug around my baby bump.

Alex and Maia have grabbed a few items but nowhere near as much as Norah.

"Are you guys staying here for the holiday?" I ask them.

Norah silently rejoins our group.

Alex answers first. "I'm going to visit my little brother in Texas. I leave very early in the morning."

Maia shakes her head. "Nolan invited me to celebrate with his family, but I declined. Now I feel like an idiot."

"It's only us girls here. Nothing said during girl time is shared with the guys. It's a given. Why did you decline?" I ask.

Norah nods in agreement.

"I'm terrified we'll mess up our friendship if I spend time with him and his family," Maia admits.

"If he's your best friend, you won't ruin anything by meeting his family. It'll show you how he became who he is and what a future together could look like," Norah offers.

I can see Maia thinking. "I'll reconsider," she states as we move onto the next store.

"What's left?" Alex inquires after opening the door to the jeweler.

"I need to pick up Christoph's gift here, and then I'm done." I meander to the counter and give my name. The perky clerk returns with my purchase and rings me out.

"All set?" Alex asks. She's softer when she isn't working. I don't mean she isn't tough or isn't capable. She absolutely is. Her guard is a little lower than when I've seen her before. Alex has shiny, long, dark hair and big, brown eyes. If I met her some other way, I would think she's a normal chick. Knowing she works for Blackthorne means something terrible likely happened to her in the past. Christoph indicated as much before I left this morning.

"Yeah, all set. How many texts have you gotten?" I ask.

She smirks at me. "He has been texting every hour."

"I'm sorry, Alex."

She sets a hand on my forearm. "Don't be. I think almost every person wants someone to love them as passionately as he loves you and your baby."

I don't miss the wistful look in her eyes. If I had to guess, she has been deeply scarred by a previous relationship. Yet she's still willing to try again. "Thank you."

As we walk to the car, Norah satisfies a baby craving with a salted pretzel from one of the food court vendors. We laugh the entire ride home about silly Christmas traditions and when things go horribly wrong.

The moment Norah pulls into the driveway, Christoph is moving to my door.

"Have fun with your brother, Alex." I state.

She replies, "Thank you."

"Good luck, Maia."

She nods.

"Norah, we'll see you at your house in a few days."

He offers me his hand and helps me to my feet. He kisses me and talks to our baby before speaking to the girls.

"Hello to you too!" Norah bellows from the driver seat.

"Sorry. I forgot to say goodbye to the baby earlier because I was worried about Madeleine."

A chorus of awwws surround us. I bury my head into his chest.

"Have a nice holiday, Alex and Maia. See you in a few days, Norah." Christoph closes the passenger door and escorts me inside and straight to the bedroom. "Did you eat? How are you feeling?" He's literally running his hands over my body. I'm sure he intends to make sure I'm fine, but it's turning me on significantly too. "What can I—"

I interrupt him with a hard kiss. Once he stops talking, I dip my hands beneath the hem of his shirt. His abs jump when my fingers glide over them. He captures my hands beneath his shirt.

"We're fine. I promise. I need you to make a choice. Either stop touching me like you're searching for a lost treasure or strip."

He raises an eyebrow, releases my hands, and lifts his shirt over his head. Within a minute, we're both naked, and he's exploring my skin inch by glorious inch. When I can no longer survive the sensual strokes of his tongue, I push him to sitting, straddle his hips, and take him in one stroke. After a few furious thrusts, we careen over the edge of carnal bliss.

I snuggle against his hot, muscled body as best I can and set my head on his forearm.

"Truly, how are you?"

I lean back so I can see his face. He's seriously asking.

"I appreciate your concern more than you could possibly know, but we're fine. I'll share with you the instant I'm not."

"Thank you." He tightens his hold on me and threads his fingers through my hair. The last thing I recall is Christoph tugging the blanket up over both of us.

The smell of bacon pulls me from our cozy bed. I tug his shirt over my head, twist my hair up, and drink the small glass of juice on the night table. I probably don't need it anymore, but I don't have the heart to ask Christoph to stop.

"Morning," I murmur when I step into the kitchen.

"Hi, gorgeous. Did you sleep well?"

I take a seat at the island as I answer. "Not really. I was thinking a lot about my mother."

"Want to share?" He sets a spinach and pepper omelet with bacon in front of me and takes a seat beside me.

"I want to reach out to her. Are we free next weekend? Maybe we can meet her halfway."

He leans over and kisses me tenderly. "If we weren't, I would clear our schedule. As long as your boss is okay with you working remotely." He winks at me. "What pushed you to your decision?"

"Mostly the content of her letters. My tears were mostly anger at Estelle not Mary Jane. She made the only choice she thought was available to her at the time. Jake's summary of one letter each month from Mary Jane was an understatement. There is at *least* two a month. Mary Jane sent a card or letter for every special occasion in my life and Estelle withheld them from me. Mary Jane did everything right, and Estelle thwarted her efforts."

"I'm sorry Estelle prevented you from a meaningful relationship with Mary Jane sooner, sweetheart."

My back bows out. "I am too. Now, though, I can attempt to foster a relationship with my mother as an adult so our first little person can have one with her from the beginning." I'm sure he didn't miss when I said first.

After dressing and starting my only cup of coffee for today, I fish the card from Mary Jane out of my purse. Christoph joins me in the kitchen and continues with the coffees.

One deep breath later and I input her phone number.

I'm taken aback when she answers on the first ring. "Hello."

"Hi." I take a few deep breaths. A myriad of things spin through my mind. Are there rules for this? What do you say to your biological mother when your grandmother kept you apart for almost your entire life? I grip the island with my free hand.

Christoph sets his atop mine and links our hands.

"Take your time, Madeleine." Her voice sounds as shaky as mine feels.

I exhale slowly. "I'm sorry. This is harder than I anticipated. First, please know I never received any of your letters, cards, or gifts over the years. I wasn't aware you were reaching out to meet me. Estelle never told me, not once." I settle myself and push down my anger toward Estelle. Simply saying her name makes my blood rush faster through my veins. "Estelle only shared about you a few weeks ago after your visit to the DC office. I needed some time to separate my anger and what I truly want. I would like to get to know you better. Can we meet you halfway between here and South Carolina at some point soon?"

A soft sob echoes in my ear. "You don't know what this means to me."

"I do. It means the same to me."

"Byron and I will make time to meet you. Do you have a few moments to talk now?"

"Yes." My response is hesitant.

"You said 'we.'"

Oh. "My... Christoph. He's my other half."

He releases my hands and slides his arms around me as he draws me closer.

"How wonderful. Estelle never told you anything until recently." It's a statement but a question too.

"No, she didn't. If it's all the same, I would prefer to talk about Estelle as little as possible. I'm angry, and it isn't likely to subside any time soon." It isn't good for the baby either.

"Of course. I understand. Frankly, I have been angry with my mother for the last twenty years. She placed roadblock after roadblock in our path to reconnecting with you. I will admit, I'm grateful she kept all our letters for you."

"Me too." Silence drifts over the line. "Can we talk again early next week to solidify plans and a location to meet?"

"I'm looking forward to it."

"Me too. Bye… I apologize. I don't know what to call you."

"Nothing to be sorry for. It isn't your fault. Let's start with Mary Jane, and we'll go from there."

"I look forward to hearing from you soon, Mary Jane."

"Until then, Madeleine." I end the call and drop my head forward against Christoph's chest. His hands move up and down my back. Tears well in my eyes, but they don't fall.

We're on the road toward Betty's soon after I compose myself. I'm crazy excited to see the farmhouse next door. Next door is a bit of an overstatement. True, the properties abut one another, but walking next door will take a decent amount of time.

Christoph produces a key from beneath a flowerpot with a snow-covered plant in it. "The only thing Lacey said was it needs updating and likely a new kitchen."

"Does she know about your cooking skills?"

He blushes. "I've only shared my cooking skills with one woman—you. However, everyone from my childhood knows Betty taught me to cook well."

I wander through the large colonial and picture what our life would be like here. We're about forty minutes from the office for Christoph and twenty for me on a traffic-free day. As Lacey suggested, the kitchen needs to be gutted. However, the bones are good. The molding and fireplaces are in impeccable condition. Modernizing this home won't be difficult, but it will take time. I climb the stairs. When I reach the top, I'm confronted with a large window overlooking the property. It's gorgeous and peaceful.

I peer into each of the three bedrooms upstairs. Each is a good size but are considerably smaller than the master.

I feel Christoph before he says anything. "There you are."

"What do you think?" I know he'll ask me the same thing. I would like to hear his opinion first. Even if he hates the idea of modernizing this home, he would do it for me if it's what I want.

"Lacey was right about the kitchen. It needs some upgrades. The downstairs needs some fresh paint and updated light fixtures."

I wrinkle my nose. "Didn't you say you don't know anything about home remodeling? Only exterior work if I recall correctly."

He smiles sheepishly. "I may have done some research after talking to Lacey. What about you?"

"It'll be perfect with a little work."

A huge smile breaks open on his face. "You could be happy here?"

"We'll be happy beside you anywhere. Can you call her now?"

"You realize it's Christmas Eve right?"

I nod furiously. "Yes, but she may answer, and it might mean a lot to her and her siblings to know we're going to take care of her father's home."

Reluctantly, he pulls out his phone and dials Lacey. Unfortunately, it goes to voice mail. I tune out his message. We walk through the house, and he starts a list of things to fix or improve. When we finish, we get back into his truck and drive to the far edge of the property before heading to Betty's.

CHAPTER THIRTY-FIVE

CHRISTOPH

I drive back toward the house as my phone rings. I recognize the number, park, and answer on speaker.

"Hi, Lacey. Thank you for calling back today."

"Of course."

"What is your proposed list price?"

"When Dad listed it two years ago, he listed for one and a half million. There were no takers given the condition of the house. The barn and stables are in excellent shape. Even the fishing cottage is in better condition than the house. Most of the buyers weren't interested in those aspects of the property. Only the house."

"No problem. If you could text me your email address, we'll send you a proposed contract for purchase over the weekend."

"I look forward to reviewing it with my siblings. Have a wonderful holiday, Christoph. Please say hello to Betty for us."

We're going to make the Stillman farm our dream home. "Happy holidays, Lacey. Please share our wishes with your family as well." I end the call and kiss Madeleine.

"I believe we found our home."

A huge smile grows on her face. "Yes, we did."

Our little person clearly feels my excitement. He or she is practicing gymnastics in Madeleine's belly. She takes my hands and places them so I can experience it too.

"Hey, tiny human. Go easy on your mama." I laugh. "Seriously, though, he or she isn't hurting you?"

"No, not at all. Not so far anyway."

We sit in silence until the baby tires out or falls asleep.

"Are we sharing with Betty or waiting?" she asks.

"I think we should wait until our offer is accepted. We won't be able to move in for a while."

"True. We should talk about how to finance this purchase as well."

I look over at her. The vast difference in our salaries doesn't bother me, but in this instance, I need to contribute. "Once we figure out the offer, we can split the down payment."

If she's upset, it isn't showing. "Okay."

My woman understands me better than I thought. "Ready for a delicious dinner and blueberry pie with Betty?"

"Yes!"

I steal a kiss and drive to Betty's. When we arrive, there's a pickup truck parked in the driveway as well as a sedan.

"Do you know who those belong to?"

"Nope, but we're about to find out." I round the car and take her hand in mine.

Betty rushes out the door with an older gentleman right behind her. "Oh, my heart! You're here already. Philip, this is my oldest grandson, Christoph, and his better half, Madeleine. Christoph, Madeleine. Philip Remington."

I extend my hand to him and shake it. He then takes Madeleine's as well. "Pleasure to meet you. I've heard so much about you and, more recently, your younger brother, Collin."

I haven't heard a damn thing about you. "You as well."

"Please go inside; it's chilly for Madeleine. I'll be right in." Betty shoos us through the door.

I heed her wishes, but I'm intrigued by Mr. Remington.

"Hey, bro! Madeleine. Great to see you again so soon," Collin states as we step into the kitchen.

"Didn't know you were off today. We could have come earlier."

"No worries. When am I going to be an uncle?"

Madeleine's eyes widen. "Did we not share with you?"

"Can't say you did," Collin acknowledges.

"I'm sorry. The baby is due in May," Madeleine answers.

"Awesome! Congratulations!"

"Thank you. Did you get the scoop on Mr. Remington?" I ask my brother.

"As far as I can tell, he's courting Betty. She isn't having any of it though. He brought a poinsettia and a box of chocolates," Collin answers.

"Does it seem recent?"

"It's none of your business." Betty steps into the kitchen.

I shake my head. "Of course it is, Grams. We love you. We're simply looking out for you."

She closes her eyes and pushes out a breath. "He's a nice man, Christoph. We met at bridge. We've been having coffee dates after bridge for about six months. It's nothing more than coffee."

"Thanks for sharing, Grams."

She smiles and checks the progress of dinner in the oven. "Dinner should be ready in about an hour."

We chat in the kitchen until Betty serves dinner.

"I'm so happy to have you all here. To my grandsons, my new granddaughter, and great-grandchild, I wish you peace and happiness in the upcoming year. Cheers." Betty raises her glass.

"Cheers."

We enjoy an amazing dinner with Betty and Collin before presenting Betty with her gift from the baby.

"We got this for you."

Tears fill her eyes, but they don't fall. "You didn't need to get me anything."

"We know, Grams."

Betty digs into the bag, tossing tissue paper left and right. It floats to the floor in a yellow, crinkly pile. She pulls out a shirt with the words *Promoted to Great-Grandma* on the front. The unshed tears plummet down her cheeks. "Thank you. It's wonderful."

"You're welcome."

Over blueberry pie and coffee, we make plans for a family dinner at the condo. Truthfully, I'm excited about the future for the first time in a very long time. Collin heads back to post a little before we return home.

"It was nice of Collin to visit Betty." Madeleine says.

"Yeah. He seems like a nice kid."

Madeleine laughs. "He's not a kid, babe."

She isn't wrong. He's an adult with a stable career and seems genuinely nice. I don't fault him for having our parents to himself. Nor am I angry with my mother for leaving me with Betty. I know it was a heart-wrenching choice she had to make.

"No, I suppose he isn't. What do you say to hot cocoa upstairs when we get home?"

"I'm never opposed to time on the patio as long as you promise to keep me warm."

"Have I ever let you down?"

Her devilish smile tells me her mind is deep in naughty territory. "No, never."

Before reaching the upstairs patio with our blankets and cocoa, snow starts to fall. We opt for watching *Home Alone* before falling into our bed.

Snow falls through the night and leaves a solid six inches. I slip out of bed and shovel the steps and clear off my truck. With a steaming cup of coffee, I sit on the edge of the bed and wake Madeleine.

"Merry Christmas, gorgeous."

"Merry Christmas. Why are you wide awake already?"

I grin at her. "I cleared the sidewalk and the truck already."

She sits up and shimmies back against the headboard. "It snowed that much?"

"Enough. Ready for some gifts?"

She raises an eyebrow. "I thought we agreed on one each."

I shrug and wrinkle my nose. "We did. I might have exceeded the limit though."

I take her hand in mine and lead her to the couch. Once she's comfortable, I present her with my first gift. She's dainty when she opens gifts, carefully slipping her finger beneath the tape and wiggling the small box from the packaging.

"It's a charm… What is it exactly?"

I chuckle. It was difficult finding what I wanted. "It's a contract. Finding an appropriate charm for your promotion was more difficult than I anticipated."

"I see it now. What else do you have for me since I followed the rules?"

I shake my head and hand her one more charm box.

"It's gorgeous." She kisses me, rises, and walks away. Only once she's returning do I realize what she retrieved. After getting the bracelet, she adds the contract and the twinkling star beside the others. "Ready for yours?"

"There's one more."

"You aren't very good at following rules, are you?"

"Not when it comes to you." I hand her my final gift for today.

She's silent even after she opens the solitaire studs. "There's no way for you to know."

My stomach is twisting waiting for her response. "Know what?"

Madeleine secures them in her ears. "There are a few small gifts in the box Estelle gave me, small in size at least. One of them is a pair of earrings like these for my sixteenth birthday from Mary Jane."

"I didn't know."

She climbs into my arms, and I hold her against me. "Thank you. These are perfect. I always wanted a pair but never bought them for myself."

"Why?"

A single teardrop slides down her cheek. "I set an amount to send to Estelle each month. When I decided I wanted the earrings, it wasn't in my budget. I never considered the purchase again."

Clearly, she has had the means for at least the last five-plus years even sending Estelle money each month. "How long ago was this?"

"Soon after I started at Scala. You should open your gift." She wipes her cheek dry and grabs the small bag beneath the tree. "It wasn't easy picking a gift for you."

"I'm sure it's perfect." He pushes the tissue paper aside and lifts out the box. He's speechless as he pulls out the Breitling watch that I had monogrammed. "How did you know?"

"You never wear it, but there's one in the box on your dresser."

"It belonged to Gramps. It was the only thing he left for me. Betty held on to it until I was eighteen. It's perfect, a*namchara*. Thank you."

While we eat a hearty breakfast, we discuss our offer for the farm and what changes we want to make.

"After our little nugget is born, can we get horses too?"

"Definitely. Anything else you want to add?" I ask.

"Not for me. I'm sure you would love a greenhouse for fresh vegetables."

"I would actually, but I don't need it right away."

An hour later, we drive to Jake and Norah's holiday party. The driveway is lined with cars. I round the car and offer Madeleine my arm. I still feel the same rush I did the first time we met. With one foot on the porch, the front door flies open. Jill plows right into me. Thankfully, Madeleine was admiring Norah's decorations.

"Merry Christmas to you too, Jill!"

"Christoph. Sorry. Hi, Madeleine."

"What's the rush?"

She looks between me and Madeleine and back to me. "You were right. I'm going to see about my mystery man." Then Jill bounds off the porch. She turns back and addresses Madeleine. "Madeleine, I apologize for my reaction to your relationship. It has nothing to do with you and everything to do with me. Welcome to our huge family. Merry Christmas." Jill doesn't wait for a response. She's in her car and pulling away shortly thereafter.

I let the door close and lead Madeleine to the bench outside the front door.

"What was that about?"

"I ran into her at the candy store earlier this week. I'm sure you recall her reaction to you at the shower. Jill had some choice words to say about our relationship. I gave her some harsh but true words right back. Apparently, over the last few days she's decided I was right."

Madeleine lifts her lips to mine. After pulling back, she asks, "What did you tell her?"

"I told her to share her feelings. It worked out phenomenally for me. Even if it doesn't for her, she'll be able to move forward."

"Sound advice."

"Thanks. Ready to visit everyone inside?"

She steals another quick kiss, and we head into the party. Hours later, after merriment and catching up with everyone, including both sets of the

Blackthornes and the Michelsons, we borrow Amara for some quality time, complete with a diaper-changing lesson from Callie. The lesson was mostly for me, but Madeleine graciously accepted the tips.

We spend the rest of the weekend relaxing after submitting our offer on the Stillman farm.

CHAPTER THIRTY-SIX

MADELEINE

The final preparations for my new office are nearly complete. We may even be able to take a few days off as originally scheduled before the new year begins. Today, Christoph is joining me at the office to go over any last-minute issues and correct them before I plan to work from here next week.

"Good morning, Miss Wilton. Mr. Anderson. Happy holidays."

"Hi, Angie. Same to you. We'll be here most of the day, but I'm not taking any appointments. Please cross-check the workers with the provided list." Her deeper background check came back fine. I truly think she was taken aback by Christoph when we arrived the first time. I completely understand; it still happens to me most mornings when I wake with him beside me.

"Of course. Have a nice day."

We enter the office and start with a tour to see the progress. While I check the aesthetics, Christoph is checking the security upgrades. The furnishings are mostly in place, and the office equipment is linked to the server and ready for us except for two guest offices, which will be complete by midweek.

When we finally make our way back to the corporate offices, we're greeted by Simon and Lucia.

"You're here! Happy holidays, Mads. Christoph," Simon croons.

"Same to you," we reply together.

"Happy holidays, Lucia."

"Thank you," her response is low, and she sounds concerned.

It takes me a moment, but then I realize why she's concerned. "No need to worry about your attire. The office isn't open yet." She's wearing jeans and a slouchy sweater. It's similar to my outfit, but she can't tell because I haven't removed my coat yet.

Lucia visibly relaxes.

"Do you guys have an update?" I inquire.

Simon rattles off an update from top to bottom. As far as he's concerned, the only thing left to be accomplished is the guest offices and stocking the lunchroom.

"Have you seen your office yet?" The sheer glee in his voice makes me giddy.

"No. My office was our next stop."

We round the corner, and I open the door to my office. Simon has seriously outdone himself. The plain, drab, boring office is now a gorgeous, comfortable space with a plush couch and modern décor on the shelves.

"Simon, this is fabulous! Thank you."

He's beaming but immediately deflects. "Lucia deserves the design credit."

"Lucia, it's amazing! Thank you so much."

I hug them both and turn slowly into my office.

Simon adds, "We're going to get out of here for a bit. The notes for your schedule are by the computer. Let me know if you need changes. We will prepare a proposed order to stock the lunchroom and supply closet before you leave today."

"Perfect."

As Simon and Lucia leave, I hang my coat in the small closet and Christoph take a seat on the couch. "Lucia has an eye for design."

"Yeah, she does. It makes me wonder if her old boss was worse than she expressed."

Christoph shakes his head. "I hope for Lucia's sake you're wrong."

"Me too." I slip into my cushy desk chair and wake my computer. I attempt my old password, but it doesn't work.

"Simon, could you come back in here for a moment?" I buzz him at his desk.

"On my way, Mads."

By the time I finish emptying my bag, Simon has returned. "What can I do?"

"My password isn't working in the new system."

Simon grins. "Sorry, my fault. The generic password is taped beneath your keyboard. The IT team suggested we change them immediately."

"Thanks, Si."

Simon leaves, and I change my password and get to work. By the end of the day, Christoph has come and gone more times than I can count, interfacing with the team from Blackthorne to complete the security upgrade.

"Ready to go home, sweetheart?"

"Yes, about two hours ago." We make our way home, eat dinner, and curl into bed until morning. The rest of the week passes similarly except for Christoph escorting me to the office. I got the surprise of all work-related surprises when Jack was waiting for me midweek to drive me to work.

"Jack, what are you doing here?"

"As the most senior driver, the company offered me the expansion gig here in DC."

"I'm so happy for you."

He smiles. "Thank you, Madeleine. Mr. Anderson gave strict instructions about your travel and to make sure there were healthy and plentiful snacks."

I can't contain my exasperation and love for him in this moment. "Of course he did."

"Congratulations on your promotion and the baby."

I smile. "Thank you."

"He also asked me to remind you about your ultrasound appointment tomorrow."

I shake my head. "Thank you. Not your job though."

Jack smiles. "I don't mind. I mean, after all, I will be driving you there."

"True."

"You don't have to answer, but are you planning on learning the gender?"

"We are, but we aren't sharing it with anyone."

"Don't want green and yellow but want it to be a surprise for the friends and family. I love it," Jack states and pulls away from the curb.

As the week wraps, the final holiday of the year is upon us. I've never had a date for New Year's Eve before. Interestingly, neither of us are interested in going out. Lacey and her brothers accepted our offer for the farm. To celebrate our new home and the holiday, we have a low-key dinner at home and snuggle on the couch watching movies until the holiday programming starts. In my early twenties, the concerts and events went all evening long. Now they don't begin until ten at the earliest. Our intentions were good, but we fall asleep before midnight. Christoph escorts me to our bed in the wee hours of the new year with a sweet kiss and murmured wishes for the best year ever. Although my brain is in a sleep fog, I recall offering the same to him.

As the next week winds down, my nerves increase as the time to meet Mary Jane and Byron in person gets ever closer. We agreed to meet in Richmond at a hotel. The drive is a bit longer for them, but they suggested the meeting place.

After a fitful night's sleep, we leave for our short road trip. This time though, Christoph is prepared with gas station candy.

"I've never seen you this nervous for anything."

I glare at him. "Not true at all."

"Really? Name one other time you were this nervous?"

"Without hesitation, when I asked you to have a drink with me at Callie's wedding."

"I may not have voiced it yet, but I knew even then you were the one for me." He leans over and kisses me tenderly. "I know this is an awkward situation, but she's your mother. You don't harbor any anger towards her. She may have made a difficult decision for your welfare all those years ago, but she has been trying to rectify it for quite some time. Now you're giving her the opportunity Estelle never allowed. This visit will be amazing for you, her, and our child. It's one step toward our baby having the childhood we both yearned to have."

I'm speechless. "Thank you."

"Always."

We check in and dress for dinner. I opt for a simple sheath dress Kelly Barnett tailored for me. Actually, Kyla, one of her designers, focuses on modern office attire. I ordered five suits to hopefully get me through the rest of my pregnancy.

With our fingers threaded together, we make our way to the restaurant. When we arrive, the hostess guides us to a table with six seats. "Could I be as lucky as you?" I wonder out loud. Did Mary Jane bring other family members?

"It's a possibility." He kisses me lightly after taking his seat beside me. "How would you feel if you have siblings?"

"It would increase my anger at Estelle, but otherwise, overjoyed, I think." I don't have much time to dwell on my thoughts as the hostess escorts two more guests to our table. There's no way for me to mistake our relationship; Mary Jane could be my twin.

"Hi. I apologize for staring. You look exactly like I did at your age." Mary Jane extends her hand to me.

I rise from my chair and slide my hand into hers. Her eyes well with tears. All I can do is nod to acknowledge our impeding new arrival.

Byron and Christoph are exchanging handshakes beside us. I greet Byron and we take our seats. After ordering drinks and small plates, Mary Jane speaks first.

"I would love to hear about you and your life now. Given the fact Estelle failed to share my letters, I'm confident you don't want to speak about her. I'll answer any questions you may have about my decision to leave you with Marcea."

I tilt my head in acknowledgement. Estelle is the last person I want to focus on right now, so I fill in Mary Jane about my life starting from adulthood. Everything from then forward are completely my accomplishments. I credit Estelle with nothing other than teaching me to stand on my own two feet. Now I have a partner to lean on if I need to. One who willingly supports me in everything I choose to do.

Our dinner is wonderful. The chairs were simply extra. I would say I felt let down there weren't more family members, but honestly, I'm perfectly content with my found family and the one Christoph and I are building. We agree to keep in touch and video chat at least once a month.

As I walk away from the table with my fingers laced with Christoph's, I feel lighter, as if all aspects of my life are as they should be. I'm not a big believer in fate, but every facet is falling into place as if I laid them out myself.

I collapse onto the bed in our room and toe off my shoes.

Christoph lies beside me on his side facing me. "How are you?"

Shifting to face him, I wiggle as close as I can. "Initially, I was worried Mary Jane would judge me. As if she would've raised me differently or better than Estelle. It didn't come across at dinner if it's how she feels."

"I agree. Mary Jane and Byron seemed genuine in their questions and attention to your responses."

I push out a breath to stifle my emotions. Our little person makes we weepy. "I'm sorry you won't get the same opportunity."

He shrugs. "After learning about them, I'm not angry. Carolyn clearly put me first leaving me with Betty. My parents afforded me the opportunity to have a relationship with my brother by sharing their painful choices with Collin. I'm grateful they admitted their shortcomings to him despite doing the right thing. Betty is my grandmother and mostly a single parent. It isn't about the number of parents or the money. Raising a child is teaching life lessons so the child can stand on their own feet. My childhood with Gramps and Betty was stable and loving. Exactly what every child deserves. Exactly what we will give to our children."

"I agree those characteristics would provide an amazing childhood and foundation for a productive adult. Until Mary Jane showed up at the office, I thought Estelle provided those things to me. I suppose she did in her way. However, the trust needs to go both ways. Estelle broke mine, repeatedly, only I wasn't aware until recently."

"I know."

With his arms around me, we sleep in the huge, comfy bed and return home the next morning after a delicious spread of room service.

CHAPTER THIRTY-SEVEN

CHRISTOPH

Madeleine left for the office about twenty minutes ago. I'm grateful Jack accepted the offer to move to the area. After eliminating the threat to me and indirectly to my family, I'm more comfortable allowing Madeleine to go to work alone. I realize how overprotective, possessive, and obsessive my feelings sound. It isn't far from the truth. My purpose is to provide her with the life she deserves. It isn't about money; no true partnership is. I'm not suggesting having an abundant amount isn't helpful. It absolutely is. Our bond is key for our growing family.

Every detail is coming together for our date this weekend. I have stealthily planned the perfect date. The only remaining detail is to confirm the flower delivery and dinner. At first, I considered asking Jill to prepare our meal but decided against it. She may have decided to chase her mystery man, but our friendship is still rocky at best.

The new members of my team will be arriving for training midweek next week. The contracts for Lane Hawkins, Barrett Beaumont, and Patton Daley were delivered to the office a few days ago. I expect to hear from Cruz by the end of the day tomorrow, his self-imposed deadline for making a decision.

My phone rings on the island. "Hi, Gemma."

"Morning, Christoph. There's a delivery here for you requiring a signature."

"It isn't meant to be there until tomorrow. Gemma, please open the package and make sure it's perfect. I don't want to hold up the delivery service."

As I grab my keys, I hear her ripping open a box. "It's a book," Gemma states.

"Yeah, there should be about twenty pages of star charts."

"Christoph, it's beautiful."

I smile even though she can't see me. "Thanks, Gemma. I'll be there in about thirty to pick it up."

"See you then."

I hustle to my truck and take off toward the office. My phone buzzes as I drive. After I park beside the building, I check my texts.

Anamchara: *Why does Simon have the late afternoon blocked off on my work calendar for a personal appointment tomorrow?*

Me: *I planned a date, and Simon made sure your schedule was clear.*

Anamchara: *Again with the subterfuge? I would have blocked it off willingly myself.*

Me: *Perhaps.*

Anamchara: *Where are we going?*

Me: *Nope. You have to wait until tomorrow. Love you.*

Anamchara: *Love you.*

The next one is from Betty.

Betty: Are you and Madeleine free for dinner with Collin on the 15th?

Me: Hi, Grams. How are you?

Betty: I'm well. The floral contract is keeping me busy, but I love it.

Me: Glad to hear it. We'll be there. Love you.

Betty: Love you too.

Next is our contractor for the farm.

Jimmy Holden: The plans for your home were approved by the town.

Me: Great! What will your best-case completion date be?

Jimmy Holden: Mid-April at the earliest.

Right before the baby is born. Perfect.

Me: Thank you.

The last one has me cheering.

Cruz: I'm in, but I need a little more time.

Me: It's yours. I'll call you in about fifteen to talk details.

Cruz: Roger.

Smiling, I make my way to the office.

"Hi, Christoph."

"Hey, Gemma. Thanks for the assist. I planned to be here to get this tomorrow."

"No problem. When do you plan on making it official?" She's perceptive like her father. I suppose it's a necessary skill in our line of work.

I drop my head. "I have no idea what you could be referring to Gemma."

"Fine, you keep your plans hush, hush. She's perfect for you."

More than I deserve. "She is. Thanks."

"Anytime."

I return to my truck and dial Cruz after pulling onto the road.

"Hey, Cruz."

"C-Top."

"Welcome to Blackthorne Security, bro!"

"Thanks. The department won't let me sign a contract until I officially use all my vacation and personal time."

I roll my eyes. "Okay. When can you start?"

"Seriously?"

"Of course. We've wanted you on the team since Jake started the company."

Cruz hesitates. "I could start early February."

"Good. We'll see you then."

"Thanks, C-Top. I need to move on from this setback."

"We're brothers. I'll send you the manual and training regime so you can study on your off time."

"Thanks." I end the call and smile. My professional life is almost set, and tomorrow night, I plan to stake a claim for Madeleine for the rest of our lives. I scurry home and stash the book in my only secret hiding place in the condo. At least I don't think she's found it yet.

A few hours later, I hear Madeleine call, "Hi, babe. I'm home," from the foyer.

"Hey. Are you still angry?"

She grins at me. "Not angry. I'm not used to Simon having another coconspirator and one against me as well."

"It isn't against you. It's for you." I draw her against me and welcome her home properly with a breathtaking, toe-curling kiss.

"I'll allow it."

With a hearty laugh, I escort her to the kitchen and dazzle her again with my cooking prowess. After dinner we discuss her call today with Mary Jane.

"Oh. It isn't time yet, is it?"

She shakes her head. "She can call whenever she wants, but Estelle was taken to hospice earlier today."

I wrap my arms tighter around her. "How did Mary Jane find out? How do you feel about her decision?"

Before answering, she moves my hand to her belly. Our little person is moving around a lot right now. We know the gender, and we're working on a name. "Mary Jane is listed as Estelle's emergency contact given she's her only surviving child. I'm surprised she didn't use my name in an effort to force me to see her again. As far as how I feel, she's dying. She can make whatever decision is best for her. Forgiveness isn't something I'm ready to give to her. I may not ever be over it, if you will. You would think her illness would rush me to forgive, but it isn't. My anger is less, but I have a lifetime of lies to forgive, and I'm not ready yet."

"You need to do what's best for you."

"Thanks. What about you?"

A huge grin breaks out on my face. "Our plans for the house were approved. Jimmy said they could be done by mid-April with our improvements."

"Really?"

I nod enthusiastically.

"Perfect timing. What else?"

"Cruz is in, but he needs more time before he can report here."

"Fantastic! Is it a big deal?"

I explain the reason for the delay and my ability to keep the slot open for him.

"Sounds perfect."

"It is. Do you know what else is perfect?"

She cranes her neck to look at me. "What?"

I lean down and kiss the tip of her nose. "Watching the snow fall snug in our warm bed naked." A short while later, we're cuddled in our bed snuggling naked.

The next morning, I shoo Madeleine off to work with Jack and hustle to finish the last-minute items for tonight. I've checked every detail three times, and I'm still nervous something will go wrong. To soothe my nerves, I text Simon.

Me: Is everything set there?

Simon: Boss lady is digging for information. I won't crack.

Me: I'm counting on you, Simon.

Simon: Your confidence is well placed. The two of you are a power couple. It's amazing to witness.

Me: Thanks, Simon. I'll be there at five.

Simon: She'll be ready.

With my nerves soothed for the time being, I decide to go for a long run to pass more time. Unfortunately, I have to use the treadmill given the snow-covered sidewalks. Six hard miles later, I head upstairs to shower and dress for my date. I take a peek at my texts to make sure everything is still on schedule.

Anamchara: *What are you up to?*

Me: You promised to let me take care of you.

Anamchara: *I give. I love you.*

Me: I love you.

I park in her designated spot and enter the building.

"Good afternoon, Mr. Anderson. Would you like me to announce you?"

"Hi, Angie. Please let Simon know I'm here, not Miss Wilton."

"Of course." Angie informs Simon, and I wait for him to let her know I'm here. I overhear Simon indicate I'm free to go back.

I approach Simon and Lucia as I enter the Scala office. "Good evening, Mr. Anderson."

"Hi, guys. Is she ready?"

"When you said you would take care of her, I was skeptical. Well done, Christoph." Simon admits.

I take his extended hand and hug Lucia. Not only did I send a manicurist to her office, but a new dress designed by Kelly Barnett with a little inspiration from Lucia as well as new Lucia approved Manolos. "I meant every word. Thanks to both of you."

"Mads, Christoph is here to whisk you away for your date."

I glare at Simon.

"It's true, and she already knows about the date."

"Fair enough."

Madeleine steps out of her office, and I'm floored once again by how gorgeous she looks. Kelly has outdone herself. I know what I requested, but it's miles beyond what I envisioned. The dress is a royal blue faux wrap dress with a beaded plunging neckline. The floor length dress also boasts a tie at the waist. Her dress skims over her new shoes.

"Wow! You're stunning."

She blushes despite the fact I tell her each morning. "Thank you. You didn't have to go to all this trouble for a date."

"I wanted to give Simon and Lucia something else to take care of."

Simon and Lucia are beaming, and Madeleine is shaking her head.

"Ready?" I hold out her coat for her and she slides it on.

"Almost." She leans in and whispers, "You look hot! I love you, Christoph."

I offer her my arm. She loops hers through mine. I lean closer and reply, "Not remotely as hot as you. I love you, Madeleine."

During the ride to our destination, she tries to pump me for more details.

"I won't relent, *anamchara.*"

A sexy pout materializes on her lips but fades quickly. "Thank you."

"For?"

Her gaze is pinned to my profile. "Being mine."

I lift her hand to my mouth and kiss the back. "The same is true for you." The surprise of our destination is about to be revealed.

"We're going to the planetarium at the Smithsonian?"

A huge grin graces my face. I knew the location was perfect given the season and my plan, but her reaction is more than I could've hoped for. "Maybe?"

I pull into the staff entrance and swipe the card my contact gave me. Two years ago, Blackthorne was hired to assess the security of some high-profile buildings in DC for a private event for one of our clients. Her daughter planned to get married at the museum. We assessed three options for her. It earned us some major favors from the higher ups at the locations. I called in a huge favor for tonight. After finding the designated spot, I round the back of the car and pull a few things from the trunk.

I open the passenger door, and she slides her hand into mine. I guide her to the side entrance, and we're ushered inside by security. So far, she hasn't uttered another word.

The only sound is the click of her heels on the tile floor.

"Thank you, Jamison."

"Have a lovely evening, Mr. Anderson. Miss Wilton. The program is all set. The control room is unlocked."

I nod and follow Madeleine inside. She's in awe. For someone who loves stars, I'm surprised she's never visited a planetarium before. Then again, I suppose it wasn't on her approved list of activities from Estelle.

"Madeleine?"

Her gaze meets mine. "I'm floored."

Wait until later, anamchara. "You deserve this and more."

"We are all I need." She steps closer and sets her lips on mine.

I motion for her to take a seat. "I'll be right back."

After turning on the projector, I bring our first course to the table. In between bites, Madeleine shifts between looking at me and the stars. We chat about the farm and the baby while we eat our main course.

"I have a gift for you. I'll be right back." I hurry to the control room and start the program. Thankfully, the steward gave me enough time to get back to Madeleine for her to follow along. "Please open it."

She pushes the tissues paper aside and pulls out a personalized book I had created for us—well, mostly her.

"The first page is the stars over where you were born. It matches the stars above your head right now. The second page is the stars over where I was born."

Slowly, the program scrolls through each location in the book. "Each page is the stars at a different location when we were together starting in Atlanta, then Crescent Bay, and every locale including New Orleans, Chicago, LA, and New York."

"We were never in New Orleans together."

I raise an eyebrow. "Physically, no. We were there together though."

She flips through the pages as the stars above her change.

"Why is this one loose?"

"The stars tonight for this location are printed on the loose sheet."

"Why are there blank pages?"

"They're for our future. I have one for tonight, and one for our new home. We can add more in the coming years." If she knows where I'm going with this gift, she isn't letting on. "We are an amazing team. I need you beside me each day. I never thought there was a woman tailor-made for me until I found you. There's nothing I won't do for your or our family."

I fish the box out of my pocket and lower in front of her on one knee. "Madeleine, I love you more than I could adequately portray in words. You fill in holes I didn't know were present in my life. Will you do me the honor of taking my last name and spending the rest of your life with me?"

She leans forward and kisses me breathless. "It would be my honor to take your last name."

I slide the Asscher cut diamond with two tapered baguettes onto her finger and kiss her breathless.

"We can't get frisky in here, right?"

This woman owns me. "No, but I did book a suite for us here in the city for tonight."

"How about we bring the chocolate dessert you have over there to our suite so we can celebrate properly?"

"As long as it means naked and numerous times."

"It absolutely does."

With expedience, I shut down the projector and hurriedly escort my future wife to our hotel suite. We spend the next two days celebrating before sharing our engagement with anyone else.

EPILOGUE

MADELEINE

Over the past few months, my client list has grown at Scala and the employees have readily accepted the numerous changes I've made. As promised, I haven't made any major policy changes. However, I learned from my meeting with department heads and agents, the staff felt Stavros was unapproachable. I plan to be different than him regarding my accessibility to the staff.

Stavros and I have spoken numerous times. Leanna is making great progress with her rehabilitation program. In the summer, I plan to visit the city to see her again.

"Madeleine, Mrs. Michelson and two bundles of bliss are here to see you."

"Thanks, Lucia. She can come back."

I rise from my chair to meet Callie. I'm surprised she doesn't have an armed guard given Connor's insane protective nature over her and the babies. The fraternal twins, Sutton Mara and Myers Connor were born at thirty-eight weeks which is awesome for twins. Callie and Connor wanted their names to reflect how they came together. Not only do they honor Connor and Mara as twins, but Callie's parents as well.

"Hey, Callie. Where's your bodyguard?"

She laughs. "He's with the guys at the office. I'm not sure how much he'll get done with Amara underfoot. How are you feeling?"

"As big as a house. This little darling can arrive whenever he or she is ready."

"Stop it! You look amazing! I remember feeling like I couldn't take anymore. They made me wait another week though. How are you holding up after everything with Estelle?"

Callie and I have grown closer in the last year. We're more friendly than we were in the past. "Estelle betrayed me in the deepest conceivable way. She left her estate, which largely included my money, to Mary Jane. There's nothing I can do about it. I'm not even bothering with it. Mary Jane knows the truth because Estelle told her on one of her last days. It's twisted, but I'm letting it go." Money that I provided to Estelle for living expenses is going to my mother and stepfather because Estelle never spent a penny of it. While Mary Jane and I are making progress with our relationship, it still stings Estelle wouldn't leave her estate to me. It means she never intended to or changed her will near the very end of her life.

"You're a better person than I am, Madi."

A harsh contraction makes me stop moving.

"How long have you been having contractions, Madi?"

"Braxton Hicks… for the last month. Real ones? Maybe the last few hours." My voice is calm and collected.

Callie's eyes widen. "You need to call your doctor and then Christoph."

Reluctantly, I call my doctor, who requests I come to the office even though it's a week early.

"Hey, are you guys about done there?" I ask when Christoph answers.

"We're done because Norah's water broke."

"Oh. Well, I need you to meet me at the doctor's office with my bag." Silence passes over the phone line. "Christoph, babe, are you there?"

"Uh-huh." I can't see him, but my protective fiancé is cursing himself for not coming to the office with me today.

"We can do anything hard together. Callie is going to bring me to the doctor's office. Why don't you have Connor drive your truck there? Christoph, we very well might make one of our dreams come true today. Please hurry. I love you."

"I love you, *anamchara*."

Callie has packed my bag and laptop from my desk. Lucia and Simon are waiting at the threshold.

"He's freaking out?" Callie asks.

"Christoph has always wanted to be a dad. It's possible he might become one in the very near future. He's ecstatic and terrified at the same time At least that is how I perceive his lack of response during our call.

He isn't in control of something for the first time in his life and there's no way to plan or gain control either.

"Makes sense. Let's get a move on. No babies born in my car."

"Simon and Lucia, I'll keep you informed when I know more."

"Good luck," they say at once.

The contractions increase in frequency and intensity as we drive to the office. Christoph is waiting impatiently at the entrance to my doctor's office. "Hi, sweetheart. How are y—"

A contraction seizes my body, and I grip his forearm. I breathe through it like the classes recommend, and then we make our way to the office.

"Miss Wilton, right this way," the nurse greets us.

Within minutes, Dr. Flagstone joins us. "Hi, Madeleine. How far apart are the contractions?"

"It's varying between ten to fourteen minutes or so."

Christoph takes my hand in his. "You should've called sooner."

Dr. Richardson chuckles. "Madeleine, you're five centimeters dilated. We're going to escort you over the maternity ward. I'll join you in a few hours."

"We're having a baby today?" Christoph whispers.

I slide the pad of my thumb across his cheek. "We're having a baby today. We've got this." My voice has more confidence than my mind.

With moderate speed, I'm escorted over to the hospital and into a room. Nurses and staff are coming and going. Christoph is staring out the window.

"Is there any chance we could have about fifteen minutes?" I ask one of the nurses quietly.

She notices Christoph's posture and answers, "Sure."

I sidle beside him and breath through a contraction. "Christoph, look at me." Only three times have I seen that look on his face. When I agreed to date him, when I shared we were having a baby, and when I accepted his proposal.

He looks over at me. The unshed tears in his eyes make my heart squeeze more.

"I need you to focus on right now. After our gorgeous daughter is born, we'll give her the life she deserves. The one we believe she deserves. I love you."

"I've never been more scared than I am right now. I have absolutely no control right now. I've faced numerous unknown militia members, close calls with IEDs, and even escaped gunfire. None of that terrified me as much as failing you or our little girl."

"You and this little girl have captured my whole heart." I set my hand on the window frame and breathe until the tightness in my abdomen eases. "I'm scared too but having you beside me makes it possible to face a blissful life without reservation." As the words pass through my lips, my water breaks.

I waddle over to the bed, and Christoph helps me sit. Aimee, the nurse who gave us uninterrupted time, returns.

"My water broke a few minutes ago," I inform her.

"Let me check your progress, and then we can talk about pain medication."

"Yes, please," Christoph pleads.

Aimee laughs. After reminding him of my preference not to have pain medication, she explains the monitor and leaves to update my doctor.

We breathe through two more contractions before Dr. Flagstone joins us in the room. "Madeleine, it's time to have a baby. When the next contraction comes, bear down and push. Dad, you can hold her foot or hand whatever she prefers."

I reach my hand out and draw him closer. When the contraction spikes, I push and breathe like I learned in class.

"Good, whenever you're ready, go again," Dr. Flagstone instructs in her smooth voice.

I follow the same pattern two more times with Christoph watching me in awe.

"On the next contraction, baby will be here," my doctor assures me.

A wailing cry fills the room after another strong push. I've never heard a sweeter sound.

"Dad, would you like to cut the cord?"

Christoph can only nod and follow her instructions. After cleaning her up a bit, they set her on my chest, and I'm dumbstruck with love and fear.

"Hi, Elizabeth Harper." Tears fall from my eyes. With one hand on our daughter, I reach up, swipe a single tear from Christoph's cheek and kiss him softly.

Aimee takes our daughter across the room to check her weight and a few tests.

"Go ahead. I'm fine."

Christoph ambles over to our daughter and watches her like a hawk. The sheer awe and joy on his face is unfathomable. He pulls out his phone to take a few dozen photos. He accepts our daughter from the nurse and takes a seat beside me in bed.

"I have a message for you from next door. Samuel Benjamin Blackthorne has made his arrival about fifteen minutes before your daughter," Aimee shares.

"Thank you. Please share the same information with them as well."

Aimee smiles and slips out of my room.

"How are you doing, Dad?"

He presses a kiss to our daughter's head and then mine. "Still terrified but overjoyed as well."

"Me too."

Thank you so much for reading *Protecting Our Forever*!

I hope you love Christoph and Madeleine. Will Cruz make the leap to Blackthorne?

Order *Protecting Us* now so you don't miss it!

Check out Frankie's HEA in *Chasing My Sunshine* coming soon!

Did you love *Protecting Our Forever*?

Thank you for taking the time to read it. I hope you loved it!
If you liked this book or another one of my books, please consider
posting a review.
A short line or two will be perfect!
I appreciate your support and feedback.

COMING SOON

Two new stories are coming soon!

A York Beach Novel
The Cappellis
Chasing My Sunshine

A Blackthorne Novel
Protecting Us

MY BOOKS

YORK BEACH SERIES:
A New Beginning with You
Taking A Chance on Me
Just One More
Kiss You Like You're Mine
Only with Him
My Once in a Lifetime

THE CAPPELLIS
Chasing Forever

MORGAN BROTHERS SERIES:
One Unforgettable Favor
Until I Kissed You
Always Have, Always Will

BLACKTHORNE SECURITY
Protecting My Forever

All my books in one place: www.nicolevidal.com/books